DEAD
EVEN

BY
C.C.
RISENHOOVER

PaperJacks LTD.

TORONTO   NEW YORK

PaperJacks

DEAD EVEN

PaperJacks LTD

330 STEELCASE RD. E., MARKHAM, ONT. L3R 2M1
210 FIFTH AVE., NEW YORK, N.Y. 10010

McLennan Publishing, Inc. edition published 1986
PaperJacks edition published July 1988

This is a work of fiction in its entirety. Any resemblance to actual people, places or events is purely coincidental.

10 9 8 7 6 5 4 3 2 1

ISBN 0-7701-0738-9

To Friends

CHAPTER ONE

Laurie was brushing her teeth when the doorbell rang. The sound startled her, caused a tingle of fear to run down her spine. She had always been fearful, but even moreso since they had moved into the big house.

At first, she was tempted to ignore the doorbell's insistent ringing, to act as though she was not at home. But if it was someone they knew and Paul found out she had not responded, he would be angry.

And Paul's anger was more to be feared than anyone at the door.

So, she quickly rinsed out her mouth, checked herself in the mirror and frowned. She thought she looked a mess, which was not an unusual evaluation. She wasn't a confident woman. She was always unsure of her appearance.

After cinching the belt of her light blue robe, the one Paul had given her for Christmas, she hurriedly ran a brush through the tangles in her shoulder length auburn hair. Then she reluctantly made her way to the front of the house.

The entire bathroom scenario had taken less than a minute, but it seemed much longer to Laurie because of the off-and-on ringing of the doorbell. The ringing had now intensified, triggering a fearful annoyance in her. And the grandfather clock in the den added its chimes to the unpleasant sound.

It was eight o'clock.

Through the peephole in the front door, Laurie identified the person interrupting her morning. Who it was surprised her and, to some extent, evaporated her earlier annoyance.

What's he doing here? she wondered.

After unlatching the assortment of locks on the door, she opened it and with attempted cheerfulness said, "Well, this is a surprise."

"Would you believe that I was just out jogging in the neighborhood?" he asked.

She forced an uneasy laugh. "Knowing your aversion to exercise, I do find that a little hard to believe. And most joggers don't dress quite as nicely."

"It is the jogger without class who doesn't wear a designer suit," he said.

"I suppose so. But where did you park your car?"

"It's parked up the street."

Laurie wasn't good at humor, but she tried. "Oh, that's real good. Some poor housewife will be having to explain to her husband and neighbors about a strange car parked in front of her house. Now, no kidding, where did you park the car?"

"I told you. It's parked up the street."

"Why?"

"I didn't want to tell you, but I'm having an affair with one of the neighborhood housewives."

"Very funny." His teasing always bothered her, always got on her nerves. But she realized it was pointless to continue questioning him about the car.

"Well, are you just going to stand there, or would you like to come in?" she asked.

While walking through the door, he again teased, "I'm never sure when I'm welcome."

Laurie shook her head in mock resignation and said, "Shut

2

the door and I'll make you a cup of coffee."

"That sounds good, if it's no bother."

"It isn't," she assured, "as long as you promise not to make fun of the way I look."

He feigned astonishment. "Me...make fun?"

His exaggerated acting triggered another uneasy laugh from Laurie.

"I sure could use that cup of coffee," he said.

She relaxed a little. "Hold your horses and I'll make you the best cup of instant that money can buy."

"I was hoping for fresh perked."

"I'm sorry to crush your hopes, but in this household you get instant. I just hope you can stand drinking it while looking at someone as grubby as me."

"You'll do."

"Thanks," she said with a tinge of sarcasm. "It's good to know that I'll do. And by the way, I'm surprised you didn't wake up the baby with all that doorbell ringing."

"Sorry about that. I forgot."

"As hard as it was for me to get him to sleep, you'd have been real sorry if he had waked up. I'd have made you take care of him."

"With that kind of threat, you can count on me ringing softly from now on."

They were in the kitchen now, its earth tone colors a reflection of the woman who lived in the house. Sunlight filtering through the curtains on oversized windows filled the room with light, giving it the aura of being a warm and cheerful place.

Looks can be so deceiving, he thought while seating himself in a chair at the breakfast table. Laurie was such a scared mouse. He knew that she hated the house, felt unsafe in it. He reasoned, though, that she would feel frightened and unsafe wherever she lived. She was a woman who was obsessed by fear.

He played spectator as Laurie filled a kettle with water and

3

placed it on one of the stove's burners. She turned the burner's dial to the high setting, then, while waiting for the water to heat, spooned generous portions of instant coffee into bright orange mugs.

He couldn't help but think that the mugs seemed out of place with her personality, but teased, "You do that well. I'm impressed with your domesticity."

"I'm really good at boiling water," she countered. "I don't know of anyone who can make a better cup of instant coffee."

Looking at her carefully, he supposed that most men would find her beautiful. The auburn hair provided the perfect framework for an angelic face that was accentuated by dark brown eyes, a small nose and well-shaped lips that defied cosmetic improvement.

He also supposed that to most men there was a definite sexual rightness to the way her five-foot four-inch body was proportioned.

The water was hot. She poured it into the mugs and it released the aroma of the coffee, permeating the room and overpowering the other kitchen smells. She then placed the kettle back on the stove and stirred the contents of both cups with a spoon.

"Do you have any Sweet'n Low?" he asked.

"Yes."

"Well dammit, I'd like some," he said with a chuckle.

She again emitted that unsure and fearful little laugh that was so much a part of her character. "OK, I'll get you some."

When she handed him a package of Sweet'n Low, he looked in her eyes and was reminded of a frightened rabbit. He liked rabbits. They were sweet animals, animals that threatened no one.

Laurie was sweet, too, certainly no threat. Still, he knew he had to kill her.

CHAPTER TWO

Matt McCall was startled into semi-consciousness by the incessant ringing of the telephone. With a groan of displeasure, he rolled over on his back and groped at the bedside table. For a few seconds, he had trouble locating the plastic-encased mechanism that was responsible for disturbing his slumber. Mentally cursing Ma Bell and AT&T, he finally located the receiver and wrested it from its cradle.

"Yeah," he mumbled into the mouthpiece.

"McCall, is that you?" a voice asked.

"Who in the hell else would be answering my phone at this time of night?" he grumbled. "Or is it morning?" He recognized the caller's voice as belonging to Turner Sipe, the *Tribune's* pudgy city editor.

"This is Turner."

"Yeah, I know," he replied with disgust.

"It's only eleven o'clock. I figured you'd be up."

"Well, you figured wrong, which isn't unusual. I had things to do in bed that you probably wouldn't understand."

"Oh," Sipe responded in his seemingly always puzzled manner.

His eyes were now accustomed to the darkness. He could see Cele lying beneath a pile of extra blankets on the other side of the kingsize bed. She was still sleeping soundly. It surprised him that she had been able to sleep right through the harsh ringing of the telephone. He made a mental note that from then on he would unplug the damn thing when they went to bed.

"What in the hell do you want, Turnip?" He enjoyed irritating Sipe by calling him Turnip instead of Turner, though he laughingly admitted to others that he felt guilty about degrading the vegetable. He really figured a Turnip had more personality than the man he often referred to as "a balding excuse for a city editor."

"There's been a murder," Sipe said.

"That's really big news in San Antonio," he responded with sarcasm, "unless, of course, you're talking about the mayor or some of the Air Force brass. Don't you have anyone else who can cover this? My ass is tired."

"This is a big one," Sipe emphasized. "Parkham wants you on it." The reference was to Ed Parkham, the managing editor.

"Tell me about it."

"No, just get your ass down here. Ed and Katie are waiting for you." Katie Hussey was the metro editor.

The fact that Parkham and Katie were at the paper this late gave McCall reason to believe it might be more than a run-of-the-mill homicide. The two editors were usually shacked up, with each other, by eleven. However, he couldn't be sure that it was a big story, because he was convinced that collectively Parkham, Katie and Sipe didn't have a thimbleful of news judgment between them.

"I'll shower and get right down," he said.

"You don't need a damn shower," Sipe said with authority. "Just get your ass down here."

"Look, you little asshole," he angrily replied, "I don't need you or anyone else to tell me what I should do in the way of personal hygiene. I'll be there when I get there, and if that's not good enough, fuck you and the horse you rode in on."

6

He slammed the receiver back in its cradle, then chuckled to himself at the knowledge that Sipe would be speechless and redfaced. He figured that either Parkham or Katie, maybe both, had been standing at Sipe's side when he made the call. Otherwise, the man would never have tried his bullshit boss routine.

He didn't particularly like authority anyway, especially when it was used unnecessarily. And he would have responded to Parkham or Katie in the same way that he did to Sipe.

Cele was now awake. "What's wrong?"

"Nothing, baby, just a murder. Go on back to sleep."

"Who was murdered?"

"I have no idea. They're being mysterious about it at the paper. But Sipe claims it's big or they wouldn't have called me."

"They probably wouldn't have."

He chuckled. "Hey, don't start taking their side."

She laughed, flashing her straight, white teeth.

Damn, she's beautiful, he thought. He wished that he had time to make love to her before going to the *Tribune*.

"Maybe we can get something about the murder on the radio," she suggested.

"That would surprise the hell out of me," he said. He figured most radio newscasters got what little news they reported from the newspaper.

Cele turned on the clock radio that was on the bedside table. Loud music blared from the speaker, the kind he considered African and inane. It was the kind of music that was loud even when the volume was turned down low.

Cele's continued efforts to find a newscast resulted in discovery of a preacher who thought the world was coming to an end, and an all-night call-in talk show.

"You listen," he said. "I've got to get a move on."

"Are you leaving now?"

"Just as soon as I can take a quick shower."

"When will you be back?"

7

"Who knows?"

"Wake me up when you come in. Maybe we can do something."

"Count on it."

They kissed and her closeness stirred him.

"Now that I'm awake, I wish you didn't have to go," she said.

"You're not the only one," he replied. "Unfortunately, duty calls." He kissed her again with greater passion, then thought, what the hell. They can wait.

When their lovemaking was completed, he rolled out of bed and barefooted it to the bathroom. While soaking himself beneath rivulets of warm water, he thought about Cele and what they had together. He wasn't sure that it was love, but he figured it was pretty close to the real thing; maybe as close as he would ever get.

He remembered Hightower's thoughts about love in Faulkner's *Light In August*. The passage read: "Perhaps they were right in putting love into books. Perhaps it could not live anywhere else."

He had met Cele the previous year, when she was twenty-two and shortly after his thirty-ninth birthday. It was at a time when he had begun to find women, especially separated or divorced women, distasteful. In fact, he had all but given up finding a woman with whom he could have anything close to a meaningful relationship.

He had begun to think that his lot in life was to provide a stud service for divorcees; spending endless hours with them in bars, going over the same old ground, listening to the same trite statements he had heard so many times before.

Going to bed with these women had become a boring chore, and listening to their endless dribble even more of an unwanted task. They all seemingly wanted to talk about their divorces, to complain about how their husbands had mistreated them.

The way he figured it, a few husbands might have gotten the short end of the stick, too.

But Cele was different. And it wasn't simply because she had

8

never been married. It was the proud, aloof way in which she carried herself. And maybe he had been challenged by a friend's analysis that she was untouchable.

His interest, however, was much deeper than merely making it with a virgin. For one thing, he wasn't sure that he considered virginity all that much of a virtue.

But he was intrigued by her moral stance, the fact that she had not yielded to pressure. Of course, he was impressed with strength of any kind, especially that of the will and mind.

Cele was five feet four inches tall, with long, straight hair that stopped at her waist. Her green eyes were rounded and very pronounced. And her complexion was so picture-perfect that she really didn't need makeup.

He thought she was the most beautiful woman he had ever seen.

After they were introduced, they were together constantly. Both had verbalized that they thought there was a special magic to their relationship, but she still kept him sexually at bay for months. It was something he would not have tolerated in any other woman.

Finally, however, her championing of virginity wore thin. He became surly and angry about it, then gave way to his passion and forced himself on her. She had experienced some emotional trauma as a result of the incident, which included a month of administering heavy doses of mental punishment to him. Eventually, though, they resolved their differences and started living together.

As anticipated, their unwedded state did not please her parents. But it was more than that. They also thought he was too old for her. And there were times when he felt the same way.

While the age difference did bother him, he tried to reconcile himself to the fact that Cele was a person, not some chronological entity.

Of late, he had even thought in terms of marriage, which was something he had not previously considered in his adult life. In the past there had been no time, and there had also been no one to seriously consider.

He turned off the shower and toweled the wetness from his body. He brushed his teeth, towel-dried and combed his hair, administered anti-perspirant and cologne, then quickly dressed in the darkness of the bedroom.

Cele had gone back to sleep, leaving the radio on. He turned it off and kissed her lightly on the cheek before going out the door. Moments later he was racing along in the Porsche, unmindful of the speed limit. The police knew his car and they knew him. They gave him some leeway because he made a better friend than enemy.

CHAPTER THREE

McCall parked in front of the Tribune Building, entered the lobby and waved at the guard while enroute to the elevator. He had often wondered what an old and gunless guard would do if a terrorist decided to machine gun the entire city room.

The elevator's movement toward the third floor, where the newsroom was located, was turtle-like; and its slowness always annoyed him. With all the money the paper was making, he figured management could afford to put in a faster elevator.

Exiting the contraption, he walked into a foyer with walls adorned by scores of award certificates and plaques. His name was inscribed on several of them.

Most important of his awards was a Pulitzer, which he knew was the only reason management tolerated his independence and disdain for authority. It was also the reason he was paid more than anyone else on the news side, including the various editors.

The *Tribune* was in a circulation battle with the city's other daily, so he was pampered for fear he might defect. He was the *Tribune's* star.

The other paper had made numerous overtures, including

the promise of more money, more freedom and more benefits. Money, however, wasn't important to him. And he already had the freedom to pick and choose his assignments. For example, if he chose not to handle the murder case Sipe had called about, Parkham and Katie would just have to accept it; which was one of the many reasons they had for not liking him.

Besides, he realized there wasn't that much difference in the philosophies of the two papers. And, if he made a switch, he would lose his leverage.

There was something else, too, something he didn't particularly care to talk about. He felt a deep loyalty and commitment to the *Tribune*.

Parkham, Katie and Sipe were waiting for him, cloistered like a package of Fruit of the Loom underwear. Walking into Parkham's office, he noted the furrowed brows of the trio, and was pretty sure they had been questioning the legitimacy of his birth.

He thought they might possibly represent everything in journalism that he hated.

"About time you got here," Parkham said.

He was amused by Parkham's attempted forcefulness, which was always attempted when Katie and Sipe were present. He never let the managing editor enjoy such moments, however, because he always acted as though anything said to him was a compliment. He knew how much his attitude pissed-off the ghost-colored man, which made the game all that much more fun.

So, he answered the attempted reprimand with, "Thanks. I raced right over after taking a shower. Turnip insisted that I clean up before meeting with you."

Sipe's face flushed beet red and Parkham answered the sarcastic reply with, "We've got a big one here, the kind of investigative stuff you can really sink your teeth in."

Dramatic, McCall thought. The man should have been an actor.

"Great," he responded without enthusiasm. "I could use

12

something out of the ordinary. Life's been pretty boring lately."

"You won't find this boring," Katie said.

"Fine, let's cut out all the preliminary bullshit and get on with it then," he said. "You don't have to jack me up for something that's worthwhile. Just tell me about it, Ed."

He noted that Parkham was, as usual, immaculately dressed; living proof, he thought, that clothes don't make the man. He also reasoned that Parkham's obsession with clothes might have to do with his otherwise drab physical appearance. The man's face was so white that it looked as though it had been powdered for burial. And his thin, brownish hair receded to the point where there was no hope for its salvation.

Parkham was not overly fat, but his body reeked of softness. He represented a kind of weakness that McCall found intolerable.

"Paul Roget's wife has been murdered," Parkham said. He paused to let the impact of his words sink in, but McCall showed no emotion.

Instead, he deadpanned, "Maybe I'm stupid, but who in the hell is Paul Roget?"

"He's an attorney who lives on the northeast side of San Antonio," Sipe said.

McCall looked through the lenses of Sipe's glasses, into the beady gray eyes above the flared red nose. "Why is this murder so all-fired different than the others we have in San Antonio?"

"It's the way the woman was killed," Katie chimed in.

She seemed so excited that McCall surmised that she was either elated at being able to get her two cents worth in, or happy about another of her gender being eliminated. He was getting a bit irritated because he was beginning to think that they had called him from the warmth of his bed to cover some piss ant story that was as routine as a morning trip to the john.

With resignation he said, "Well, fill me in on this mysterious murder. Or do we have to sit here scratching ass all night. Before we get started, though, I need some coffee."

Parkham went to the door of his office and summoned a copy boy. "Bring us four coffees," he ordered.

"I'll need some Sweet'n Low," McCall said.

The copy boy nodded acknowledgment.

"Mrs. Roget was strangled to death with a macrame cord," Parkham said, "but the strange thing is the message the killer left on the mirrored bedroom wall. It was written with Mrs. Roget's lipstick and said, 'Thanks Paul, now we're even.' And that's just one of the mysterious elements in this murder."

McCall calmly asked, "Why don't you tell me some of the others?"

Katie took the cue with, "We've also had a report that Mrs. Roget had semen in her mouth."

In his relaxed off-the-wall manner, McCall asked, "Have you ever had any semen in your mouth, Katie?"

His crudeness shocked her, which he expected. And even Parkham's white face showed a tinge of color.

"I don't think that was necessary," the managing editor said.

"No more necessary than this meeting," McCall said. "The final edition has already been put to bed, and you could have given me all this information by phone. Better still, we could have discussed it in the morning."

The copy boy interrupted before Parkham could answer. "Here's the coffee, sir."

McCall emptied half a pack of Sweet'n Low in his coffee, then watched while Parkham, Katie and Sipe sugared and creamed theirs.

"Damn it, McCall," Parkham said, "we called you down here because it's important to discuss how this story should be handled. You seem to forget that we operate as a team at this newspaper."

"Bullshit."

"What's bullshit?" Parkham asked, the irritation obvious in his voice.

"This damn team concept you're so hung up on. We're not the Dallas Cowboys. There's no need for a team here. All you

14

need to do is to keep some dumbass from screwing up what I write."

Parkham's face colored. "Damn you, McCall. You seem to have a lot of trouble knowing your place at this paper."

"My place?" he asked. "Just what is my place, Ed?"

"Maybe that wasn't a good choice of words," Parkham said, "but as long as I'm managing editor, we'll do things my way."

"The fact that you're managing editor doesn't impress me one damn bit," McCall said. "If you want me to handle this story, I'll handle it my way. My way has always been good enough in the past and it'll have to be good enough for this one. You can help by keeping your asshole editors from screwing up the copy."

In any confrontation, McCall always attacked, which generally put his adversary on the defensive. And, as usual, his method worked with Parkham. He knew Parkham would have gotten great joy from firing him, but he also knew that he didn't have the balls to do it. The top brass would have taken a dim view of Parkham's decision to fire the paper's most noted journalist. And the competition would be more than happy to have a Pulitzer prizewinning journalist on its staff, because it would mean a promotional edge in advertising and circulation.

McCall knew Parkham was well aware that he had to be careful in handling him. He knew the brass considered him the paper's greatest promotional resource. And Parkham wasn't about to get his tail in a wringer with top management. He wanted to someday be a part of it.

So Parkham said almost apologetically, "Look, let's not haggle about all this. This could be one of the biggest stories of the year."

"Maybe," McCall said doubtfully. "Right now we just have another bizarre San Antonio murder, which is about as common as the bad coffee we get here. But once I sort out all the characters, maybe we can get a better reading."

It was strange, he thought, how tension could come and go so quickly; as though it never actually existed.

"By the way," he asked, "what time was Mrs. Roget killed?"

"Our source at the coroner's office tells us they can't pinpoint the exact time of death," Sipe answered. "The coroner is saying it could have happened anytime between six a.m. and six p.m."

"Doesn't the coroner watch television?" McCall quipped. "Those guys give you the time right down to the exact second."

Parkham chuckled. "Television and the real thing are always a world apart, aren't they?"

"Always," McCall answered. "By the way, what time was the body found?"

"It was a little after six this evening," Parkham replied, "but the police didn't arrive until about seven-thirty."

"Why the delay?"

"They weren't called immediately."

"Am I to assume that the husband found the body?" McCall asked.

"Yeah," Parkham answered, "but he had a friend call the police. And they weren't called until after seven."

"So, the husband is a prime suspect," McCall said.

"You know he is," Parkham agreed, "but our sources tell us the police haven't talked to him yet. He is supposedly grief-stricken and in seclusion with friends."

McCall said, "There may not be a mystery then."

"Roget is supposed to have an airtight alibi," Sipe contributed. "He was on jury duty all day."

"How convenient," McCall replied.

"You know," Parkham said, "him being on jury duty really surprised me. I didn't know that lawyers could serve on a jury. In fact, I'm pretty sure they can't where I come from."

Parkham was from up east, which was, McCall thought, the reason he had been hired. The buffoons who managed the *Tribune* figured the fountainhead of journalistic knowledge was in the east. The fact that Parkham's job with an eastern paper carried little, if any, responsibility made no difference to the powers that be; he was from the right part of the country.

"Welcome to Texas," McCall said with a laugh. "Down here we allow lawyers the same rights as normal people."

"I don't think it's a good idea to let lawyers serve on a jury," Parkham continued.

"You won't get any argument from me," McCall said, "and you probably wouldn't get any argument from most lawyers.

"But if the coroner can't pinpoint the time of death a bit closer, then the husband's alibi isn't worth a damn. Unless, of course, the man can prove he left the house before six a.m."

"It's usually always the husband in a case like this," Katie lamented.

"Let's hope it's not on this one," Parkham answered.

The bastard, McCall thought. He doesn't give a damn about the woman who was killed. He just wants a big story.

However, in analyzing his own feelings, McCall realized he wasn't all that pure himself. He, too, wanted a big story. The very prospect of a big story got the adrenalin flowing.

"Is there anything else?" McCall asked. He sensed that they had not told him everything.

Parkham shrugged his shoulders, glanced at Katie and Sipe before replying. "Not that I know of. We routinely intercepted the police call regarding the murder, but the cops have kept a pretty tight lid on details. It was all we could do to come up with a few sketchy facts for a final edition story. When we started piecing together some of the bizarre details, we called you.

"Oh, there is one other thing. Did we mention that there was a baby, the Rogets kid?"

McCall downed the last of the coffee from the styrofoam cup and answered, "No, you didn't. Is the kid alright?"

"As far as we know," Parkham said.

"Maybe the coroner should have checked the baby's diaper for a clue as to when the mother was killed," McCall said matter-of-factly.

"I'm sure the coroner thought of that," Katie said.

"You have more confidence in public servants than I do,

17

Katie. But anyway, the kid does add another element to the story.

"Now, is there anything else that you haven't told me. I'm going to be questioning the cops, the neighbors, the coroner, the relatives, anybody and everybody connected with the Rogets in any way. I just don't want egg on my face because of something you haven't told me."

"We've told you everything that we know," Parkham assured. "Now, who do you want working with you?"

McCall pondered a moment, then answered, "I'll take the spic kid, Ramirez."

He had counted on agitating Katie with the label he put on the young Mexican reporter, and she didn't let him down. He saw the corners of her mouth curl downward, read the disgust in her eyes.

McCall saw Katie as having a sixties mentality, knew that she envisioned herself as a great liberal, a spokesperson for the downtrodden. She had worked diligently to convince the minority journalists employed by the paper, including three out-of-the-closet homosexuals, that she was their benefactor.

Unfortunately for Katie, her attempts to lift up the oppressed were not looked on favorably by the persons she was allegedly trying to help. McCall had heard some of the blacks and Mexicans talking about her with disgust. They considered her patronizing.

It was something they couldn't say about McCall.

McCall knew it would be impossible to explain to Katie why most of the blacks and Mexicans liked and respected him. They understood that his racist remarks were bullshit, his way of indicating that color meant absolutely nothing.

As for Ramirez, he liked the kid and thought he had the potential to be one helluva good reporter.

McCall knew his relaxed attitude about race bothered Parkham, too, but the managing editor merely said, "Do you think he's experienced enough?"

Ramirez was twenty-four, had been working for the paper

18

for slightly more than a year. He had taken the job immediately after graduation from college, a victim of a minority hiring policy.

Parkham's question gave McCall a chance for a little needling, so he replied, "Hell, all I need is someone to handle a few details. Even Turnip might be able to do it."

McCall knew his sarcastic remark angered Sipe, but he also knew the city editor didn't want to get into a pissing contest with him.

Parkham, ready to halt the discussion, asked, "When do you get started?"

"I've already started," McCall replied. "I'll have a major story ready tomorrow night."

"Good," Parkham said. "Just keep us posted."

McCall laughed. "Sure, no problem." He had no intention of telling Parkham or anyone else any more than was necessary. At the moment, he just wanted to get home to Cele.

"And," Parkham continued, "try not to let that temper of yours get us in another lawsuit."

"No guarantees on that," McCall replied.

CHAPTER FOUR

Ed Parkham was forty-two years old, five-feet nine-inches tall. He wore black horn-rimmed glasses that accentuated his orblike face, a face that served as a foreground for deepset and pale blue eyes; and as a background for almost colorless eyebrows, a pug nose and an oversized mouth.

During the time he had been with the *Tribune,* he had developed an intense dislike for Matt McCall. Part of the dislike had to do with McCall's physical appearance, which pretty well matched the reporter's personality.

McCall was a ruggedly handsome man, with the facial coloring of one who had spent considerable time in the outdoors. His ruddy face showed a few lines, but no wrinkles; and the prominent nose, high cheekbones and strong chin were granite-like in visage. There was a small cleft in the chin that went virtually unnoticed, possibly because piercing brown eyes discouraged too close an observation.

McCall's salt and pepper colored hair always appeared windblown, which caused most persons to think he was taller than six feet. But the misinterpreted height was also a result of his bearing. He carried his one hundred eighty pounds in an erect fashion, like a soldier on parade.

Yet he always seemed relaxed, very laid-back.

Parkham had found out early in their association that McCall's laid-back appearance was deceiving. In McCall, he had discovered a tense, quick-tempered man; one who had a short fuse that could easily be ignited. When anger took control of McCall, he was an altogether different person; frightening, at times, to those around him.

Not that his anger was all that visible. It was more like a controlled fire, but Parkham could sense it, and it gave him an uneasy feeling. Parkham knew that under certain circumstances, McCall was not adverse to settling an argument with his fists.

So, McCall's appearance was not the only reason Parkham found for disliking him. He actually feared the man.

He also resented McCall's disdain for authority, especially his cavalier attitude toward the title of managing editor. At the newspaper where Parkham had previously worked, the managing editor was like a god. He had anticipated that kind of reverence from the *Tribune* staff, and by and large had received it; from everyone other than McCall.

Katie Hussey was not a Matt McCall fan, either. She didn't like the way he looked right through her, the way his eyes checked out her soul.

Katie liked to think of herself as a self-made woman, but when McCall looked at her she knew what he saw: a woman who had literally screwed her way up through the ranks. She had, after all, been a society page writer until Parkham arrived at the paper. It was after she started dropping her pants at his command that she moved up to the metro editor position.

Katie knew she didn't love Parkham, knew she didn't even particularly like him. But she loved power, and being an editor gave her some power. And Parkham was a way to keep that power.

She hated confrontations with McCall because he didn't give her credit for knowing anything about news. In fact, he

21

had once told her that she wouldn't know a good news story if it jumped up and bit her on the ass.

The funny thing was, in spite of her hatred for him, Katie felt a certain sexual attraction for McCall. He stirred her, even though she detested his chauvenism. She was quite aware that he had some very old-fashioned ideas about a woman's place, and that place wasn't in the newsroom.

Though she didn't consider herself a beauty, Katie also didn't think of herself as hopelessly ugly. She did carry a bit too much meat on her five-feet three-inch frame. And though she was just in her early thirties, her oversized rear was drooping too much. Her tits were also beginning to sag, complimenting, she supposed, her thick ankles and heavy legs.

The eyes were nice enough, though, emphasized greatly by a nose that was too pointed. And while she did not have buck teeth in the classic sense, they did protrude slightly. She also had a weak chin and what some might refer to as a mean mouth. It was small and straight, the lips narrow.

Her face was framed by shoulder length hair that was straw colored.

Turner Sipe was another who didn't care for Matt McCall, but subconsciously he wished for some of the same characteristics. For example, he would not admit it but he admired McCall's strong opinions on issues, especially his willingness to fight for his beliefs.

Sipe had never been a fighter, had just kind of rolled with the punches that life dealt him. Now in his late fifties, he had started working for the *Tribune* immediately after graduation from college.

Since he was considered to have minimal writing ability, he was initially somewhat of a rural reporter. That entailed visiting small towns surrounding the San Antonio area for the purpose of gathering inane tidbits of information. Occasionally, he even got the opportunity to cover an unimportant college football game.

Sipe was quite aware of his inadequacies, so he played the

game the way it was supposed to be played. He never offended any of the small town readers of the *Tribune,* and he earned his reputation as a "good ol' boy." All his copy read like it had been approved by the Chamber of Commerce.

Eventually, his propensity for putting his nose in the right place paid off. He was awarded a position as assistant to the president of a Baptist university, enabling him to get tuition-free college educations for his two siblings.

When the president of the university tried to sabotage his school's journalism department, he had a willing ally in his assistant. Sipe had never been one to get all hung up on freedom of the press and journalism ethics. The most important thing to him was his relationship with the person in charge.

Sipe would have been quite content to have spent the rest of his days at the university, but when the president retired his successor gave Sipe the boot. He felt very fortunate that the newspaper took him back.

Sipe was quite aware that McCall considered him a weakling when it came to journalism, or for that matter, when it came to anything. He knew McCall thought his return to the newspaper was just another testimony to incompetence being rewarded.

Sipe's reluctant admiration for McCall was tempered by hatred because so many persons on the news staff thought the reporter was so great. They talked of McCall like he was Moses, the only man around with conviction.

And Sipe was bothered by the fact that McCall was such an outstanding investigator and writer, a rare combination. Indeed, it seemed as though McCall had no weaknesses.

There were even those who thought, because of his looks, McCall should have been a television journalist. But Sipe knew, as did anyone who would listen, how much McCall detested television journalism. He was a print man, through and through.

As for ego, Sipe thought McCall had more than enough to

spread around. But Sipe reluctantly admitted to himself that McCall never allowed his ego to become bigger than the story he was covering.

McCall could be faulted for a lot of reasons, but news judgment, the way he covered a story, wasn't one of them.

Sipe saw McCall as an enigma. He seemed outgoing enough, but there were times when he seemed to be an unwilling participant in what was happening. He had been described by another journalist as a gregarious introvert, a description, Sipe thought, that was quite appropriate. McCall seemed to shun friendships and maintained certain acquaintances only because his work demanded it. He was such a private person that most peers knew him only in the context of his work.

McCall's past was shrouded in mystery, and Sipe, like others, had nosed around in an attempt to find out more about the reporter. There were rumors that he had served with an elite group in Vietnam, which was supposedly CIA connected. But McCall always dismissed any questions about his personal involvement.

He would, however, express bitterness about America not winning the war; crediting politicians with the no-win policy and for all the body bags occupied by American soldiers.

And McCall had no sympathy for Vietnam veterans who claimed the war had affected them mentally, or who had become victims of drug abuse. He despised that kind of weakness, often said such persons used the war as an excuse for their ineffectiveness in coping with life.

McCall had served three tours in Vietnam, plus a stint as a journalist. It was his writing about the war that had earned him a Pulitzer.

Unlike the majority of his peers, McCall was a political conservative. Sipe had heard him say often enough that the reason most journalists were liberals was because it was fashionable to be liberal. Sipe had also heard McCall say that journalists, like most people, were unthinking sheep; that they were ready to believe anything the politicians told them.

Sipe figured that, in truth, McCall was apolitical.

But all that aside, Sipe knew that most co-workers admired McCall because he was never intimidated by management or anyone else. It was not a macho thing for him, just a way he chose to live life.

Sipe had always thought reporters should be detached from the stories they were covering, but McCall was always telling him that was bullshit. McCall was quite vocal regarding his subjectivity on issues, wasn't adverse to calling colleagues liars when they claimed to be totally objective. McCall called the journalistic concept of objectivity "mindless buffoonery."

CHAPTER FIVE

McCall awoke early from a fitful sleep. He normally slept soundly after lovemaking with Cele, but during the four hours he was in bed his subconscious had been disturbed repeatedly. It was as though his mind was over-anxious to plot a course of action for covering the Roget murder.

Funny, he thought, I don't really know if there is a major story. Maybe I'm just having premonitions of things to come.

As usual, he felt anticipation and excitement; emotions that were always present when he was covering a big story. It had always been that way, since he had covered his first story.

There was something about the Roget case that bothered him. Maybe it was simply because he knew so little about it, or his suspicion that Parkham hadn't given him all the information about the murder. As to why Parkham might withhold information, he wasn't sure. The possibilities were that Parkham and his cronies were just playing a game with him, or that they were too stupid or careless to realize the importance of every minute detail.

It really didn't matter. He figured that by day's end, he would have more information on the murder than anyone else, including the police.

Though he respected the police, McCall had very little confidence in their plodding investigations. He thought most detectives were unskilled in interviewing witnesses and in powers of deduction and logic. After all, rank in the police department was primarily based on passing some inane test. The entire purpose of the police department seemed to be that of getting the paperwork in order. The department was always inundated with paperwork.

McCall tried to quell the feeling that the Roget murder might be a special story. It could, after all, be just a simple case of a husband murdering his wife; or having it done.

He really couldn't buy the latter, because he figured a paid killing would be cleaner. Unless instructed to do so, a hit man would not have written on the mirror. And it was also unlikely that a professional would have had oral sex with the victim, forcibly or otherwise.

It was more likely that the killer was someone Mrs. Roget knew, and definitely a pervert. Someone like that might have ejaculated in the victim's mouth after she was dead.

There was even the possibility that it could have been a ritual murder.

But the more he thought about it, the more convinced he became that Mrs. Roget knew her killer. He knew he was jumping to some conclusions, but what the hell.

Of course, his theorizing did make the husband a prime suspect. And the fact that Roget had not immediately talked to police, had gone into seclusion, bothered him. But maybe Roget had talked to police later in the evening, or he might possibly even be talking to them now. People did handle grief differently. Maybe he was too shocked and grieved to talk to police right after discovering the body.

But most people, especially under such circumstances, didn't know they had a choice. And the police could be pretty demanding.

McCall's mind wandered to how he might react if Cele were

murdered. He was fairly certain that his grief would be tempered by anger, that he would be most anxious to avenge her death.

A shower and shave, the usual chores associated with getting ready for work, did not distract him from his thought processes. Getting ready for work was something he did in a semi-conscious state anyway.

After he had finished dressing, he kissed Cele on the forehead and left the bedroom, closing the door behind him. She was still sleeping soundly.

She could sleep through an earthquake, he thought.

That was one of the many ways in which they were opposites. He, more often than not, found excuses for not sleeping. And she slept far more than he thought was healthy.

It was still too early to begin contacting his sources, so he went to the kitchen and heated water for instant coffee. After putting a teaspoon of instant and a half package of Sweet 'n Low in a mug, he poured in the steaming water and stirred it.

After one swallow of coffee, he realized that he was hungry. He began rummaging through the refrigerator, but found nothing that appealed to him. For some reason, he craved cold fried chicken.

The craving caused him to recall a humorous minister story, it being that the way a man knew he was called to preach was that he woke up with a hard on craving fried chicken.

When closing the refrigerator door, he noticed a paper taped to it with Cele's handwritten selection of diet meals for the week. He had been too preoccupied to notice it earlier.

Though he didn't think it necessary, she was always on a diet; which meant that when he was home, he was on a diet, too. Her diet.

When he read that she planned to have tuna and asparagus for lunch, he smiled. He planned to have a couple of chili dogs with lots of cheese. He couldn't get chili dogs at home anymore, even when he was watching a ballgame on television.

A further check of the menu showed that fillet of sole was

28

scheduled for the evening meal. Why the hell all the fish? He hated fish. He made a mental note to work past dinner.

It had started to rain. He sat at the breakfast table, drank coffee and watched the raindrops hit and streak down the windowpanes. He liked rain, though at times it reminded him of death. He couldn't remember ever attending a funeral when it wasn't raining.

Of course, it had been different in Vietnam. There, his theory would have required a perpetual rain. But in thinking about it, he realized that he had never actually attended a funeral in Vietnam. He had simply seen dead American soldiers stuffed in body bags and carted off.

For a long time, he had figured that was also his destiny. Or that he would be butchered by the enemy and left to rot somewhere.

Then he remembered that Parkham had not told him Mrs. Roget's first name, nor had he seen a picture of the dead woman. He figured, however, that the paper had gotten the story too late to secure a picture.

Trance-like, he got up from his chair and went to the front door. He opened it, retrieved the newspaper and returned to the kitchen.

The brief story about Laurie Roget's murder was on page one, but there was no picture. And there was absolutely nothing in the story that Parkham hadn't told him.

He left Cele a note that he might be late, suggested that she have dinner without him. He wondered how long it would be before she caught on that he never showed up for dinner when fish was on the menu. He had told her on numerous occasions that he hated fish, but she simply ignored his dislikes in food. She insisted that he eat things he didn't like because they were good for him.

Of course, while it was bad enough to eat certain things, there was also the jogging. She insisted they jog practically every night, in spite of his contention that they could burn up plenty of calories through sexual activities.

He was soon maneuvering the car through traffic, enroute to police headquarters. He was almost certain that Detective Lieutenant Bill Haloran would be handling the Roget investigation, which he thought would be to his advantage. He and Haloran were both adversaries and friends.

After parking the car near the station, McCall was soon entering the lobby of the headquarters building and exchanging greetings with some of the officers he knew. He then made his way through the maze of desks, clutter and noise to Haloran's office. Through the open door, the burly, crewcut detective saw him coming.

"I figured you'd be showing up," Haloran said. "How the hell are you, McCall?"

"I'm fine, Bill. And if you figured it would be me, then you must also figure the Roget killing is something out of the ordinary."

"Yeah, you might say that," was the reply.

McCall couldn't help but notice that Haloran was wearing the same dark blue suit he'd seen so many times before. Actually, the coat to the suit was thrown carelessly across the end of the desk, partially covering a stack of file folders. The detective was wearing a short-sleeve white shirt that needed pressing, accented by what McCall thought was a strange-looking, multi-colored tie that defied description.

"Have time for a cup of coffee, Bill?"

"No, but I'll take it if you're buying."

McCall laughed, the quipped, "Is this some kind of a shakedown? Freebies give you cops a bad name."

"I'll just have to risk some discretion on your part. I don't have a damn cent."

Haloran's revelation of his financial plight didn't surprise McCall. "What in the hell do you do with your money, Bill? It's obvious that you don't spend any of it on clothes."

The detective laughed. "That's tacky. Not all of us can drive a Porsche and wear a two hundred dollar jacket."

"Four hundred dollar jacket," McCall corrected.

"Well, screw you very much," Haloran retorted with a grin. "I certainly didn't mean to belittle you."

"See that you don't," McCall jokingly warned. "I happen to be a very heavy taxpayer."

Haloran chided, "I did notice that you're beginning to get a bit of an innertube around the middle."

"Bill, you could wish that you were as firm as I am all over. And I mean all over."

They enjoyed jousting with each other, but neither let it get in the way of their jobs. McCall knew, for example, that Haloran had once run a check on him. He was pretty sure that the detective had been acting on orders from the chief of police, but also figured Haloran was pro enough to have done it even without orders.

The police chief, like a lot of other city officials, didn't like the idea of a reporter who was as independent as McCall. And they were all a little more than curious about where he got his money, since his lifestyle definitely required more than he received from the newspaper.

The check didn't bother McCall. The Agency informed him of it, and the fact that the chief was trying to get an edge amused him. In fact, he figured the inquiries into his background worked to his benefit.

The inquiries made him even more of a mystery.

For one thing, police discovered that his parents were of modest means. They also could find no record of an inheritance from a deceased relative.

The IRS turned a deaf ear to the police inquiries, and in the attempt to check McCall's military records the problems became insurmountable. It soon became obvious that most of the records about McCall were falsified, which led police to conclude that he had worked for the Agency; and possibly still did. That made him one of them, someone to be trusted.

Haloran, in particular, liked the idea that McCall had been, and might still be, with the CIA. He had, on numerous occasions, pumped McCall for information on his background. However, he soon discovered that McCall was a master at fending off questions and, that more often than not, he was the one who ended up being interrogated.

The detective also liked the fact that McCall's philosophical and political views were closely atune to his own, something he concluded following numerous conversations with the reporter. Though not now obvious because of the midrift and graying hair, Haloran had once been a very lean sergeant in the Marine Corps. So, when McCall launched one of his tirades against Jane Fonda types and liberal politicians, Haloran was a sympathetic ally.

They walked from the police station to a diner they often frequented. It had no name. There, Haloran ordered coffee, orange juice and a couple of donuts.

"What the hell...are you trying to break me?" McCall asked.

"You can afford it, big bucks. Us public servants have to get whatever we can from you citizens."

"What do you have on the Roget murder?" McCall asked.

"Not much at this point."

"Were you at the scene?"

"Yeah, but I didn't get much. We went through all the normal procedures, but haven't gotten anything back from the lab yet."

"Have you talked to the husband?"

"No."

"Where is he?"

"I don't know that, either. His best friend tells us he's too distraught to talk to anyone."

"Don't you think that's a little strange?"

Haloran answered, "Hell, I don't know. I've been at this business too long to think anything is all that strange. Besides, I imagine we'll probably talk to him today."

The typical police way, McCall thought. Just plodding along, in no particular hurry.

"Who's this best friend, Bill?"

"Francis Reynolds. He's an attorney, too."

"Know anything about him?"

"Not really."

"You don't know a helluva lot, do you?"

Haloran laughed.

"You did say you were at the crime scene, didn't you?" McCall reiterated.

"Yeah, I was there."

"Are you going to tell me about it, or do I have to pry it out of you?"

Haloran motioned to the waitress for a refill on the coffee, then answered, "There's really not much to tell."

"Let me be the judge of that," McCall said. "You guys tend to overlook a lot of things that are important."

"And you newspaper types tend to exaggerate unimportant things," the detective countered.

"Bullshit, Bill. You're the most nitpicking guy I know. Don't give me that crap about unimportant things."

Haloran, who knew he had been complimented, replied, "I call it thoroughness." Then, with a grin, he continued, "I'll fill you in on all the nitpicking details on one condition."

"What's that?"

"That you'll brief me on whatever you find out." Haloran knew McCall had sources that were not friendly to the police, that more often than not he uncovered relevant material that law enforcement couldn't.

McCall laughed. "I can't believe you'd think I wouldn't fill you in on everything I discover."

"You asshole," Haloran responded. "If I believed that, then I could convince everyone that I'm another Sherlock Holmes."

"You might be, if you snorted coke," McCall said. "Besides, I already think you're better than Sherlock, so give me what you've got."

"You know, of course, that she was strangled with a macrame plant hanger," Haloran began.

"Yeah, I knew that."

"Did you know that she was nude and that her hands and feet had been tied?"

"I didn't know about the tied part, but I did get a report that she had semen in her mouth."

"That's true."

"You said her hands and feet had been tied. Are you saying that the murderer tied her up, killed her and then removed the ropes?"

"We're not sure about the sequence of events, and we're not sure that rope was used to tie her. But yes, whatever she was tied with had been removed. We're hoping the lab can give us something."

"Had she been raped?"

"Other than giving us information about semen being in the mouth, the coroner hasn't said. But we're talking preliminary report here. I'd have to say, though, that if Mrs. Roget had sex with anyone, other than oral, it wasn't rape."

"Why do you say that?"

"Because she had coffee with someone during the day, and there was no evidence of forced entry. I have to think she knew the killer."

"Maybe she had coffee with her husband before he went off to jury duty."

"So, you know about the jury duty alibi."

"Yeah, and that's a helluva good alibi, especially if the coroner can come up with a time of death during the period when Roget was at the courthouse."

"I can tell you this," Haloran said, "if Roget had coffee with his wife, he must have been wearing gloves."

"The cup was wiped clean, huh?"

"As a whistle."

"If the killer took so much care in cleaning his fingerprints off the cup, I wonder why he didn't just clean up all evidence of having coffee with Mrs. Roget?"

"You tell me," Haloran answered. "You think more like a criminal than anyone I know."

"Very funny. Do you have any idea when this coffee break took place?"

"The preliminary report indicates that it was fairly early in the morning."

"You might be able to be a little more specific if the coroner was more specific about the time of death."

"It would make my job a lot easier," said Haloran. "But then, we're talking preliminary. Maybe he'll be able to pin it down better when we get all the pieces together."

McCall smiled. "Doc Rodale sure doesn't want to get cornered, does he? I'll bet it took him a couple of hours to declare the victim dead."

"Maybe it's because so many defense attorneys have nailed his ass," Haloran replied with a chuckle. "But you're right. He puts a disclaimer on everything."

"The man overdoes it," McCall said. "He's afraid to confirm when he took his last crap."

"He's weak," Haloran admitted. "Real weak."

Dr. John Rodale, in his mid-fifties, was a tall, gaunt Icabod Crane looking individual who had been county coroner for fifteen years. He was cautious to a fault, and his often vague autopsy reports had on numerous occasions stymied police investigations. Police had pretty well quit counting on his reports to substantiate evidence presented at murder trials.

"You know when we can expect the final autopsy report, don't you?" Haloran asked.

"Probably in two or three weeks," McCall joked. "I'm surprised you got the preliminary so quickly."

"One of his assistants did it. Rodale's playing golf this morning, so he wanted everything out of the way."

"I take it that you're not expecting the final report to be much help?"

"Hell no," Haloran answered. "You know how he is. The final won't be that much different than the preliminary. The bastard's a master of vague generalities."

"What can I say? We all have our burdens to bear."

"Mine are a little heavier than most," the detective complained. "By the way, who's your source at the coroner's office. You seem to get information from there before we do."

"Hey, you don't expect me to blow the whistle on one of my sources?"

"Hell, I'm not out to nail him. I just want to use him."

"Well, I can tell you this," McCall said, "Rodale's got some good young people working in his office, but he's so threatened by them that they can't take a shit without his approval.

"But back to Mrs. Roget, what's your theory as to the identity of the mysterious coffee drinker?"

"I definitely think it was the killer because of the absence of fingerprints on the cup. That's about the only thing that makes sense."

"And the husband would have no reason to wipe his prints off a cup," McCall concluded.

"That's true," Haloran said. "I just wish I could talk to that sonofabitch."

"So, what's stopping you?"

"C'mon McCall, you know we're dealing with a lawyer here, one who obviously has some powerful friends. The same rules don't seem to apply that apply to everyone else."

"Bill, I'm not in the mood to listen to all your lamentations about lawyers. We both agree that they are the assholes of the world, but we have to live with them. Do you even know where Roget is holed up?"

"Not exactly."

"What in the hell does that mean?"

"We think he's staying at the home of one of his law partners, but we're not sure."

"Can't you find out?"

"We're trying, but we're having a helluva time getting information."

"So, the legal profession gets away with hiding one of its own under the pretense that he's grief stricken."

"Let's not jump to any conclusions," Haloran cautioned.

"Maybe it's not pretense."

McCall laughed and said, "Sorry, Bill. God forbid that I should be anything other than totally objective."

"All you newspaper clowns claim to be objective," Haloran chided.

"Not me," McCall denied. "You've never heard me say that I'm objective, and you never will."

Haloran grinned. "Come to think of it, you haven't said anything about being objective. And from personal experience, I'd have to say you're one of the most pigheaded, prejudiced bastards who ever lived. You're right. You're not objective."

"Boy, look who's talking," McCall said.

"I need to get back to the office," Haloran said. "I can't sit around here drinking coffee with you all day. I have work to do."

McCall slurred the word, "brother," then joined Haloran in exiting the booth. He paid the bill and they began walking back to the police station.

"Bill, was there any other physical evidence in the kitchen?"

"Nothing," Haloran said. "Just the two cups and a half empty pack of Sweet'n Low. I thought about you, because you always use half a pack."

"Maybe Mrs. Roget used it."

"Naw, it was used in the cup that was wiped clean."

"You mean there was still some coffee in that cup?"

"In both cups."

McCall shook his head in bewilderment. "Why in the hell didn't the murderer wash out the cup? Why just clean the outside of it?"

"Don't ask me," Haloran said.

"Did you get anything from the neighbors?"

"We checked the neighbors and couldn't find anyone who had even been in the Roget house."

"Don't you think that's strange?"

"I don't know," Haloran answered. "Do you visit with your

neighbors? Have you been in the home of just one of your neighbors?"

McCall laughed. "You got me there, but I'm not a family man. And I live in a condo, not a house. Besides, everyone knows I'm a little weird."

"Little weird, hell. Your weirdness doesn't have any boundaries."

"Whoa, William. Keep up that kind of talk and I'll sue you for slander."

"Why sue me? I'm more complimentary of you than anyone else is."

McCall feigned hurt. "That's not true. I happen to be one of the most beloved and respected newspapermen in this town."

"Whew! If that's the case, newspapermen should never go anywhere without bodyguards."

"Enough," McCall said. "Did any of the neighbors notice anything unusual at the Roget house on the day of the murder?"

"A kid said he thought he saw a department store van in front of the house, but wasn't sure."

"Was there anything else about the murder scene that was peculiar?"

By now they had entered the police station.

"Yeah, the victim's clothing was all folded and neatly stacked."

"You mean the clothing you think she was wearing?"

"Well, I'm pretty sure the robe, nightgown and panties belonged to Mrs. Roget. I don't think the killer wore them to the house."

They entered Haloran's office and the reporter plopped himself down in a chair. Haloran took the chair behind his desk.

"Do you think it was the killer who folded and stacked the clothes?" McCall asked.

"Who else?"

"There's always the husband or his friend, the one who

38

called the police."

"You're right, but I'm ninety-nine percent sure it was the killer, and I'm guessing he did it after she was dead. And yes, before you ask, I do find that kind of neatness a bit strange."

"How about the lipstick message?"

"Who knows?" the detective answered with a shrug of the shoulders. "Maybe it's just an attempt by the killer to confuse us. Maybe it's just the work of a sick mind."

"The killer must be an amateur," McCall quipped, "or he'd know that it doesn't take anything that elaborate to throw you guys off the trail."

"Kiss it, McCall."

"What about the baby?"

"He's with his grandparents."

"The mother's or father's?"

"Hers."

"Is there anything else you can tell me?"

"Only that the house was too clean."

"What do you mean?"

"I'm saying it was abnormally clean," Haloran replied. "Things you'd expect to find in any house just weren't there."

"Such as?"

"Bills, magazines, stuff like that."

"Do you think someone did a little housekeeping before the police arrived?"

"It sure looks that way."

"Maybe the killer is a neatnik."

"I can't buy that."

"You think the husband may have done some cleaning?"

"Yeah, him or his buddy. But I can't figure why he felt it was necessary."

"Well, don't ask me, you're the cop. By the way, are you going to provide me copies of the police reports?"

"You know I can't do that," Haloran said. Then he reached in a desk drawer and brought forth a buff-colored envelope, which he handed to McCall. "It's all there. You expect too much, though. Do you know that?"

McCall grinned. "Yeah, but I'm obviously getting too predictable."

"It didn't take any great detective work to know that you were going to ask for that stuff. Just promise that you won't quote me. I don't want to get my ass in a sling with the chief."

"Don't worry," McCall assured. "Are you going to let me see the pictures?"

"Why in the hell do you want to see pictures of a dead woman? Never mind answering that. I've got to get rid of some of this coffee."

As he was leaving, Haloran pushed a folder of photos across the desk in McCall's direction. When McCall opened the folder and saw the nude, lifeless body of Laurie Roget, the story became more personal.

He knew the victim.

He had known her very well.

CHAPTER SIX

McCall had first met Laurie Roget about three years before. She had been wearing a nurse's uniform, rummaging through a supermarket's produce section, selecting the ingredients for a salad.

Liking what he saw, and not being the bashful sort, he had approached her and tried to strike up a conversation. It had been difficult. He recalled her shyness during that first encounter. She reminded him of a scared rabbit.

"The lettuce leaves a lot to be desired," he said.

She seemed startled by his voice, and probably by the fact that his eyes practically undressed her. "It does," she responded. "It certainly does."

"Tell me," he said, "how important is it that I eat this kind of junk?"

"What do you mean?"

"Well, you're obviously a nurse, probably know a lot about nutrition. I just want to know if I need any of this green stuff to support my normal diet of chili dogs and potato chips?"

"Yuk," she responded. "I can't believe anyone eats chili dogs." She had trouble looking in his eyes.

41

McCall had laughed and said, "Chili dogs are what makes this country great."

It was smalltalk. Meaningless, really. Laurie had later told him that she knew he wasn't talking to her to ask advice, that it was his real motive that had made her so nervous. She had also said that she would have walked away, ignored him, had it not been for the fact that he was so pleasant. The store was also crowded, and she said the numbers made her feel safe.

"If the only meat I could get was in a chili dog, then I'd be a vegetarian," Laurie had said.

"You'd be a beautiful one."

"Thank you."

"You're more than welcome. By the way, my name's Matt McCall."

"My name's Laurie. Laurie Fuller."

Fuller. That was the only last name he had ever known her by. Maybe she hadn't been married at the time. He recalled that he had checked her left hand. There had been no wedding band.

"Now that we have been formally introduced," he had said, "how about joining me for a cup of coffee?"

"No, I don't think so."

"Is it because you're too busy, or are you afraid that I might attack you?"

She had laughed. "If you were going to attack someone, I'd think you would want a little more privacy."

"So, why not have a cup of coffee with me?"

"I just feel funny about it. I don't really know you, just your name."

"How are you ever going to get to know me?"

"You're being argumentative," she had countered with a touch of exasperation in her voice.

"Yeah, here we've known each other for maybe a minute and we're already engaged in a lovers quarrel. Let's kiss and make up."

The ridiculousness of his statement had made her laugh, put

her at ease. He had even shown her his press card, to further relax her.

"I thought your name sounded familiar," she had said.

"You've probably never read anything that I've written."

"Oh, yes I have."

"So, are we going to have that cup of coffee?"

She had laughed and sighed with resignation. "I suppose so."

There was a deli in the store, complete with booths. They found an empty one and, while Laurie seated herself, McCall went to the counter and ordered coffee. He recalled that while the uniformed girl behind the counter was pouring the coffee into styrofoam cups, he had turned to Laurie and asked, "Do you want anything in yours?"

"No," she had responded. "I drink it black."

McCall's recollection of that first encounter with Laurie was as clear as though it had just happened. He even recalled that when he had put a half package of Sweet'n Low in his coffee she had said, "That stuff's not good for you."

Had McCall been aware when questioning Haloran that the murdered woman was the Laurie Fuller that he had known, he would not have asked who had used the Sweet'n Low in their coffee. The Laurie he knew didn't use any type of sweetner in her coffee or tea.

"So, what's it like being a writer for a big city paper?" she had asked.

"Probably like being a nurse, except for the nobleness of purpose."

"You don't consider your profession noble?"

"Idealistically, yes. Realistically, no."

"Why's that?"

"Management, idiocy. A lot of complex reasons, none of which are very interesting."

"Oh, what do you find interesting?"

"You. You're the most interesting thing I've stumbled onto in a long time."

43

She had blushed. "There's nothing interesting about me."

"To the contrary, I find everything about you interesting. Your face, your body, your..."

"Stop. I agreed to have a cup of coffee with you, not to listen to a breakdown of my anatomy."

He had laughed. "There you go with that doctor word. I should warn you that I don't have a lot of respect for the medical or legal professions. I refer to doctors and lawyers, not nurses."

"Well, I'm glad you're not down on nurses, because that could make this conversation more tense than it already is."

"I'm not tense."

"I am."

"There's no need to be. I'm harmless."

"I'll bet. Maybe it's because I'm just not used to being picked up in a grocery store. To tell the truth, I'm not used to being picked up at all."

"I wouldn't call it being picked up."

"What would you call it?"

"Just an opportunity to expand one's range of acquaintances."

"I like that, but I guess I should expect such interpretation form someone who deals in words."

"Maybe. But the simple truth is that I saw someone who I wanted to meet, so I initiated contact."

"Do you initiate such contact often?"

"No."

"I'll bet," she said, then continued with the question, "So, Mr. McCall, are you satisfied with your new acquaintance?"

"More than satisfied."

"With the way I look today, I find that hard to believe."

"You look beautiful."

Thinking about that first encounter and all the subsequent ones, McCall remembered that Laurie was always unsure of her appearance. She was, in fact, a woman who was desperate for reassurance. And he gave her that.

At that first meeting he had asked for her home address and place of employment, the phone numbers for both. While she had refused to provide that information, she did agree to a time and place where they could meet again for coffee.

Had he been so inclined, McCall could have gotten the information he requested from Laurie. He could have followed her, run a check on her automobile license plate, or used any number of investigative procedures at which he was an expert.

But he hadn't bothered.

It was more than just a matter of respecting her privacy. He realized that he was dealing with a fragile psyche, and initially it hadn't made any difference anyway. He had not been interested in developing a longterm relationship.

Laurie had been like so many other women in his life, nothing more than a temporary diversion. And in recalling their first and subsequent meetings, he reasoned that she could never have been anything more.

They had met a couple of times for coffee before she agreed to an evening date. As for the date, he remembered that she had insisted that it be on a Wednesday night. And she had also insisted on meeting him. She had never allowed him to come to her house or apartment, wherever she lived at the time.

He had thought then that she might have been married, but figured that if she wanted to play games it was her business. After all, his reason for wanting to see her had not been a noble one. He had merely thought of her as a welcome change from some of the dreary dredges he often bedded down with at night.

She had not been easy. There were several Wednesday nights together before he was able to coax her into his bed.

Trying to recall how she had been sexually was impossible. He did remember that she was frightened and inexperienced.

Their weekly Wednesday night ritual had lasted for some time, always at his apartment. She never told him where she lived or worked, and he never asked.

He had begun to become a little concerned that Laurie might be falling in love with him, a complication that he didn't want. He simply wanted a Wednesday night from her. Nothing more.

So, on that first Wednesday night when she didn't show up, it didn't particularly bother him. And when she didn't show up on subsequent Wednesday nights, that didn't bother him, either. He had, instead, been relieved. He figured their relationship had run its course anyway, that there was no place it could go.

On the fourth Wednesday night when Laurie didn't show, McCall did not sleep alone. He replaced Laurie, though he couldn't recall the name of the replacement.

Of course, he had forgotten Laurie, too. Until he saw the pictures. Then he remembered her as a sweet woman, one who didn't deserve to die the way she did.

CHAPTER SEVEN

McCall had considered telling Haloran that he knew the dead woman, but thought better of it. The information would have served no worthwhile purpose. Besides, excess information tended to confuse police. He might tell Haloran about it in time, but not now.

As McCall raced his car northeast toward the Roget residence, he wondered it anyone knew about his relationship with Laurie. Did anyone at the paper know? Did Parkham know?

If Parkham was aware, it might be the real reason for his insistence that McCall cover the murder. It might also account for the mysterious game playing by the trio of editors.

No, they couldn't possibly know, he thought. His and Laurie's affair had been most discreet. And Parkham, Katie and Sipe played games with him only because they were stupid, collectively and individually.

No one knew.

And if someone did know, what difference did it make?

His only real concern in the matter was Cele. Even though the affair with Laurie had occurred before they had met, Cele was not the most tolerant and understanding of women. Even the slightest hint of his past indiscretions caused her to turn cold.

And McCall needed and wanted her warmth.

Two police cars were parked on the street in front of the Roget house, a house McCall estimated could be valued from three to five hundred thousand dollars. It was hard to tell.

But he found it intriguing that Laurie had, at least for a brief time, chosen to escape her husband and her affluent surroundings.

McCall had learned from Haloran that Laurie had been married to Paul Roget for eight years. He hadn't been all that surprised by the information. But in recalling his relationship with Laurie, he couldn't help remembering that he had never noticed any telltale evidence of a ring. And he figured any married woman living in this neighborhood would have a rock big enough to choke a horse.

Maybe Laurie had a ring like that and didn't wear it because she was a nurse. That would account for the lack of an impression on her finger.

Of course, the fact that she was a nurse didn't jive either. Not when she lived in this kind of neighborhood.

McCall parked his car behind the two police cars. He knew the cops wouldn't let him inside the Roget house, but he wanted them to be aware that he was in the neighborhood. His snooping always created a little paranoia, which pleased him a great deal. The police always worried that McCall would discover something they hadn't, which he usually did.

As McCall exited his car, he had to make a decision; whether to talk to one of the Rogets next-door neighbors, or one of the neighbors from across the street. He planned to talk to all of them eventually, but considered the first interview the most crucial. It would set the tone for the way he questioned all the other neighbors.

The importance of the order in which persons in a crime environment were questioned was critical.

Quickly analyzing what he saw, McCall determined that his best source of information would probably be the persons living in the house south of and next-door to the Roget residence. They would have the best view of the victim's backyard and patio.

In the midst of his analysis, it shocked McCall to realize that he had been thinking of Laurie as a victim, not as a flesh and blood person who at one time had been a part of his life. The fact that he had thought of her in that way bothered him, and it caused some questions about himself that he didn't want to answer.

He wondered, have I become such a cold, noncaring sonofabitch that no one means any more to me than just another story?

He remembered that he had become that way in Vietnam, insulating himself against caring about the dead and dying. There were so many, the carnage so great that the aura of death pervaded his senses. He had to disassociate himself from it. It was the only way he could retain his sanity.

The morbid flashes weaving an irregular pattern in his mind were jangled into reality by the doorbell he was ringing.

The woman who opened the door was tall and strikingly beautiful. She was wearing a short-sleeved white blouse and yellow shorts that tightly hugged her thighs. The tan, all that he could see of it, was perfect. So was the body.

Flashing his identification he said, "I'm Matt McCall, with the *Tribune*."

She smiled and said, "A newspaperman. I knew you weren't a policeman. You're dressed too nice."

He laughed. "Bill Haloran must have been here."

"I believe that was his name."

"Bill's not going to win any awards for the way he dresses, but he's a good cop."

She shrugged her shoulders. "He seemed nice enough. Did you say your name was McCall?"

"That's right. Matt McCall."

"I knew that you looked familiar. I've seen your face on some billboards around town. You have a pretty famous face."

"Only locally," he replied. He hated the hype being used in the circulation game the *Tribune* was playing against the other paper. He would have been pleased if the woman had said that she read his stuff, but no one mentioned what he wrote. It was just the billboards and television commercials that they remembered.

"Would you mind telling me your name?" he asked.

"Oh, I'm sorry," she replied. "I'm Lanelle Rogers."

"Well, Mrs. Rogers, I hope I'm not interrupting anything, but if you're agreeable I'd like to ask a few questions."

"I'm quite agreeable, but I've already told the police everything that I know."

"Unfortunately, they haven't shared their information with me," he answered with a grin, "nor do I think they will."

She smiled. "I would have guessed as much, Mr. McCall. I'll bet you give the police pure hell."

If she read my stuff, she'd know that I do, he thought.

"The police and I are not enemies, but we do have somewhat of an adversary relationship," he confessed. "I'm completely cooperative, but they're often petty and try to hide things from me."

She laughed, showing her straight white teeth. The laugh was one of those infectious kinds, which was totally congruent with what he surmised was an outgoing personality.

"Mr. McCall, I really don't know you, but I'm sure the reason your eyes are brown is because you're full of it."

"Actually, my eyes are hazel," he replied with a grin, "but I can't imagine what you're talking about."

"Well, I think it probably comes in hazel, too."

He liked her. The sense of humor, the sensuous mouth, the dark eyes, the shoulder-length hair. There were no imperfections except for the smallish tits. A woman like Lanelle Rogers deserved to have big tits.

"All of that notwithstanding, which is a word I use rarely,

50

and never when it lends any particular meaning to a sentence, what can you tell me about your neighbors?"

"I'd just made a fresh pot of coffee and was about to have some when the doorbell rang. Would you care to join me, Mr. McCall?"

"I never turn down a cup of coffee, Mrs. Rogers."

"I'll bet there's a lot that you don't turn down," she teased.

"That's obvious, huh?"

They laughed together. He had met women like her before, those who quickly interpreted his sexuality, who were seemingly unafraid of it. As he followed her through the house and toward the kitchen, he admired her shapeliness, especially the legs. And he couldn't help but be stirred.

"Sit," she commanded when they arrived at their destination, pointing to a small table and two chairs just off the kitchen. It was an intimate little area that might be described as a breakfast nook, but the candles on the table suggested that in the evening it might better lend itself to wine and serious conversation.

McCall positioned himself in a chair where he could watch her activities in the kitchen.

"Do you want anything in yours?" she asked while pouring the coffee into mugs."

"I'll take a little Sweet'n Low, if you have it."

"I've got it. I couldn't live without it."

"Do you know whether or not Paul Roget uses Sweet'n Low?"

She paused in the midst of opening a package of the sweetner, looked puzzled and replied, "How would I know?"

"Well, I thought possibly that you and your husband might have had coffee with the Rogets. Maybe even dinner."

"Hardly. How much of this stuff do you want in your coffee?"

"Half a package."

"That's how much I use."

"I knew that we had a lot in common," he joked, "but I had

51

hoped for something more meaningful."

She deposited a mug on the table before him, sat down in the other chair, and with a smile said, "Give us time."

McCall tasted the coffee and then in a somber tone said, "Maybe I should begin by asking just how well you knew Mrs. Roget?"

"I really didn't know her all that well, and I certainly don't know him. When I saw Laurie outside, I always spoke to her. Sometimes we even chatted briefly, but never about anything important.

"My husband and I have always spoken to him, too, but he always acts as though it's an inconvenience to say hello. In fact, my husband tried to start a conversation with him three or four times without success, so he finally just said to hell with it."

"So they kept pretty much to themselves?"

"That's a real understatement," she replied. "You're going to find that no one in this neighborhood knew her, or knows him. And I think everyone in the neighborhood made a conscious effort to make them feel welcome."

"When did the Rogets move here?"

"It was a couple of years ago. We even had a cocktail party to welcome them, but they never reciprocated in any way."

"Are you sure that they had no contact with any of the neighbors?"

"Mr. McCall," she said emphatically, "none of us have ever set foot in the Roget house."

"Do you consider that unusual?"

"In this neighborhood, yes. We have crime watch meetings, block parties, so much neighborliness that it makes me ill."

"And the Rogets never attended any of those things?"

"You got it. To my knowledge, the party we had welcoming them to the neighborhood was the only thing they ever attended."

"Well, did you notice anything unusual around the Roget home?"

"No. Not unless you consider the lack of activity as being

unusual."

"What do you mean?"

"I'm just saying that they never seemed to do any of the things that are normal for most of us."

"Such as?"

"Well, they have a swimming pool, but to my knowledge they never used it. And they never cooked out or ate on their patio. That's strange to me, because most people here in San Antonio take full advantage of the sun."

"It's obvious that you do. You have a beautiful tan."

"Thanks," she said. "I'm glad that you approve."

"I most definitely do," he replied with a chuckle. "Do you have a complete tan?"

"I think it best that you just wonder about that. It can be another mystery for you to solve."

There it was, the invitation. Or was it?

"You can bet that I'd like the opportunity of working on it."

"Consider yourself assigned to the case. Do you want another cup of coffee?"

McCall glanced down at his empty cup and said, "Sure."

She got up from her chair, took the cup and walked into the kitchen. As she poured the coffee their eyes met. It was unspoken communication, but understood by both of them.

When she returned and put the mug on the table, he pulled her to him and kissed her. She responded for a moment, then quickly pulled away with, "My god, I've got a kid running around here somewhere."

He laughed. "I don't see one."

"Well, he's around here somewhere, and I don't want him to see his mother acting like a fool. My god, McCall, what in the hell are you doing to me?"

"What do you mean? I'm not doing anything." He considered her sudden surge of righteousness a bit melodramatic.

"Do you think that I kiss every stranger who comes through the door?"

53

He figured that she kissed enough of them, but responded as he knew she wanted with, "No, of course not." If she wanted him to think that he was special to her, it was fine with him.

"I'm not sure what came over me," she said.

He raised his arms in mock surrender and replied, "I don't know what came over both of us, but I'm willing to give up to whatever it is."

She smiled. "Kind of nice, huh?"

"You bet. By the way, how old is that kid of yours?"

"He's ten."

"It's hard for me to believe that you have a child that old."

"Flattery will get you everywhere."

"I'm counting on it."

She sat down and said, "I think we'd better get back to talking about the Rogets."

"Probably, though it sounds as though I'm not going to get much information from you or anyone else in the neighborhood.

"But you did say that you talked to Mrs. Roget on occasion. Where did most of your conversations take place?"

"I'd say that most of the time it was in their front yard. Laurie liked to work in the yard, so when I saw her there I'd usually walk over and chat awhile."

"What did you talk about?"

"Nothing in particular. Maybe about her flowers, how they were doing. The baby. Stuff like that."

"So you've seen the baby?"

"Of course. She usually brought him out in the yard with her."

"Did Paul Roget ever join in any of the conversations?"

"No. He was never home when Laurie was working in the yard. When he was home, I don't believe she ever came out of the house."

"He sounds pretty anti-social for a lawyer."

"As I told you, the only time I ever talked to him was at the cocktail party. I thought then that he was a pretty cold fish.

Howard, that's my husband, tried to make friends with him, but the guy is just a real asshole."

"Asshole and lawyer seem to be synonomous terms."

She laughed. "My husband's a lawyer, too."

"Whoops, I guess I put my foot in my mouth."

"Like you say," she agreed, "asshole and lawyer are synonomous terms."

They laughed together.

"I don't have any trouble understanding your description of Roget," McCall said, "but what about Laurie?"

"A frightened woman."

"What do you mean?"

"I mean that Laurie was like a scared rabbit. A lot of women in the neighborhood think that he beat her."

"What do you think?"

"I don't know. I never saw any marks or bruises."

"But you say that you never saw her all that often, either."

"That's true."

"Besides her being a frightened woman, what other impressions did you have of Mrs. Roget?"

"I thought she was beautiful, in a sweet and simple way. You know what I mean."

McCall nodded affirmatively.

"And I think she really wanted to be friends with me and some of the other women in the neighborhood," Lanelle said. "I think he was the problem."

"Any other impressions of him, other than that he's an asshole?"

"It's kind of hard to get an impression of someone you never talk to, only see from a distance. But I do have some impressions, mainly from what I've seen and what I picked up from Laurie."

"Such as?"

"Well, I have to admit that it bothers me to see a man driving an expensive sports car and his wife driving a dinky old car that's several years old:"

"I don't find that unusual," McCall said. "I'm sure that professionally Roget is expected to maintain a certain affluent image. Detective Haloran told me that Roget is in a firm that specializes in corporate law."

"I'm not saying that it's unusual," she replied with emphasis. "I'm just saying that it bothered me."

"Do you mind if I ask you a question?"

"That's kind of a ridiculous question, since all you've been doing is asking me questions."

"Admittedly poor phrasing, but this one is on a more personal level."

"Shoot. If it's too personal, I don't have to answer it."

"I just want to know what kind of car your husband drives?"

"He drives a new Mercedes."

"And you?"

"I drive a dinky old station wagon."

McCall laughed. "I rest my case."

"But I've already told you that my husband is an asshole, too. Besides, it wasn't just the car. It was Laurie's wardrobe, her attitude, everything."

"Explain."

"Well, from things she said I got the impression that she didn't have many clothes, and that she was on an unbelievably tight budget."

"Maybe they had over-extended themselves. That's not uncommon, either."

"You'd certainly never know it from the way he dresses. He's a high-roller, I can tell you that."

"Again, that could be part of a required image."

"No, what I'm talking about is different. He left the house a lot at night, and he was strictly dressed to party. He's one of those open-neck, silk shirt types who wears a lot of jewelry."

"Necklaces and such?"

"Yes. I don't object to a man wearing a chain or medallion, but Paul Roget overdoes it."

"The last time I wore anything around my neck, it was

56

government issued," said McCall. "And its only purpose was to identify you if you were dead.

"But on these night trips, did Roget ever take his wife?"

"Rarely," she said. "And when he did take Laurie, he was wearing a suit."

"So you think the times he took her along were business-related?"

"That would be my guess."

"Do you have any idea where he might have been going when he went out alone?"

"No."

"Did Mrs. Roget ever mention to you anything about her husband's outside activities?"

"Only that he played tennis a lot."

"For someone who doesn't know Roget all that well, you've kept pretty good tabs on him."

"Not by choice," she said. "As I told you, we spend a lot of time in our backyard. And since our yard is elevated considerably higher than the Rogets', it's impossible for us not to see him going to and coming from his garage. His garage is detached from the house and a sidewalk connects it with the patio."

"So Roget is aware that you see his comings and goings?"

"Of course. We've always waved to him and he waves back. Reluctantly, I might add."

"Can you recall anything unusual at the Roget house yesterday?"

"No, nothing. I didn't see Laurie anytime during the day, but that wasn't unusual."

"Any strange cars in the neighborhood, anyone walking around that didn't belong?"

"The police asked that, too, but I can't say for sure. There was a van, maybe a repair truck, that's been parked in front of the Roget house several times recently. It may have been there yesterday, but I can't swear to it.

"One of the neighborhood kids said it was there. And

another one said she saw a man walking in the neighborhood. The kids probably see more than adults. When they're out of school like they are now, they're constantly zipping from one house to another."

"What's the kid's name that saw the man?"

"Barbara Walker. She lives across the street."

"And the kid who saw the van?"

"Ronnie Hollis. He lives next door."

"How old are they?"

"Barbara's eleven and Ronnie's ten."

"I don't believe you told me your son's name."

"Howard, like his father. We call him Howie."

"Well, did Howie see anything?"

"No."

"Can you think of anything else?"

"No, I think I've told you everything that I know."

"By the way, wasn't Mrs. Roget a nurse?"

"That's right, she did work for a doctor before she had the baby. A urologist, I believe."

"Do you remember his name?"

"I'm sorry to say that I don't."

"Do you know where he officed?"

"No, I don't know that, either."

"Well, I can't think of anything else to ask you. And as much as I'd like to spend the rest of the day here drinking coffee and talking to you, duty calls. I need to talk to some of the other neighbors and especially to those two kids, Barbara and Ronnie."

She reached across the table and took one of his hands in hers. "I'm sorry that you have to leave, but if you care to come back tonight, perhaps I will have remembered something else."

"I guess it would give me a chance to talk to your husband."

"I'm afraid not. Howard's leaving town this afternoon. He'll be gone for a few days."

McCall smiled. "Well, maybe young Howie will have remembered something."

She shook her head in mock sorrow. "I'm afraid your luck just isn't running very well. Howie's leaving for camp this afternoon. I'm going to be the only one here. If you get anything, it's going to have to be from me."

"I'll bet you'll think of something for me."

"I'd say the chances are very good."

"What time would be best for you?"

"Why don't we say about nine o'clock."

"That's perfect. By then I'll have filed my story for tomorrow's paper."

"When you arrive, just drive down the alley and park your car in the garage. Our garage is more private than the Rogets' is. It's attached to the house."

"Sounds good to me. By the way, while I'm thinking about it, how about showing me your backyard? I need to see the kind of view you have of the Roget house."

"Sure." She led him through a well-furnished den and through a sliding glass door that opened onto the yard.

The yard was as immaculate as the house. The swimming pool was large, the grass and shrubbery manicured to perfection. The furniture on the patio was tasteful and comfortable-looking, matching the aura of the environment. There was even a redwood-encased hot tub inside a gazebo-like structure.

It was obvious that the Rogers knew how to live well.

The view of the Roget house was as she had told him. The terrain sloped in such a way that the Rogers' eight-foot high fence protected their privacy, but from their vantage point a similar fence around the Roget backyard did nothing more than provide a picture frame effect.

"See what I mean?" Lanelle asked.

"I sure do."

She led him back through the house to the front door and they embraced. The passion within both of them begged for release, but after a few moments she pushed away and whispered, "Tonight."

"Tonight," he agreed.

After McCall left he didn't immediately question the other neighbors. Instead, he drove to a convenience store to make use of the pay telephone. He knew Lanelle would not have objected to his use of the phone in her home, but he had a thing about privacy. He figured the fewer people who knew his business, the better.

His first call was to Eddie Ramirez, the young reporter assigned to work with him on the story. Ramirez was obviously elated at the opportunity.

"Thanks for asking for me," he said. "I won't let you down."

"I didn't think you would, but you might not be so thankful when you find out how much shit work you're going to have to do."

"It doesn't matter," Ramirez countered. "Anything's better than interviewing some Mexican or black who's pissed off at the system. I can't figure why they think I enjoy covering shit about minorities."

"Beats the hell out of me," McCall sympathized. "But if you were really covering minorities in San Antonio, you'd be covering white folks."

Ramirez laughed. "What do you want me to do?"

"Mrs. Roget was a nurse, or at least she worked for a doctor and wore a uniform. I want you to find out where she worked. It may have been a year or so since she was last employed, so consider that."

"Any suggestions on how I should go about this?"

"Yeah. Check with the nursing organization first. And if you draw a blank, check with all the urologists listed in the phone book. Her neighbors said she worked for a urologist."

"Anything else?"

"Plenty. I want you to start building a file. Get all the information you can find on the victim, her husband, parents, everyone connected in any way with the Rogets.

"And stick by the phone. I'm going to be calling you from time to time."

"I'll be here."

"Good. Eat your lunch there, too, because there's no telling when I'll be getting in touch with you. Make sure you have a couple of phone lines available and keep one of them open."

"You got it."

"And find me the name of that doctor, pronto."

Ramirez chuckled. "You speak good Mexican, McCall."

His next call was to Haloran. "Bill, I need a little information."

"So do I. Have you found out anything?"

"Not yet. Nothing that you don't already know."

"What do you want?"

"I want to know about Mrs. Roget's clothes."

"I told you about 'em. They were neatly stacked."

"That's not what I'm talking about. I'm talking about the clothes in her closet. Her wardrobe."

Haloran's tone turned suspicious. "Why do you want to know about that? Are you onto something?"

"I really don't know. Right now I'm just trying to put some pieces together. Now, what about her wardrobe?"

"I don't remember much about it. Is it important?"

"Maybe. And if I knew for sure, I'd sure as hell tell you. What about letting me look in her closet, Bill?"

There was a brief silence before the detective responded. "I don't know. Do you really think that it's important?"

"Like I said, maybe."

"I'll tell you what I'll do, McCall. If you'll fill me in on everything you have, I'll let you take a look."

"You have a deal."

"I'll meet you at the Roget house in twenty minutes," Haloran said.

"I'll be there. By the way, Bill, have you talked to Roget yet?"

"Not yet. I'll see you in a few minutes."

McCall drove back to the crime scene, but this time parked across the street from the Roget house. He read the newspaper while waiting for Haloran. He checked the baseball standings

61

and read what he considered an inane story about a managerial change.

He wondered why San Antonio couldn't attract a major league team. The city certainly had the population, and a lot better fans than could be found in cities like Oakland and Dallas.

His pondering was interrupted by Haloran's query, "What in the hell are you doing, McCall, playing with yourself?"

"That's exactly what I was doing," he deadpanned, "but my hand went to sleep."

Haloran shook his head in resignation and said, "Let's get this over with. I've got work to do."

"I thought this was your work."

"Hell no. My primary job is filling out reports. No one gives a damn if a crime is ever solved. The important thing is having the paperwork in order."

McCall followed Haloran past a uniformed officer and into the house. The furnishings were pretty much what he expected. If he hadn't known better, he would have thought that the same decorator and furniture store were responsible for the furnishings of all houses in the higher echelons of society. Everything looked interchangeable. The pictures on the wall looked as though they had been mass-produced by whoever that entity was that determined good taste in art.

McCall felt as though he had been in the Roget house many times before. He surmised the reason was that he had been in so many like it.

His feeling of knowing the house grew as they entered the master bedroom. He wondered if it was because he knew Laurie had slept there; and it was here where she had made love to the man who was her husband.

The message the killer had left, "Thanks Paul, now we're even," was scrawled across a large mirror hanging on the wall at the head of the bed.

On the carpet was an outline showing the location and position of Laurie's body. But other than the outline and lipstick message, the room looked undisturbed.

"Do you see anything unusual?" Haloran asked. "I mean anything other than the obvious?"

"The neatness of the room bothers me," McCall said. "It doesn't look lived in."

"I know what you mean. Our bedroom looks like a disaster area, but then, my wife isn't going to get any prizes for housekeeping."

"But this is the way you found the room?" McCall questioned. "The bed made and everything in its place?"

"I sure as hell didn't clean the place."

McCall crossed the room and opened the door to a large walk-in closet. Its contents were more of a surprise than he anticipated.

"Bill, did you look in this closet?"

"Sure."

"Did you notice anything unusual?"

"I didn't make a study of the thing, McCall. I just glanced in there. I didn't want to mess up anything before the lab boys had a chance to go over it."

"There's not a stitch of women's clothing in this closet."

"I'll be damned. I guess I was just too preoccupied to notice last night."

What was in the closet was a large selection of designer suits, sportcoats, slacks, ties, shirts and shoes. McCall couldn't say much for Roget's taste, but the stuff was expensive.

"The guy must spend a fortune on clothes," he observed.

"Well, there's no law against that," Haloran said. "I think it's pretty obvious from this place that the man has the money to spend."

"Oh, I wouldn't argue that point, Bill. But I do find it strange that his clothes occupy the entire master bedroom closet. How much space does your wife allow you in the master bedroom closet?"

Haloran laughed. "Hell, I don't need any space. I'm wearing my wardrobe. Seriously, though, I know what you're saying.

63

It's strange."

"I'll bet that I can show you something else that's strange."

"What?"

"I'll bet there's no women's stuff in the master bathroom."

An examination of the bathroom showed that McCall was right. There was a large assortment of expensive men's cosmetics, but nothing that could have been Laurie's.

"I think what we'll find here is somewhat of a role reversal," McCall said. "Hell, Cele took the whole master bedroom closet for herself. And she took the master bathroom, too. I get what's left over, the second bath and the spare bedroom closet."

"That's your own fault, you silly asshole," Haloran said with a grin. "But, of course, I have the same situation at home."

"I'd guess that we're not alone in that respect. Most women want their own closet and bathroom."

"I'd have to say that you have more experience with 'most women' than I do," Haloran said.

It was in another bedroom where they found Laurie's clothes.

"I saw these last night," Haloran admitted, "but I didn't pay much attention. I'm still not convinced, though, that this has anything to do with the murder."

"Neither am I," McCall said. "But would you look at this. Laurie Roget didn't have more than a dozen outfits, and only a couple that could be called dressy."

"I admit it's strange," Haloran replied. "My wife even has a better wardrobe than this. About twenty or thirty times better in fact."

Rummaging through Laurie's clothes and checking the labels, McCall continued with, "Not a designer label in the bunch. These are bargain basement brands. And what's really weird here is the lack of shoes. What have we got here, three pair? You know how queer women are for shoes."

"I know that I get pissed everytime my wife buys another pair," Haloran said. "They're already stacked in the closet like a cord of wood."

"Did you notice, though," McCall asked, "that Roget had at least two dozen or so pairs of shoes?"

"I noticed, but again I have to say that there's no law against a man having more shoes and clothes than his wife."

"That's true, but when you're trying to piece together a puzzle you need all the pieces, even those that don't seem important at the time."

"The problem is that the extra pieces can sometimes do more to confuse than to help," Haloran analyzed.

"I'm willing to take my chances on that."

"It seems to me, McCall, that you've already built up a bad case of animosity toward Mr. Roget."

"Maybe so. But at least part of that animosity is directed toward the police department. It pisses me that Roget is getting special treatment, the kind most citizens wouldn't get."

Haloran's face colored a bit. "You think that I like this kind of shit? I hate these lawyer sonofabitches and all their legal garbage."

"Damn it, Bill, smoke the prick out of hiding."

"I would have done that last night," he said, "but you know how fuckin' concerned the chief is about public relations. He told me to back off. It seems that everything we do offends some special interest group. Evidently, you've become one of those groups."

McCall laughed. "The chief's an asshole. I really do understand your problem, but it still pisses me."

"Your understanding and fifty cents will get me a cup of coffee in a few places."

"Not many."

"Anyway," Haloran said, "I've tried a little public relations with you by letting you see the victim's home. Now, I hope you're going to support your local police by sharing any information you happen to turn up."

"Like you share it with me?"

"Did I detect a bit of sarcasm in your voice? I've given you everything I've got."

"Well, I happened to notice a couple of nurse uniforms in the closet. You didn't say anything to me about Mrs. Roget being a nurse."

"Hell, she wasn't. At least the way I understand it, she hasn't been for some time."

"Do you know where she worked?"

"We haven't checked yet," the detective said, "because we thought some other things were more important. I just thought I'd ask the husband, if I ever get a chance to talk to the asshole."

"I'm sure you'll talk to him eventually. Just remember not to offend him in any way."

"Shithead."

"But a lovable one."

It didn't surprise McCall that the police hadn't yet checked on Laurie's former employment. Nor was he surprised that Haloran was content to wait until he could get the employer's name from the husband. The police were not noted for what they considered unnecessary investigative work. They generally opted for the easy way, which often accounted for their lack of thoroughness. McCall knew that Haloran was a good cop, but he was caught up in the system. And he couldn't do everything on his own.

"If I discover the name of Mrs. Roget's employer, I'll let you know," McCall volunteered.

"I'd appreciate it. Now, if you're satisfied, McCall, I'd better get back to the shop."

"We haven't looked at the other bathroom."

A quick survey of the bathroom Laurie used revealed that she didn't have a lot of cosmetics, and what she did have were of the cheaper variety. A search of bureau drawers also revealed very little in the way of lingerie.

"OK, I'm satisfied," McCall said. "Do you have to go back to the office right away?"

"Why?"

66

"Hell, I was going to buy your lunch."

"In that case, I guess I can spare a little extra time."

They drove to a nearby cafeteria where, in spite of McCall's harassment, Haloran loaded his tray with starchy foods.

"Damn it, McCall," the detective complained, "if you're into mothering, do it with somebody else. Besides, your diet isn't going to win any health awards."

"Hey," McCall challenged, "my gut isn't in the shape yours is in."

Their mealtime conversation was light, laced with the trading of good-natured insults. And though Laurie Roget's murder occupied a large area of the subconscious of both men, for the moment they were content to let any discussion of it rest.

After lunch, Haloran headed back to the police station and McCall telephoned Ramirez.

"What do you have for me, Eddie?"

"The lady worked at Medical City for a doctor named Franklin Barrington," was the reply. "You anglos have weird names."

"Thanks, not for your evaluation of names, but for identifying the doctor."

"I've also got the phone number of the victim's parents. Do you want it?"

"Not now. If I talk to them, it'll be later. They need some time."

"Sipe's been by a half-dozen times asking when you'd be in to do the story."

"I'll be there about six, but there's no point in telling Turnip that. He needs to sweat off some of that baby fat. If he asks you again, tell the sonofabitch that you haven't heard from me."

"You're a cruel man, McCall."

"Thanks."

McCall decided his next step would be to talk to the neighborhood kids who had seen the man and the van. He drove back to the neighborhood and again parked behind the

67

police cars.

His doorbell-ringing at the Walker residence was answered by a short, dumpy woman that he guessed was in her mid-thirties. The shorts she was wearing called attention to her overly-fat legs and buttocks.

"Mrs. Walker, I presume?"

"Yes."

"I'm Matt McCall, with the *Tribune*.

"Oh, yes, I recognize you. Lanelle said you would probably be coming by."

"Then you know that I'm here to talk to Barbara. You, too, of course, if you have any information about what happened yesterday."

"I'm afraid that I don't know much, but come on in and I'll get Barbara for you."

She led him into one of those typical immaculate living rooms, the kind he was sure was never used except to make the guest feel uncomfortable.

"Have a seat," she said, pointing to a Victorian-style couch. "Can I get you something to drink? Coffee? A soft drink? Tea?"

"No thanks, I just finished lunch."

"I'll be right back."

She was gone no more than a half-minute, returning with a chubby-cheeked girl that McCall was sure would one day be a mirror image of her mother.

"Barbara, this is Mr. McCall. He's with the newspaper."

"Hi, Barbara," McCall said. "How about sitting down here and telling me about the man you saw yesterday?"

The girl obeyed, positioning herself at one end of the couch. The mother took a high-backed chair at the end of the coffee table.

"I just saw him walking up the street," the girl said.

"Can you tell me what he was wearing?" McCall had read the interview Barbara had given to the police, but thought they might have missed something.

"He was wearing a blue shirt and blue pants."

68

"Was the shirt light or dark blue?"

"Light blue."

"Was it long-sleeve or short-sleeve?"

"Long-sleeve."

"Do you remember anything about the collar? Did it button down? Do you know what I mean?"

"Yes, it was the kind of shirt my daddy wears to work sometimes."

Oxford style. That was something not in the police report. The only information the report contained was that it was a light blue shirt.

"He wasn't wearing a tie, right?"

"No, he didn't have a tie," Barbara said.

"And the pants were dark blue?"

"Yes."

"Do you remember anything about the man's hair?"

"Brown, I think."

"Was it long, short, thick or thin?"

"Like yours, I think?"

"About medium then. How tall was he?"

"I don't know. Not as tall as daddy, though."

"My husband is six feet tall," Mrs. Walker contributed.

"Was he a lot shorter than your daddy, or just a little shorter?"

"A lot shorter."

"Two inches, six inches?"

"I don't know, maybe a head shorter."

Taking into account that children usually saw their fathers as much bigger than they actually were, McCall figured the man to be anywhere from three to six inches short of six feet.

"Was the man fat, medium or skinny?"

"He was skinny. No, maybe he was about medium. I'm not sure."

"Was he wearing glasses?"

"Sunglasses."

"Can you remember anything about his face?"

"He had a moustache, I think."

"Was his face thin, tan, anything like that?"

"I couldn't tell. He wasn't that close to me."

"Do you recall whether the moustache was thick or thin?"

"I couldn't tell that, either."

"Would you recognize the man if you saw him again?"

"Maybe. I'm not sure."

"Well, I'll say this, Barbara, you're a very observant young lady. You're able to recall more than most adults could under similar circumstances."

His words pleased both mother and daughter.

"Thank you," Barbara said.

"There's one other thing. The wind was blowing pretty hard yesterday, even in the morning when you saw the man. Do you remember if his hair was messed-up, wind-blown, anything like that?"

"It didn't look like the wind was bothering it."

Hairspray. Maybe significant, maybe not.

Before leaving, McCall talked to Mrs. Walker about the Rogets. She recited pretty much the same impression that he had gotten from Lanelle Rogers. She said that from what she knew of Laurie, she liked her. But as for Paul Roget, she was contemptuous.

The woman who answered the door at the Hollis residence was a considerable improvement over Mrs. Walker. Mrs. Hollis was a statuesque brunette, probably the closest thing in the neighborhood to competition for Lanelle Rogers. She was friendly enough, but businesslike in her manner. She led McCall into the den, offered him refreshment, which he declined, then summoned ten-year-old Ronnie to join them.

She was also wearing shorts, and she looked good in them.

"Ronnie," McCall began, "tell me about the van you saw in front of the Roget house yesterday."

His mother interrupted with, "He's not sure that he saw it yesterday. He just thinks that he did."

"Yeah, I understand that," McCall acknowledged. "So what

70

about this van that you might have seen yesterday?"

"It was light green," the youngster replied.

"The van's been there more than once," Mrs. Hollis contributed. "It's a Nichol's Department Store repair truck."

Nichol's was a large regional chain.

"Did you see the van?" McCall asked the woman.

"Not yesterday, but I have seen it there a few times. Laurie told me they had bought several things from Nichol's. A washer and dryer, I believe, and maybe a television set."

"Are you sure that the van Ronnie saw belonged to Nichol's?"

"It did," the boy said. "The name was on it."

"I believe the police report said that you thought you saw it in the afternoon?"

"Yessir."

"Mrs. Hollis," McCall said, "you say that you saw the van there more than once. Do you have any idea as to why it was there?"

"Laurie mentioned something about trouble with one of the appliances, but I really didn't pay much attention."

"Did you have occasion to talk to Laurie Roget often?"

"No, but probably more than most of the neighbors. My oldest daughter babysat for them."

"I wasn't aware that you had other children."

She laughed. "I'm surprised that Lanelle didn't tell all. But I do have twelve and fourteen-year-old daughters."

"I suppose your oldest daughter spent quite a bit of time at the Roget house?"

"No, she was never in it. She did all her babysitting here."

"Don't you consider that a little strange?"

"I really didn't give it much thought. I preferred it that way."

"So, you suggested that Mrs. Roget bring the baby here?"

"No, she's the one who suggested it. But I was glad."

"Why's that?"

"I'm not sure, except that Paul Roget gives me the creeps."

"Anything in particular about him that makes you feel that

71

way?"

"Nothing I can put my finger on, but you know how some people can affect you."

"Yeah. I've got a few editors who give me the creeps."

She laughed.

"By the way," he continued, "were you around Paul Roget much?"

"Very little, but again, probably more than most of the people in the neighborhood. Even though their house is close, they always drove over here to bring and pick up the baby. I would sometimes go out to the car and say hello to Paul, but he never got out. Laurie always brought the baby in and she always picked him up."

"How often did your daughter babysit for them?"

"Probably about once every two weeks. Laurie didn't get to go out much."

"How would you describe Paul Roget?"

"He's slightly built," she said, "maybe five-feet eight or nine-inches tall. And he has brown hair and a moustache. I can't tell you much else about him. I never looked at him for any prolonged period of time."

"Can I use your phone?"

"Of course."

"Do you happen to know the Walkers' number?"

She did.

He dialed and moments later there was a voice at the other end of the line. It was Mrs. Walker.

McCall identified himself and asked, "Do you know whether or not Barbara would recognize Paul Roget if she saw him?"

"I don't know, but I'll ask her."

Through the receiver he could hear an inaudible conversation between mother and daughter. It lasted only a minute or so.

"Mr. McCall, Barbara can't recall ever having seen Mr. Roget."

CHAPTER EIGHT

While Barbara Walker's description of the man walking in the neighborhood might fit Paul Roget, McCall thought it unlikely that they were one and the same. Roget supposedly had a perfect alibi for the day of the murder, though the coroner certainly wasn't providing him any help. Still, at the time when Barbara remembered seeing the man, Roget would have definitely been at the courthouse.

Besides, if the man had been Roget, and if Barbara could identify him, it would be too neat a package. It had been McCall's experience that the solutions to most murders, especially the mysterious ones, were never quite so simple. He had, of course, covered his share of homicides where the identity of the killer was obvious. But he was convinced that Laurie's killer was clever, perhaps to a fault.

He considered questioning some of the other neighbors, but decided their stories probably wouldn't be much different from those he had already heard. Dr. Barrington, he thought, might be his best bet for something new. The doctor might at least give him something personal about Laurie, something that would add meat to the story that he would soon be writing.

Before driving to Medical City, McCall telephoned Haloran and Ramirez. Neither had anything to report. The police still had not talked to Roget, and Ramirez told him that Sipe was on the verge of panic.

At Barrington's office, McCall identified himself to a shapely blonde named Denise. After talking to her a few minutes, he surmised that she was in her mid-twenties both chronologically and in terms of IQ. He finally got across to her, however, just why he wanted to see the doctor.

That prompted an inner-office call and Denise's statement that, "The doctor can't see you now, but his nurse is coming right out."

Denise spoke with a twang, which McCall was willing to forgive because she had nice tits. But upon closer observation he noticed a gap in her teeth. He was unwilling to abide anything less than perfect teeth in someone as mindless as Denise.

"Mr. McCall." The sound of his name came from the mouth of a heavy-set woman wearing a nurse's uniform. She was not all that obese, though she obviously carried some fat on her tall, wide frame. "I'm Mary Murphy, head of nursing for Dr. Barrington."

"Pleased to meet you, Ms. Murphy." He assumed she was unmarried. Since she didn't correct him, he figured he was right about her marital status.

"If you'll come with me," she said.

It was a common but incomplete sentence, which was one of McCall's pet peeves. Her sentence usage was, perhaps, the reason why, when following her down the hallway, he couldn't help but envision an aircraft carrier. The *U.S.S. Elsie,* he thought.

She led him into a sparsely furnished office, the kind with the usual uncomfortable vinyl-clad chairs that give evidence of a medical environment. He had often wondered why the only thing austere in the life of a doctor was his office. And, of course, his first wife. The one who had worked to put him through medical school.

The nurse took the chair behind the desk and McCall took one facing her.

"I understand that you're here to talk about Laurie," she said.

"That's right."

"Well, Mr. McCall, she was not only one of the best nurses who ever worked for me, she was also one of my dearest friends."

"I didn't realize," he sympathized. "I came here to talk to Dr. Barrington, so if this is difficult for you I can just wait until he's free."

"Dr. Barrington wants to talk to you as soon as he takes care of a patient. But I don't mind talking. Maybe it'll help."

It was quickly apparent to McCall that Mary Murphy's sorrow and grief were genuine. It made him like the woman. It also made him ashamed that he had mentally crucified her appearance.

"Tell me, Mary, when was the last time you saw Laurie Roget? By the way, I hope you don't mind if I call you Mary. I'd prefer that you call me Matt."

"I don't mind. As for Laurie, I saw her just last week. She usually came by every other week, brought the baby and had lunch with me and some of the other girls. She was close to them, too."

"I'd like to talk to them, too."

"It was Annette who told me Laurie was dead. She called Laurie last night and Francis Reynolds told her. When she called me, she was hysterical. At first, I thought Annette was trying to tell me that her husband had died."

"Francis Reynolds, that's the husband's best friend, right?"

"Yes."

"Since you were obviously very close to Mrs. Roget, would you mind telling me a little about her?"

"No one can imagine how I feel," the nurse said, tears filling her eyes. "Losing Laurie is like losing a sister or daughter. She was such a sweet and beautiful person. She gave her friendship to everyone. She was a super nurse, a lovely lady."

"How long has it been since she actually worked here?"

"I guess it's been a year and a half. She quit three months before the baby was due."

"So, she was working here when they moved into the current house?"

"Oh, yes. Paul certainly wasn't opposed to her working. I think it would have suited him fine if she had gone back to work right after the baby came.

"And as for the big house, that wasn't her idea. Laurie wasn't the pretentious type, which is more than I can say for Paul Roget."

"I take it that you don't like the man?"

"The feeling's mutual. He detests me and Laurie's other friends."

"Why is that?"

"We're not high enough on the social ladder to suit Mr. Roget," she replied with sarcasm. "He's a prime example of a 'have not' who suddenly got something and let it swell his head."

"He didn't come from an affluent family then?"

"No way. Laurie worked and sent him through school. I think he despised her because deep down he knew she was responsible for his success."

"Whoa," McCall said. "This is something I hadn't heard until now. What makes you say that he despised her?"

"The way he acted the few times I was around both of them," she related. "Besides, it's certainly not unusual for a professional man to despise the person who helped him achieve success. That's why so many lawyers and doctors dump the wife who put them through school."

"I'm sure what you say is true."

"Listen, Matt, I'm an expert. I've got the scars to prove it. I might not look it now, letting myself go as I have, but there was a time when I was a really good-looking woman. And I married a pre-med student who was destined for greatness.

"For almost ten years I busted my buns as a nurse, working the worst shifts and sometimes double shifts so he could concentrate on his studies. And as soon as he didn't need me anymore, he kicked me right out the door.

"Now he makes more money in a year than I'll make in a lifetime. He's got himself a young, good-looking wife who has a Mercedes to drive and a big house to live in. So, I know something about the subject."

"Obviously," he agreed, thinking that if Mary's well-rounded bitterness could be cut into pie-shaped slices there would be enough to feed an army. He wondered how much of that bitterness she had implanted in Laurie, and whether her evaluation of Roget was more personal than factual.

"If I sound bitter and angry," she continued, "it's because I am. I'm no women's libber, but I do hate men who take advantage of women. And Paul Roget used Laurie.

"None of us can really believe this happened to her. All day this place has been like a morgue. We all loved her, and when she was nursing the patients loved her. There wasn't a cruel bone in Laurie's body.

"And as for Paul Roget, those of us who know him think he had something to do with Laurie's death."

"Why do you say that?"

"I just believe it. I can't help but believe it."

"From what I understand, he has an airtight alibi."

"I don't care what kind of alibi he has," she said. "The man is evil and he had something to do with Laurie's death."

"Those are pretty serious charges, Mary. The police are interested in just one thing, and that's proof."

She stared blankly at him. He realized that she wasn't listening to anything he had said, that her mind was locked in on a frequency that exluded input from the outside. He had on many occasions dealt with expressions of remorse, most of which were usually shallow and meaningless. But this woman was genuine. She was hurting. He could not help but feel compassion for her, because he knew in that moment that Mary really had thought of Laurie as the daughter she had never had.

"I've got pictures of her when she was pregnant," the nurse said. "It was me she called when she went into labor. It was me she called and trusted about everything."

"I'm sorry, Mary." It seemed an appropriate response, even though he knew that she was not listening. She was too engrossed in the articulation of her grief.

Mary went on with, "She died of what she feared most. She was cautious. I know she was. Her father taught her to be cautious. She has three sisters and he taught them all.

"I know she didn't leave anything unlocked. She locked everything. She was that way. She was afraid."

"The way I understand it, everything was locked, Mary."

"Then how did the killer get out? And how did he get in, if she didn't know him?"

"All the deadbolts were locked," McCall said, "if we are to believe Francis Reynolds. Roget discovered the body, but Reynolds is the one who talked to police. They haven't been able to talk to Roget yet."

"Matt, I knew this girl in and out, and I can tell you that she was very afraid when she was alone. She would even put things against the door when she heard a noise. She was so frightened that I just can't believe that she would let someone in that she didn't know."

"I can't argue that. And there was certainly no sign of forced entry."

She shook her head in disbelief. "That's why it doesn't make sense. That's why I'm convinced that Paul had something to do with it. Maybe he gave someone a key.

"Anyway, I can tell you that you'd have to kill her to get her clothes off."

"Someone did."

She ignored the remark and continued, "Laurie was such a private person that even the doctor had difficulty getting her to

78

undress for an examination. She didn't want anyone to see her naked, but I guess that's hard for most people to believe. Maybe it's hard for you to believe."

"Why do you say that?"

She just stared at him for a few moments before going on. "I can remember that when Laurie worked here there were some mornings when she would come in looking just awful. I'd ask her what was wrong and she'd tell me that she was just dead tired, that Paul had been out all night and that she hadn't slept. She said she heard noises all night."

"Was Paul gone a lot at night?"

She ignored his question and said, "I've got my own theory about the noises. I think Paul Roget took delight in frightening the poor girl."

"Why would he do that?"

"The man has a sick mind. He made demands on Laurie that just weren't normal. They went far beyond the bounds of what's considered normal for man and wife."

"What kind of demands?"

"I'd rather not say," she replied.

"I don't mind telling you," another voice said.

McCall rose from his chair to greet a smallish, white-smocked man who extended a hand in greeting.

"I'm Franklin Barrington," the doctor said while shaking hands, "and what Mary seems reluctant to tell you is that Paul Roget is a homosexual."

If the doctor had expected some emotional reaction from McCall, he was disappointed.

"Are you sure?" McCall asked matter-of-factly. The doctor's revelation surprised him, but he had been well-trained to exhibit a calm demeanor even when taken off-guard.

"As sure as you can be without actually being involved with one of them," Barrington replied, the distaste obvious in his tone. "Of course, I'm also going on the basis of what Laurie told me about her relationship with Paul. And I can tell you that she didn't even realize what she was telling me. I doubt that she even knew he was homosexual. She was a pretty naive lady."

"I guess the obvious question is, how can a wife not know when her husband is homosexual?" McCall asked. "But I suppose that's fairly common."

"Very true," Barrington said, "and in Laurie's case we're talking about someone totally unaware of proper sexual behavior."

"Hell, I don't even know if I'm aware of what's proper," McCall said.

Barrington laughed. He had taken a chair, leaned back in it, and had plopped his feet on the desk.

"Roget obviously had intercourse with his wife," McCall continued.

"Yes," Barrington said, "but very infrequently. In fact, they did not have intercourse on their wedding night, nor anytime during a two-week honeymoon."

"Mrs. Roget told you this?"

"Yes, but only because she thought her husband's lack of desire was in some way her fault. She was the kind of person who tended to blame herself for everything. Maybe it was because of the kind of Baptist background that she had."

"What's Roget's religion?"

"He's a Catholic," Mary contributed.

"That's sort of a strange union in itself," McCall opined. "But if Roget is homosexual, why did he bother getting married?"

"He needed someone to work and put him through school," Mary said, disgust in her voice.

"What Mary says has some merit," the doctor agreed, "but you also have to remember that Paul Roget is a closet homosexual. That's often the case with those who are in a profession. They like to have a cover because they're paranoid, afraid they'll be discovered."

"I can tell you this," Mary injected, "Paul Roget would do anything to be a full partner in that law firm he's in. And he'd

80

do it no matter who got hurt. That's why he doesn't have any friends."

"He has at least one," McCall reminded.

"Francis Reynolds," she snarled. "Birds of a feather."

"So you think Reynolds is Roget's lover?" McCall asked.

"There's very little doubt about that," Barrington said. "Reynolds is a closet homosexual, too. And, like his lover, I doubt that he has many friends.

"Homosexual lovers may have a few acquaintances, but rarely do they have many real friends outside their relationship. Both are usually too jealous of the other to tolerate either partner having a close friend. Any friendship would have to be mutual."

"What about one of them having a wife?"

"Neither would feel all that threatened by a woman," the doctor said. "It would be understood that a relationship with a woman was only for the sake of appearances."

"Some of this is pretty heavy stuff, doctor. And, of course, it's unlikely that I can use any of it. But you said something earlier about the Rogets having a strange sexual relationship, that Paul Roget made unusual demands on his wife.

"As far as I'm concerned, the deal about not having intercourse on the wedding night and during the honeymoon is strange enough, but what else?"

"It was Mary, not me, who said that Paul Roget made strange demands on his wife," Barrington corrected. "But I would have said it if she hadn't.

"What I'm about to tell you falls into the category of patient-doctor confidentiality, but it can't hurt Laurie now. And maybe what I'm about to tell you will help in some way to nail that bastard, Paul Roget. Because as sure as there's a nose on your face, he had something to do with Laurie's murder."

"Maybe you should be telling this to the police," McCall counseled.

"I intend to," the doctor said. "All of us, everyone here who cared anything about Laurie, intends to tell the police

81

everything we know. But we're not stupid, Mr. McCall. We know that what we have isn't proof of anything. And we also know that the police have hundreds of cases to contend with other than Laurie's murder. So they're not going to get too excited and expend a lot of energy on the speculation of Laurie's friends. Unless, of course, they're prodded a little by the press."

"I'm not sure that anything I write would encourage the police to do anything different than they usually do."

"Tell someone else that," Barrington said. "There's no need for false modesty with me. I know a lot of people in city government who cringe when you get on their case, and the police chief is no exception."

McCall shrugged. "Tell me more about Roget's strange sexual behavior."

"Laurie's life must have been a living hell, but she was determined to make the marriage work," Barrington said. "Earlier you said that they obviously had intercourse but from what Laurie told me those times were few and far between. When Paul chose to have sex with Laurie, it was normally anal sex. Not all the time, mind you, but most of the time. When she talked to me, she couldn't recall one time during their marriage that they had sex when she was lying on her back."

McCall interrupted with, "Pardon me, but I meant to ask you why Laurie talked to you about this?"

"I'm not sure," Barrington replied. "It was about two and a half years ago, and I know she was troubled about something. She talked to you, too, didn't she, Mary?"

Two and a half years ago, McCall thought. That's when I was seeing her.

"Even before then," Mary said, "she told me some things that made me know Paul was strange."

"What sort of things?" McCall asked.

"I can't remember specifically," she said.

"According to Laurie," Barrington continued, "the last time Paul kissed her was at the wedding ceremony."

"That's incredible," McCall said.

"It's true, though," Mary injected. "Laurie mentioned it to me on several occasions. She couldn't understand why he refused to kiss her or touch her. He even made her sleep under the bed when he was mad."

"That's hard to believe," McCall said. "I don't know any women in this day and time who would tolerate something like that."

"Laurie wasn't most women," Barrington informed.

"And she was afraid of him," Mary said.

Thinking back on his moments with Laurie and the strangeness of their situation, listening to the doctor and nurse speak of her marriage to Roget, McCall could now better understand some of the things she said and did. It was as her friends said, she was living a nightmare. And he was but a moment of escape from the harsh reality of a bitter life.

"Still, we're talking about a human being here who had some choices," McCall argued.

"Did she?" Barrington asked. "What you're doing, Matt, is thinking logically. There was no logic to Laurie's life. Roget robbed her of that. It wasn't allowed."

"It's really hard to accept."

"I know," the doctor admitted. "Ever since I heard what happened to Laurie, I've tried to analyze why she stayed in that situation. There's just no logical explanation.

"One of the things he forced her to do before having sex was to watch porno movies. And I'm talking about the hardcore stuff, too. From what she told me, there weren't any females in those movies.

"As I told you earlier, it was almost always anal sex, and she said he turned on a lot of lights when he performed the act. She said he sometimes looked at nude men in magazines while he was doing it."

"If all that Laurie told you and Mary is true, then your statement about extreme demands is an understatement," McCall said. "But my god, we're talking about a nurse here.

83

She had to be more knowledgeable than you indicate."

"Matt, she didn't live in our world," Barrington said. "I'm just sorry that I didn't do something to get her out of that situation. I'm not sure what I could have done, but I should have done something."

"You can't blame yourself," Mary said. "If anyone should have done something, it was me."

"Well, it's too late now," Barrington said. "I'm sorry, Matt, but I have a patient waiting. I think Mary can fill you in on anything else that you need to know."

"I appreciate your time, doctor."

"Listen, we appreciate your coming here," Barrington replied. "We want to help get Laurie's killer, no matter who it is."

After the doctor had left, McCall said, "Good man."

"The best," Mary replied. "Knowing him has kept me from thinking that all men are assholes."

McCall laughed. "I don't guess most of us have many redeeming qualities."

Without disagreeing she began, "Laurie was really scared. The big house scared her and Paul scared her. She didn't tell me that, of course.

"She thought it was her duty as a wife to believe everything that he said. Whatever he said, she thought she was duty-bound to believe it."

"You'd think a man would treasure a wife like that," McCall said.

"Matt, I happen to know that the girl worked her fingers to the bone trying to be a good housewife. Her house was so clean that you could eat off the floors, but her hands looked as though they belonged to a sixty-five-year-old woman. She scrubbed everything."

"From what you and some of the neighbors said about Roget's pretentiousness, I'd figure him to want a maid."

"Are you kidding? Laurie was his maid. He spends plenty on himself, but he never spent it on Laurie. And he didn't give it to her to spend. Besides, if there had been a maid in the house she would have discovered all his porno trash."

"The police didn't find any of that stuff," McCall said.

"Of course not. If it hadn't already been hauled off when he planned Laurie's death, his good friend Francis Reynolds carted it away before the police got there."

"I checked Laurie's closet," McCall said, "and she didn't have much in the way of clothes."

Mary grunted. "She didn't even have any decent underwear."

"Was Roget having any financial problems?"

"No, none whatsoever. He sure doesn't deprive himself of anything. They didn't always have money, but he makes plenty now. In fact, Laurie told me that he told her not to get too attached to the house. He wanted a bigger one."

"He sounds like a man with ambition."

"He's that," she said, "and he doesn't care who he hurts to get to the top."

"Since they were allegedly poor when they got married, did Laurie ever say who paid for that two-week honeymoon?"

"Her parents."

"Tell me about her parents."

"They're good, kind people of modest means. Very strict from what Laurie told me. Paul didn't want to be around them after he finished using them. He wouldn't let them visit Laurie, either. He's an ungrateful dog."

"What about his folks?"

"Poor as church mice. He doesn't have anything to do with them, either. He doesn't think his or Laurie's folks are smart enough to be in the same room with him."

"Does he keep Laurie's parents from seeing the baby?"

"He even tries to keep his own parents from seeing the child. He insisted that the baby be raised a Catholic, but he doesn't give a damn about any religion. He just figured raising the baby a Catholic would hurt Laurie's folks, and he likes to hurt people."

85

"I know there's a lot more you could tell me, Mary, but I've got a deadline to meet. I'd like to talk to you again."

She nodded agreement.

"Here's my business card with my office and home number. Call anytime. If I'm not in the office, they'll transfer you to a guy named Ramirez. I check in with him periodically, so he'll give me your message."

"I'll call," she said, "because I'm going to do everything in my power to see that Laurie is not just another statistic."

"You can count on me to do the same," he said.

"I know I can," she said. "You see, I know about you and Laurie. She told me."

CHAPTER NINE

The fact that Mary Murphy knew about his relationship with Laurie was a bit unsettling. Mary had told him, though, that she had no intention of making Laurie's indescretion known to anyone. Mary didn't want a blemish on her friend's memory.

"And I can't fault her for what she had with you," the nurse had said. "It was probably the best thing she had in her entire life. At least, that's what she told me."

"If that was the case," he had asked, "why did she disappear out of my life?"

"Maybe I'll tell you why someday, but not now," Mary had replied.

Thoughts of his conversation with the nurse bounced around in his mind as he tried to crank out a story for the next day's edition. But for the moment, the screen of the video display terminal was blank. He didn't particularly like working on a computer system. He figured his old Royal typewriter would help him come up with a lead. A lot of stories had been cranked out of it. But the VDT stared back like a blank television screen.

"When are you going to have that story for me?" Sipe asked.

"Get away from me you little asshole. You'll have the story in an hour, if you leave me alone."

Sipe made his way back to the city desk, hoping no one other than Ramirez had heard the exchange.

"Anything I can do?" Ramirez asked.

"No thanks, Eddie, you've done a helluva job putting a lot of these facts together."

"Could I at least get you a cup of coffee?"

"That I could use."

"Half a pack of Sweet'n Low, right?"

"Right."

McCall had called Haloran and found that the police still had not talked to Roget. It didn't surprise him. Someone was pulling some strings and he would damn well find out who.

His brain started the fingers moving and the first graphs of the story began to appear on the screen. Nothing fancy, just the gory details of the murder. However, the unique sentence structure and pace of the story was vintage McCall, the kind of narrative *Tribune* readers expected from him. He had a way of writing that made the reader feel as though he or she was reading a personal letter.

He was also master of inuendo, calling special attention to the fact that police still had not questioned Roget, suggesting that there might be some hidden reason. The wording would create a little smoke in the right places.

It was a good story. Factual, questioning. It captured the essence of what was still a mystery.

"Call it up," he hollered across the room to Sipe. "And if you change a word I'll kill you, you old sonofabitch."

McCall took his cup and made a beeline for the closest coffee pot. He filled it, added the usual sweetner, and made his way to the city desk.

"Good story," Sipe said grudgingly.

"Thanks, Turnip."

"I see you're sharing the byline with Ramirez."

88

"He deserves it. He did a lot of work."

"Well, that's up to you."

"I would hope so."

McCall went back to his desk and telephoned Cele. The phone rang several times with no answer, but he didn't give up. He figured she was either asleep or soaking in the tub. Finally, there was a voice on the other end of the line.

"Is this the lady of the house?"

"It is."

"Ma'am, you've just won a fifty dollar gift certificate to be applied to the purchase of our famous sewing machine."

"Just what I needed. Where are you?"

"I'm at the paper."

"Are you on your way home?"

"Afraid not, baby. I'm going to work late."

"You're going to miss a good dinner. Should I save you some?"

"No, don't bother," he replied, remembering that fish was on the menu. "I'll just grab a bite somewhere around here."

"Now Matt, don't eat any junk food," she cajoled.

He laughed. "Of course not."

"I'll wait up for you."

"You don't have to." He knew that she liked to stay up late anyway, watching late night movies on television.

"I want to."

"OK, I love you baby."

"Love you, too."

After hanging up the phone, he checked his watch and saw that he had a couple of hours to kill. He called Haloran.

"Have you talked to Roget yet?" he asked, already knowing the answer to the question.

"Damn it, McCall, are you going to call me every hour to ask about that?"

"Well, you obviously haven't talked to him or you wouldn't be so testy about it," McCall kidded.

"No, I haven't talked to him," Haloran confessed. "And by

89

the way, Mary Murphy called and said that you suggested that she get in touch with me. I appreciate that."

"For whatever it's worth, you're welcome."

"I'm going to talk to her tomorrow. Also a Dr. Barrington."

"Yeah, I talked to them earlier today. Can you break away for awhile, maybe meet me at the diner?"

"I don't know why not. It looks as though I'm going to be here for the duration."

"I can be at the diner in ten minutes," McCall said.

"I'll be there."

McCall caught all the lights exactly right and parked in front of the diner at the predetermined time. Haloran had already taken up residence in a booth.

"I've already ordered us some coffee," the detective greeted, "which you're buying."

"Hey, I wouldn't have it any other way."

"I was hoping, too, that it being the dinner hour and all, that you'd be kind enough to buy a weary policeman a hamburger."

"You've got to be the biggest damn mooch I know."

"I can't help it if I'm hungry and penniless."

"The truth is that I haven't eaten, either, and I was going to offer to buy you some dinner even before you asked. With inflation and all, it's not often you can bribe a cop for a couple of bucks. It's probably the biggest bargain in town."

"What can I say? We all have our price."

The waitress brought the coffee and asked if they were ready to order.

"Sure," McCall said. "I'll have a couple of chili dogs with cheese, no onions, a large milk and some potato chips."

"That sounds good to me," Haloran said.

"You shouldn't be eating that kind of junk, Bill. Not with that gut of yours."

"Is that going to be all?" the waitress asked.

"I'll have a piece of lemon pie, too," Haloran said.

"Nothing else for me," McCall answered.

After the waitress had left, he asked, "Bill, would it surprise

90

you to know that Roget is queer?"

"Nothing surprises me, but where did you get this information?"

"I got it from Mary Murphy and Dr. Barrington."

"And how would they know?"

"Frankly, I don't think they do know for sure, but they've put a lot of pieces together from things Mrs. Roget told them."

"Such as?"

"I'd rather not say. You're going to be talking to them tomorrow, so I think it best that I not give you secondhand information. I want you to hear what they have to say, then we'll get together and compare notes."

"That's probably a good idea. Going in cold, I might stumble onto something that you missed."

"Exactly. I was pressed for time when I talked to them, and I'm sure that Mary knows a lot more than she told me."

"Of course, whatever they say might not make any difference. He's got one hell of an alibi."

"That doesn't mean he didn't have a part in the murder. Honestly, do you have any idea when you might be able to talk to him?"

"I don't know. So far I haven't been able to get through Winnow. He tells me that Roget will come in as soon as he's able, that right now he's so torn up about his wife's death that he just can't talk to anyone."

"Bob Winnow, huh? He's the head honcho of the law firm where Roget works, right?"

"Yeah."

"What do we know about him?"

"I don't know anything about Winnow or his partner, Darden, except that they specialize in corporate law. And they obviously have some pull in the right places."

"A little pressure, huh?"

"All I know is that the chief told me not to push this business of questioning Roget, that he would come in and talk to us when he was up to it."

91

"Nice."

"In the meantime, Bob Winnow is doing all the talking for Roget."

"And you still don't know where Roget is holed up."

"We're pretty sure he's at Winnow's house."

"I'd think that he would be staying with his friend, Francis Reynolds."

"Yeah, that would make sense. But we also haven't been able to talk to Reynolds since last night when he was at the Roget house. He didn't go to work today, and if he's home he's not answering his telephone."

The waitress brought their food.

"Fast," Haloran observed.

"The age of microwave," McCall said.

They ate in silence until the reporter asked, "Doesn't Reynolds work for Nichol's Department Stores?"

"You know damn well he does. He works in their legal department. And I know what you're thinking."

"Well, it does seem a strange coincidence that he works for Nichol's and that a kid thinks he saw one of the store's vans at the Roget house the day of the murder."

Haloran laughed. "Nichol's doesn't hire attorneys to drive vans. But you'll be glad to know that we ran a check today.

"All vans are checked out on a daily basis and logged in with Nichol's security. Reynolds didn't check out a van yesterday. In fact, he's never checked out a van. Their security people told us they'd consider it strange if he even tried, because only authorized drivers can check'em out."

"I'm sure that you have a list of people who did check out vans yesterday."

"You know we do, but there was no scheduled visit to the Roget residence."

"But I'll bet you know when there was a scheduled visit to the Roget house."

"Of course. It was last week."

"Why must I pry this information from you?"

"Because I don't like for anything to be easy for you, McCall."

"I still think it's a strange coincidence."

"That's all it is. And you have to remember that the phantom van was seen by a kid."

"I've always found kids to be more observant than adults."

"Maybe so, but they don't hold up too well as witnesses. When you have a kid witness, a smart attorney usually destroys his or her testimony."

"That has nothing to do with being observant. That has to do with a stupid system that gives criminals more rights than their victims."

"I can't argue with you on that."

"In this case, though, I don't think the kid really knows when he saw the van."

"That's the way I see it."

"I do think the girl saw a man walking in the neighborhood."

"Yeah, there's not much doubt about that," Haloran agreed. "I just think it's going to take some time to get all the pieces of this case together."

"You won't have all the pieces until you talk to all the suspects."

"You're talking about Roget again. We haven't determined that he's a suspect."

"C'mon, Bill, none of that bullshit with me. No matter how good his alibi is, the man has to be a suspect. Even his pal, Reynolds, has to be a suspect."

"Just see that you don't quote me in the paper as saying they're suspects."

"You know I wouldn't do that."

"That's where you're wrong. Hell, I never know what you'll do."

McCall laughed. "That's good to know. I wouldn't want to become too predictable."

"That should be the least of your worries."

"Would you mind calling me when you talk to Roget?

Reynolds, too, for that matter?"

"Why? You're probably going to call me every hour until I do talk to them."

"Damn it, will you call me or not?"

"Conditional."

"What are the conditions?"

"That you get me four tickets for the Houston Astros series with Los Angeles."

"You bastard. You must have invented the word graft."

"Screw you, McCall. It's not going to cost you anything. You can get the tickets from your sports department."

"It's not the tickets, it's the principle of the thing, asshole. But I'll get'em for you. Just don't think that you're bribing a respected member of the press. This is just more dirt that I can add to the file I have on you."

"Thanks. I don't give a shit about the file, but I appreciate the tickets."

"I also can't believe that you'd drive all the way to Houston to see the Astros play."

"I'm going to see the Dodgers play."

They bantered back and forth for awhile, until McCall announced that he had to go.

"I'll probably see you tomorrow, Bill."

"I can hardly wait," the detective said.

Moments later he was herding the Porsche through traffic, enroute to the northeast part of the city. It was a quarter until nine, and he didn't want to keep Lanelle Rogers waiting.

As she had promised, the garage door was open. He pulled his car in beside her station wagon and killed the engine. That was no sooner done than the door from the house into the garage opened. She stood there in the doorway, wearing a bikini swimsuit.

"My, you're punctual," she said.

"That's not unusual for a man whose entire life is governed by deadlines."

McCall's eyes showed his obvious appreciation of her body,

a fact, he was sure, which did not escape her.

"Well, come on in," she beckoned. "I just opened a bottle of very good wine."

"I should warn you that with a couple of glasses of wine, I become quite amorous," he said.

"That doesn't frighten me," she replied. "If you're being truthful, I'm going to pour the whole bottle down you."

It seemed very natural to kiss her, as though it was something he did on a regular basis. There was passion in their embrace, a longing that seared through their bodies like an uncontrollable fire.

She abruptly pulled her mouth away from his, put her hands on his chest, and tried to push away.

"Not now," she whispered. "Don't be so impatient."

"I'm always impatient," he replied, kissing her neck.

"Let's have some wine and talk awhile."

Typical woman, he thought, programmed to expect some game playing before sexual submission. They all wanted a form of mental foreplay before getting down to the basics. That's why at times he really missed the Vietnamese girls, especially the ones who couldn't speak English. You didn't have to jack around with them to get what you wanted.

"You didn't invite me over here to tease me, did you?"

"No," she replied with a laugh, "but my god, let me come up for air. I might even enjoy your company as much as I'm sure I'll enjoy some other things."

He laughed. "I doubt it. To tell the truth, I'm pretty boring most of the time."

He had released her, and she stood a foot or so away examining his face.

"I don't think so," she said.

"You don't think what?"

"That you would ever be boring."

"Don't make me prove it."

"I won't," she promised. "Now, are you ready for some wine?"

"Why not?"

She led him into the den and they sat down beside each other on the couch. On the coffee table in front of them was an ice bucket containing a bottle of white wine. Two empty glasses stood at attention beside the bucket.

"Would you pour, please?" she asked.

"Glad to. Hope you don't mind if I don't sniff the cork or hold a glass of wine up to the light. I just know how to drink the stuff, not evaluate it."

The wine was good. He hadn't bothered to check the label. But then, he wasn't into being educated about wines, thinking that people who dabbled in such bullshit were hardpressed for something to do.

"Do you like it?" she asked.

"It's good, but it can't compare with the company."

"I'm glad you were able to come."

He responded with, "Me, too."

"Were you able to find out anything else about the Rogets?"

"Quite a bit." He had put an arm around her shoulders and was nibbling on one of her ears. Though she was trying to appear impassive, he could tell that it was exciting her.

"Your job must be pretty exciting."

"It is now."

She turned toward him to protest his attempted humor, but his mouth found hers before she could speak. Her protest turned into a passionate whimper, then she became totally responsive to his embrace.

While his hands were exploring her body, she again pulled away from him and said, "Let's get in the hot tub and drink our wine."

He immediately halted his exploration, thinking, here we go again.

"Why?" he asked.

"No particular reason. I just think it would be nice out this evening."

He was about ready to say to hell with it. After all, he had something nice waiting for him at home. But he decided to play out the hand.

"I don't have a swimsuit."

"My, aren't we modest."

Now she was sounding interesting. He was glad he hadn't folded.

"Well, I'm not all that modest, but I'm not an exhibitionist, either."

She laughed. "You can wear one of my husband's swimsuits, though you might have a little trouble keeping it up."

"I would hope so."

"I'm talking about the waist size."

"He a little pudgy, is he?"

"About like Mamu the whale."

"That slim, huh?"

"C'mon, let's go into the bedroom."

"I've been waiting for you to say that ever since I got here."

"Don't get overly excited. I'm just going to get you the swimsuit."

"Somehow, I guessed that."

"What does that mean?"

"Nothing. I'm just practicing perception."

He followed her into the master bedroom, where she rummaged around in a bureau drawer and came up with a brown swimsuit.

"Here," she said, tossing it to him.

"Thanks, just my color."

She laughed. "Sorry, but my husband is about as colorful as that suit."

"Hey, I wasn't kidding. I like faded brown."

"I'm sure you have an entire wardrobe of it."

"How did you guess?"

She shook her head with resignation. "I'll bet you can be exasperating at times."

"All the time."

"I'm going to get the wine and go out to the tub. Join me

when you get that brown thing on."

After she had left, he undressed and put the swimsuit on. She had been right. It was so big in the waist that he had to hold it up to keep it from falling down around his ankles.

McCall checked himself in the bathroom mirror and grinned. Bill Haloran might fit the suit, he thought, but Lanelle and I could both get in it, which isn't a bad idea.

His mind shifted gears. He wondered if Haloran had talked to Roget.

He waddled through the house and out to the hot tub, holding the swimsuit up with one hand. He was greeted with laughter.

"My, aren't you the dapper one," she said.

"Never mind," he responded with a mock grumble. "Just scoot over and let me in the tub."

After he had submerged himself chest deep in the warm, pulsating water, Lanelle handed him a glass of wine. They touched glasses, then sipped the cool liquid.

"Isn't it a beautiful night?" she murmured.

"It is that," he agreed.

They drank the wine and looked at each other. There really wasn't anything left to be said. He had long since loosed his grip on the swimsuit and it now rested on the bottom of the tub. Simultaneously, they set their empty glasses on the side of the tub and he reached for her. She came willingly into his arms.

Their kisses were passionate, each of their tongues struggling to be master. She whimpered as he removed the top to her swimsuit, then emitted short bursts of ecstatic pleasure when he began kissing her breasts.

He pulled the bottom part of her swimsuit down over her buttocks, and she worked her legs until it sank to the floor of the tub. When she was totally free of it, she pressed all her nakedness against him while her mouth sucked at his.

For a few moments they kissed, pressing and rubbing their bodies together in a ritual of familiarization. Then he reached down and placed a hand between her legs, his fingers searching for the spot that would soon unify them.

With his hands he grasped Lanelle's buttocks and lifted her. She wrapped her legs around him, groaned with pleasure as he penetrated her, then attempted to coordinate her movements with his.

"I didn't know it could be so different," she whimpered.

He didn't respond. He had heard those same words before, and from a number of women. It was as if they all went to some class to learn what to say during intercourse. He didn't give a damn whether it was different or not.

They moved together for at least five minutes before she came.

"Oh, my God," she groaned. "That was wonderful. I've never had an orgasm like that before. You have fantastic control."

He had heard that before, too. But that he believed. He had heard from too many women that a lot of men couldn't control themselves, that they didn't give their partner a chance to come.

"Is your old man too quick?" he asked.

"Let's just say that thirty seconds is a long ride for him," she replied. She had again adjusted to his rhythm.

"Do you know what I want to do?" he asked.

"What?"

"I want to take you to the bed."

"Now?"

"Right now."

She began kissing him and said, "Whatever you want."

They didn't bother to dry off before getting in the bed, but neither of them noticed the wet sheets. McCall began kissing Lanelle passionately on the mouth, then moved down her body.

"C'mere," he said, pulling her up on him. He wanted to be inside her.

They made love for thirty minutes or so, time enough for

Lanelle to have a half dozen more orgasms. Finally, he could stand it no longer and exploded inside her.

As a matter of courtesy, he lay with her for a few moments. He knew a woman was fragile after intercourse, that she wanted to be held.

"Did you enjoy it?" she asked.

"Of course. Did you?"

"It was fantastic. We're magic together."

He laughed. "Well, I am going to have to disappear."

"You're leaving?"

"I have to."

"Damn it, Matt, I forgot to ask whether you're married or not."

"Does it matter? You're married."

"Well, are you?"

"No, but you might say that I'm spoken for."

"You're engaged?"

"Something like that. I live with someone. Why, does it make a difference?" He knew that it did, that a woman like Lanelle didn't want to share a man.

"Of course not," she lied.

He had no trouble reading Lanelle. He knew that if he saw her with any degree of regularity, she would become possessive and jealous, in spite of the fact that she was married and probably wanted to stay that way.

She pouted while he showered and dressed. When he kissed her before leaving, she was unresponsive.

"I wanted you to spend the night," she said.

On the way home he stopped at a small restaurant for coffee and donuts. Cele would expect as much from him as he had given Lanelle.

CHAPTER TEN

McCall was at the paper by six o'clock the following morning, rummaging through the files for information on Bob Winnow and his law partner, David Darden. He didn't expect to turn up much but figured anything that would help him get a fix on the guy would be worthwhile.

Winnow was obviously pulling someone's string, and McCall wanted to know the who and why of the situation.

There was the usual society stuff, Winnow hosting a law school alumni function, his appointment to a United Way committee and so on. McCall did make note of the fact that Roget and Winnow graduated from the same law school. Nothing unusual there. It figured that Winnow, being an influential alumnus, would try to get new blood from his alma mater.

Parties and more parties. That's what the pile of clippings in front of McCall revealed. Winnow was a real social butterfly, along with being a strong supporter of the local, state, and national Democratic Party. It was all there in the clippings, the story of a man committed to social exposure.

But just when McCall thought all the clips would deal with

an elite social circle mentality, he came across a batch that was different.

"Bingo," he said aloud in the empty file room. "Gotcha, you sonofabitch."

The story had taken place while he was in Vietnam, which accounted for McCall not knowing about it. Or about Winnow's involvement. It had to do with County Commissioner Clark Ramsey being accused of bilking a woman out of some property, land that later became the site for a large shopping center. Ramsey had sold the land for several million dollars.

And Winnow had been Ramsey's attorney.

Ramsey was now the district attorney, which certainly might account for Winnow's influence with law enforcement.

Winnow had been the man who fielded questions from the press and assured that there was no substance to the accusation against Ramsey. He had stated that everything his client did in dealings with a Mrs. Helen Webster was legal and aboveboard.

The story gave Mrs. Webster's address as the Sunnybrook Nursing Home.

The accusation against Ramsey had been made by Harold Webster, the woman's son. He had retained a lawyer named David Darden to represent his mother's interests.

Damn, McCall thought, it's hard to believe that these assholes are so blatant.

There were only three brief clips about the alleged swindle, none carrying a byline. He checked the cross reference and discovered that this was the paper's entire coverage of the incident.

It didn't smell right.

He found the phone in the file room and called Ramirez at home. After several rings, a just-awakened voice answered.

"Eddie, get down here right away. I need you."

"McCall?"

"Yeah. Now come on and get moving. We have work to do."

McCall went back to the clips, again checking the society

articles. He checked the clips on Ramsey and found that the D.A. and Winnow moved in the same social circles, were members of the same clubs and served on the boards of the same charitable organizations.

Bosom buddies, he thought.

It probably accounted for the police dragging their feet in questioning Roget. Pressure on the chief from the D.A.'s office. But why? The chief was appointed by the city manager, and the district attorney was elected, supposedly by the people. The fact that district attorney was a political office had always bothered McCall.

If the people only knew, he thought, that the criminals on the streets are Girl Scouts compared to those on city and county payrolls. On any government payrolls for that matter.

He checked the files for information on David Darden. There were a few clips mentioning his name, the most interesting being the one about Darden joining Winnow's firm as a full partner. It was less than three months after the alleged swindle had taken place.

McCall was eager to talk to the reporter who had covered the story. Also to Howard and Mrs. Webster, if she was still alive. It had, after all, been a few years since the incident took place. And the story had given Mrs. Webster's address as a nursing home.

Finding the name of the reporter who had covered the story would not be difficult. He would simply ask Sam Capece. The old guy remembered everything and everybody. Capece had been with the paper for forty years, the last twenty or so as a copy editor.

The problem was that Capece didn't come to work until four o'clock in the afternoon. And McCall wasn't in the mood to wait for the information. He decided to call Capece at his home.

The phone rang only a couple of times before a female voice answered.

"This is Matt McCall. I'm sorry to bother you this early, but

103

I need to speak to Sam. I hope that I didn't wake you folks up."

The voice laughed. "No, we've been up for quite a while. Sam's out working in the yard. I'll get him for you."

While he waited for Capece to come to the phone, McCall made a mental list of questions he wanted to ask. He was pleased that, even after working late, the old guy was up and about. Some of the younger people at the paper could take a lesson from Capece. Cele could sure as hell take a lesson from him.

"Hello."

"Sam, this is Matt McCall."

"Oh, how are you, McCall?"

"I'm fine, Sam, but I'm calling you because I need some information."

"Well, I'll be glad to tell you anything I know."

"This goes a few years back, but do you recall the paper covering a story about Clark Ramsey beating an elderly woman out of some property?"

"Yeah, the shopping mall property."

"Sam, you're a marvel. How do you remember all that crap?"

"Well, I wish I could remember all that people give me credit for, but it would be hard for me to forget that particular story."

"Why?"

"Because it became such a hush-hush affair, even around the paper. I wasn't even allowed to edit the little bit of copy we got on it, but worse still, management dictated that we drop the whole thing. And I happen to know there was a lot more to the story than was ever told."

"Do you recall the name of the reporter assigned to it?"

"You bet I do. He ended up being fired for doing too good a job, but he wouldn't back down. Damn good kid. His name is Dan Wilkens, but I don't know where he is now."

"Who turned up the story?"

"Wilkens. When the woman's son came to the paper looking for help, Wilkens listened. He even suggested that the guy get a

104

lawyer."

"Some kind of legal action was filed, wasn't it?"

"Sure," Capece said, anger in his voice, "but you can search through the court records from now until doomsday and you won't find any record of legal action."

"How do you know that?"

"Wilkens told me. Like I said, he was a damn good reporter to be so young. A bit opinionated, but good."

McCall laughed. "I can't understand people like that, can you? Why weren't you allowed to edit the stories?"

"You know how it is down there. They get a case of the runs every time a reporter turns up something a little controversial on a public official. The paper's lawyers ended up doing more editing on the story than any of the copy editors."

"And being lawyers, they would probably be friends with Clark Ramsey," McCall concluded.

"You said it."

"I noticed there was a lot of basic information missing from the story, so I knew you didn't have anything to do with it."

"I'm sure you can guess who handled everything."

"Turner Sipe."

"You win the cigar."

"I noticed there was no mention of how much Ramsey paid the woman for the land."

"Wilkens had it in his story, but Sipe cut it out. He had a helluva lot of good stuff that didn't make it into print."

"Do you recall how much Ramsey paid for the land?"

"I think it was ten thousand dollars."

"You've got to be kidding."

"No, I'm pretty sure that was the amount. Wilkens was really pissed that it was cut out of the story."

"Hell, I can't blame him. That was the story. It's downright ludicrous because I'm sure Ramsey sold the property for millions."

"Fifteen million if I'm not mistaken. But then, no one ever said life was fair, McCall. But why are you messing in this? I thought you were working on the Roget murder."

"I am, but some of my characters strayed into this area."

"I have to hand it to you," Capece said with a laugh, "you dig so deep that one of these days you're going to involve all mankind in one massive story."

McCall knew Capece's kidding was a form of admiration. "You can't be too thorough, Sam," he replied. "By the way, I'd appreciate it if you'd keep this call confidential."

"You got it. And there are a lot of cases like this Webster thing, McCall. I've often wanted to bring some of them to your attention, but it seems that you're always up to your ass in alligators."

"Damn it, Sam, when I finish up with this murder, let's get together for lunch and you can fill me in."

"I'll look forward to it."

"One other thing, Sam. As rich as the sonofabitch is, why would Clark Ramsey run for district attorney?"

"The only thing I can figure is that he's a man who loves power. You can make a real name for yourself as a district attorney, cracking down on dope and prostitution. The man may have aspirations for the governor's mansion."

"I wonder if there's any such thing as an honest politician?"

Capece laughed. "Honest and politician are contradictory terms."

After he had hung up the phone, McCall thought about Sam Capece. The man was one helluva source.

Ramirez arrived a bit later.

Handing a piece of paper with his scribbling on it to the young reporter, McCall said, "Get me everything you can on these people. The woman's last known address was the Sunnybrook Nursing Home. The home will probably have the son's address.

"Wilkens used to work here, so personnel will probably have an address and phone number. And I want bios on Winnow, Darden, and Ramsey. Make us a file on each of them."

"You want a file on the district attorney?"

"That's what I said."

"How do these people tie into the Roget murder?"

"I don't know how some of them tie in. Maybe they don't tie in at all. But I'm trying to get a little leverage, so just get on it and I'll explain later."

"Are you leaving?"

"Yeah, but I'll be in touch. And keep what you're doing to yourself. Let's not cause our peers any unnecessary worry."

After getting Ramirez squared away, he called Haloran. "Bill, have you had breakfast yet? I'm buying."

"Hey, easy money, if you keep this up, I'm going to save enough to buy a new suit."

"It would be worth it from my standpoint not to have to look at some of the crap you wear."

"You're an easy man to dislike, McCall."

"Thanks. I'll see you at the diner in ten minutes."

This time he beat the detective by a couple of ticks of the clock. When Haloran arrived, coffee was already on the table and the waitress was waiting to take their order.

"Go ahead, Bill."

"Hell, I haven't even had time to look at the menu."

"You already know what you want, so don't waste this lady's time."

Haloran grumbled something inaudible and said, "I'll have two eggs over easy, bacon, hash browns and toast. And bring me a large glass of orange juice."

McCall shook his head in mock disbelief. "You're going to grow to building size if you don't watch it."

"Don't worry about me," Haloran replied while patting his stomach. "I'm solid as a rock."

"I'll have a couple of fried chicken breasts, gravy and biscuits," McCall told the waitress.

After she was out of earshot, Haloran said, "Damn it, McCall, you're always knocking what I eat, but the shit you ordered is more fattening than what I'm getting."

"The difference is that I exercise."

"I don't know about any other kind of exercise that you do, but you sure as hell exercise that mouth of yours."

"That hurts," McCall said with a grin. "I'm only concerned about your welfare."

"Screw you, asshole."

"There's nothing worse than a man with a limited vocabulary."

"A descriptive word is a descriptive word. How many letters it has is immaterial."

"Speaking of descriptive words," McCall interjected, "when are you going to be talking to Mary Murphy and Dr. Barrington about our man, or whatever, Paul Roget?"

"I'm supposed to talk to them at about ten-thirty this morning, and just for grins I'm taking Dr. Sprite with me."

Lewis Sprite was a psychiatrist with the police department, a man McCall had often accused of being a quack. There was no love lost between the two.

"That's great. It'll help Sprite to meet a real doctor."

Haloran laughed. "I think you're too tough on Lewis."

"The hell you do. You think there's about as much validity to a psychiatrist as I do, which is slightly below none.

"By the way, has Sprite come up with one of those psychological profiles of the killer? Those are always good for a laugh."

"Not yet, but he's working on it."

"Remember that I want to talk to you after you've talked to Mary and Barrington."

"Yeah, let's make it at about three o'clock. We can meet in Sprite's office."

"I'm sure he'll be elated at the opportunity to talk to me," McCall said.

The waitress brought their breakfast and gave them coffee refills.

"There's more here than I want. How about taking one of these breasts?"

"Well, if you're sure you can't eat it."

"I'm sure."

When McCall returned to the newspaper, he found that Ramirez had been busy.

"I've got a good bit of the stuff you wanted," the young reporter said.

"Hit me with it."

"Mrs. Webster, she's dead. So's her son, Harold."

"Whoa," McCall said. "This is interesting. Do you have any details about the cause of death?"

"The old lady died of natural causes about five years ago. She died at the nursing home."

"What about the son?"

"He was in some kind of accident. Did you know that he was in the Army?"

"No, I didn't."

"He died two or three years before his mother."

"Where did you get your information?"

"From the nursing home. They couldn't give me the exact date of the son's death, or a last address. They just had him down as deceased on Mrs. Webster's records. But one of the women in the office remembered that he died two or three years before his mother.

"Of course, I'm not surprised that they didn't have his last known address."

"Why's that?" McCall asked.

"Because until I insisted, they couldn't find Mrs. Webster's records. For awhile they were claiming that she never lived there."

"Do you think they were trying to cover something up?"

"No, nothing sinister like that. I think they're just lazy and inefficient."

"Remind me about this again when we've terminated this story and we'll do a little expose' on nursing homes.

"Try to get me some details on Harold Webster's death if you can. And what about Dan Wilkens?"

"His folks live in Portland, Oregon. I called and talked to his

109

mother. She gave me home and office numbers in Phoenix. He's in some sort of public relations there."

"I wonder how in the hell he ended up in San Antonio in the first place?" McCall asked.

"I don't have any idea."

"Maybe he was in the Air Force here."

"Maybe." Ramirez handed McCall a piece of paper with Wilkens' telephone numbers scribbled on it and said, "I should have all the bios by this afternoon."

"Eddie, you do good work. Why don't you go get yourself some breakfast?"

"I could use some."

McCall dialed Wilkens' work number and, after going through a number of female voices, got him on the line. He introduced himself and said, "Because of your experience here, I'm sure there are a lot of things you'd rather do than talk to someone from the *Tribune.*"

Wilkens laughed. "Well, I can't say that I have any love for the paper or for some of the people running it. But I've pretty well put all that behind me. I'm a bit surprised to get a call from you, though."

"Why's that?"

"Hell, you were already a legend when I was working for the paper, McCall. I used to sit in the Alaskan Palace with guys from the newspaper and listen to McCall stories."

The Alaskan Palace was one of San Antonio's more famous bars.

"There probably wasn't much truth to the stories," McCall said.

"It didn't matter. They were good stories. I remember one about you throwing a typewriter at the managing editor, and another about you beating the hell out of a guy who came in the newsroom and threatened you."

McCall was amused. "Well, I guess those stories are true. But I was acting strictly in self defense."

"How about the one where you beat the hell out of a child

110

molester?"

"Well, the guy was caught in the act, but he got off on a technicality because of some sloppy police work. I wasn't able to administer the punishment he deserved."

"I have to admit that I was a bit envious of you."

"I hope it wasn't because I spent more time brawling than writing during my younger days."

"No, it was because you were the best writer I had ever read, and you stood for something."

"Well, Dan, I appreciate that. I've heard some really good things about you, too. Do you remember Sam Capece?"

"I sure as hell do. Great old guy. Does he still work for the paper?"

"Yeah. He's the one who put me on to you. He told me you covered that story about Clark Ramsey beating a woman out of some land."

There was no response, just dead silence on the line.

"Dan, are you still there?"

"Yeah, I'm still here. Damn, McCall, all that happened years ago."

"Are you saying that you don't remember it?"

"Are you kidding? I remember every detail, just as if it happened yesterday. That's the story that got me canned. What's your interest in it?"

"Let's just say that I'd like to see justice done."

Wilkens laughed. "Good luck. I understand that Ramsey's now the district attorney."

"I'm afraid so, but that makes it more fun. I am surprised, though, that you've kept up with local politics after all these years."

"I have some good friends in San Antonio and visit them occasionally. How can I help?"

"Listen, the next time you're here, I want to buy you a drink."

"I'd like that."

"As for how you can help, I want to verify how much

Ramsey paid Mrs. Webster for her land."

"A whoppin' ten thousand dollars for twenty prime city acres."

"That's really unbelieveable. I thought Sam might have been wrong when he told me that. But why in the world did the woman sell that kind of land for so little money?"

"The old woman was senile, McCall. She wasn't competent to engage in any type of business transaction."

"What about her son? Relatives? Why weren't they involved?"

"The son is her only relative, and when she signed the papers he was in Vietnam. He's a career Army man and almost as senile as his mother."

"I'm sure you didn't know, but both of them are dead."

"I didn't know, but I sure don't understand your interest now. With no heirs, Ramsey's home free."

"Don't count on it. I'm coming at him from a different direction than the land swindle, but knowing about it gives me some leverage."

"How and when did Harold die?" Wilkens asked. "The last time I saw him he was in good health and talking about what he was going to do when he retired. He was planning to be a thirty-year man."

"We don't know how he died yet, but I understand it was seven or eight years ago. His mother died five years ago."

"Damn, I'm really sorry about old Harold," Wilkens lamented. "As I said, he was a long way from being smart but he was a decent guy. He wasn't interested in anything for himself, just for his mother. He was genuinely concerned about her."

"Was he ever married?"

"No. I got the impression that he was uncomfortable around women. Except for his mother, of course. Not that he was a fairy or anything like that. He was just shy."

"Do you recall his rank?"

"He was a sergeant, always wore his uniform. At first I

112

thought it might be because he didn't have any other clothes, but later I realized that it was because he was so proud of being a soldier. One thing puzzles me, though."

"What's that?"

"With his limited mental abilities, I can't figure out how he became a sergeant."

McCall chuckled. "Look at it this way. Is it any harder to understand than Turner Sipe being a city editor?"

Wilkens laughed. "Since you put it that way, it's more than understandable. That sonofabitch still at the paper, huh?"

"Where in the hell else could he go?"

"I heard that right after I left he took a job at a university."

"That's right, but they finally wised up and kicked his ass out. But what in the hell brought you to San Antonio anyway?"

"When I was a kid, my dad was in the service there. And my parents got the idea that Trinity University was another Harvard or Yale, so I went to school there."

McCall laughed. "Well, I went to Baylor because I wanted to lead them to a Southwest Conference Football Championship."

"You obviously didn't. They won one back in the twenties and then again recently, didn't they?"

"Yeah, it was a pretty long drought."

"Do you have much contact with Baylor?"

"Are you kidding? They don't even know my name there."

"I figured you'd be a celebrity."

"Too earthy, I guess."

"But back to Sipe," Wilkens said. "I can't think of a media person I despise more."

"I can certainly understand your attitude," McCall replied. "But speaking of despicable characters, what about David Darden?"

"That no good sonofabitch."

"I take it that you're not enamored with him?"

"I'm the one who recommended the bastard to Harold, but

he flat-ass sold out."

"So you know about Darden joining Winnow's firm?"

"Yeah, but that's not the half of it. He agreed to take Harold's case on a contingency basis, but Winnow and Ramsey obviously got to him. After a couple of weeks of supposedly working on the case, Darden presented Harold a bill for almost seven thousand dollars."

"I would mention ethics at this point," McCall said, "but I know it's a word that doesn't apply to most lawyers."

"I can't disagree."

"What did Harold do?"

"Harold had thirty days leave when he got all this started, so he was running out of time and he sure didn't have seven thousand dollars. I think he did pay Darden a couple of thousand, but because of time and money limitations, he dropped everything."

"But, from what Sam told me, you tried to keep it alive."

"Yeah, and I wonder if I did that simply because I felt guilty."

"There was nothing for you to feel guilty about."

"Well, Harold trusted me, and I'm the one who recommended Darden. I think Harold blamed me for what Darden did."

"Why did you recommend Darden?"

"When I first met him, he was a struggling lawyer who convinced me that he was committed to justice and to protecting the underdog. And he was a veteran, so I figured he'd empathize with Harold. He sold me a real bill of goods."

"What happened to the ten thousand dollars that Ramsey paid Mrs. Webster?"

"Funny you should ask, because no one seems to know. The check Ramsey gave Mrs. Webster was cashed at the same bank it was drawn on. And the check was supposedly endorsed by Mrs. Webster. But she never left the nursing home, so she's not the one who took it to the bank. It wasn't Harold because he was in Vietnam at the time. None of the nursing home employees would admit to cashing it, and none of the bank employees could recall handling the transaction. The money never turned up in any form or fashion."

"You're sure there was a check?"

"That I saw. At least I saw a copy of it. What I can't be sure of is whether the endorsing signature was Mrs. Webster's. Darden said it was and I believed him, but at the time I didn't know that he had sold out. It could have been a bogus check. Someone at the bank could have been in on the deal."

"It's good to know that human nature doesn't change, isn't it?"

Wilkens laughed, then his voice turned somber. "I only know that neither Mrs. Webster nor Harold ever benefited in any way from the sale of the property. Harold was paying quite a bit of the cost of keeping his mother in the nursing home, so he was strapped."

"Where did the Websters get the land anyway?"

"It had been in the family for years," Wilkens said. "It was part of a farm Harold's grandfather worked."

"Progress sure is wonderful," McCall said. "I guess we've put concrete over a lot of old farms."

"Like I said, Mrs. Webster was senile when she deeded that property over to Ramsey. There's no telling how he induced the old woman to do it."

McCall thanked Wilkens for the information and told him that he might contact him again. He was relatively sure that he would think of some additional questions for the former reporter.

"I've always wanted to know, McCall, how you ended up in San Antonio?" Wilkens asked. "With that Pulitzer and all the other awards you've won, I know that you could go to one of the biggies."

"I first came here in the military," he said, "liked the place and decided I wanted to call it home."

He had no sooner hung up the phone when Ramirez said, "Call for you."

It was Lanelle.

"I just wanted to tell you how much I enjoyed last night," she said.

"The feeling's mutual."

"Would you be interested in another glass of wine tonight? About nine o'clock."

"I'll be there."

After agreeing, he regretted it. After all, where could a relationship like this go? He was often filled with remorse after the fact.

"Are you going to call Mrs. Roget's folks?" Ramirez asked.

"That can wait until after the funeral. By the way, when is it scheduled?"

"Day after tomorrow."

"Make sure we get some photographic coverage of it. Outside stuff, of course. I want to know who's there. Try to get copies of the pages in the memorial book that people sign. I want the names of everyone who paid their respects."

"You got it."

"Right now," McCall said with a grin, "I'm going to pay my respects to Mr. Bob Winnow."

Ramirez laughed. "I'm sure you'll be welcomed with open arms."

It took McCall about fifteen minutes to drive to the building that housed Winnow's law firm. It was one of those tall, modern structures that gives the appearance of being a mirror.

When he entered the Winnow and Darden suite on the fifteenth floor, McCall was pleased to see that it was typically ostentatious. He would have been disappointed if Winnow had shown any taste.

The receptionist was also typical, a perfect match for the surroundings. She was attired in a tailored business suit, her hair pulled straight back and laced in a bun. He guessed her to be about thirty, probably divorced, and as cold as a well digger's ass.

"May I help you?" she spouted out coldly.

116

"I need to see Mr. Winnow."

"Do you have an appointment?"

"No, but I think he'll want to see me. I'm Matt McCall, with the *Tribune*."

"Just a moment, please." She dialed a number and said, "A Mr. McCall with the *Tribune* is here to see Mr. Winnow." A pause. "Yes, thank you."

Addressing him, she said, "Please have a seat. Mr. Winnow's secretary is telling him that you're here."

"Thanks."

He plopped down on the couch and watched the receptionist try to give the appearance of being busy. She wasn't a good enough actress to pull it off.

"Pretty busy, huh?" McCall teased.

"Yes," she replied frigidly.

The damn woman doesn't have any fun in her, he thought.

He was about ready to test her again when a door opened and a shapely blonde entered the room.

"Mr. McCall," she said, "I'm Celeste Grigg, Mr. Winnow's secretary."

"Pleased to meet you Ms. Grigg."

"I'm afraid Mr. Winnow is not going to be able to see you."

"Why?" He liked the way she looked.

"Well, you don't have an appointment. And Mr. Winnow is busy."

"Is anyone with him now?" Her legs looked superb.

"Not at this moment."

"Then it doesn't seem to me that he's all that busy." Her mouth was very sensuous.

She smiled. "There's more to being a lawyer than just talking to clients."

"I would certainly hope so," he agreed, "but it's real hard for me to comprehend what a lawyer does." The hair was naturally blonde, the eyes a sparkling blue. She was a truly beautiful woman.

"Well, Mr. McCall, I'm afraid there's nothing I can do. Mr.

Winnow just doesn't have time to see you."

"When do you think he'll have time?"

"I'm not sure. Why don't you call later. Perhaps we can arrange an appointment."

"Never mind. I guess he's afraid I wanted to talk to him about Paul Roget."

"I wouldn't know."

"Well, what I wanted to discuss was the alleged Webster land swindle, but if he doesn't have time to talk to me I'll just have to go with what I've got. You might tell him that."

"I will."

He gave her his business card and watched her walk back through the door, snapped off a salute to the receptionist and left.

By the time he got back to his desk, there was already a message to call Winnow's office. He ignored it.

"Have you got anything on Harold Webster's death yet?" he asked Ramirez.

"Not yet. I've got some calls in, but it's going to take some time to cut through the red tape."

"Maybe I can speed it up a bit. Why don't you go out and get us a cup of coffee."

While Ramirez was gone, he called the Agency and asked one of his contacts to check on Webster's death. He hated asking the Agency for help, because for every favor they expected one in return. Still, when you were in a hurry, there was no substitute for the Company's efficiency.

Ramirez returned with the coffee and asked, "What now?"

"Let's just let things simmer awhile. After I finish this coffee, I'm going to take my daily constitutional and read the paper."

"What do you want me to do?"

"Just hang loose and let things start developing. We've baited enough hooks. I'm sure we'll get a bite."

McCall was in the newspaper lunch room drinking more coffee and reading the paper when Ramirez came in and told him that he had a call.

"The guy who's calling sounds like some double-o-seven type. He wouldn't give his name, just said he had the information you requested."

"Thanks, Eddie. Making his way back to the desk and phone, McCall thought, the dumb shits never learn. They want to play cloak and dagger with everyone.

"Hello," he said into the mouthpiece.

"McCall, Arnold here. I have the information you wanted on Harold Webster."

Arnold, the Ol' Man's number one boy. "Good," McCall said. "Hit me with it."

"Looks like your man got drunk and ran a car off a cliff. The car blew and the body was burned almost beyond recognition."

"Where did it happen?"

"Near Fort Ord."

"Anything strange about the accident?"

"Not according to the Army. They treated it routinely. Do you think there might have been more to it?"

"I really don't know, Arnold. Do you have time to check it out thoroughly?"

"I can handle it."

"I'd appreciate it."

Before hanging up, Arnold told him the date of Harold Webster's death, which was fairly close to the time of the alleged land swindle. McCall wondered as to whether he was off-track in thinking Webster's death was anything other than an accident. The fact that he had died at a time close to when the land swindle occurred, however, added to his suspicions. Logic told him that Laurie's death was in no way connected with Webster's, but his instincts wouldn't let him rule out the remotest possibility.

His thoughts were interrupted by the ringing of the telephone. It was Winnow's secretary.

"Mr. Winnow could see you anytime this afternoon," she said.

"It's not necessary that I see him at all," he replied. "But I sure can't see him this afternoon. The only time I have open is seven o'clock in the morning, and it would have to be here at the newspaper office."

If the sonofabitch wanted to see him now, it would be on his own turf.

"I'm not sure that he can see you then, or that he can come down to the newspaper office," she said.

"It doesn't matter to me. I'm not coming back over there."

"He does want to see you."

"Then I guess he'll be at the newspaper office in the morning. I'll pencil him in on my calendar, but hey, it doesn't matter to me whether he shows or not."

"Well, I'll give him your message. Will you be where I can reach you later to tell you whether he will be there or not?"

"What time do you get off, Ms. Grigg?"

"Five o'clock."

"How about just meeting me for a drink after work?"

"I don't know about that."

"Ms. Grigg, are we to be like two ships that pass in the night?" he joked. "Surely, you can spare an aging reporter a few minutes of your time."

"I'm not trying to be difficult," she replied with obvious good humor, "but I tend to think association with you might not be a wise career move."

"So, the die is cast. You'll meet me then?"

She laughed. "Did you hear anything that I said?"

"Do you know where The Plum is?"

"Yes."

"Do you think you could make it from your office to The Plum by five-thirty?"

"I'm sure that I could if I was going there, but I'm going home."

"I could get a good bottle of wine and meet you at your place."

"No, you couldn't. Besides, you don't know where I live."

"You could tell me, or I could just check with the phone company."

"My number's unlisted."

"Please, Ms. Grigg, don't play naive with me. I'm sure that your boss can get an unlisted number as easily as I can."

She laughed. "He has my number."

"Very funny. Well, I'm going to be at The Plum at five-thirty. If you change your mind, meet me there."

"I'll think about it."

"Think real hard."

"You could see Mr. Winnow at five-thirty if you wanted to."

"But I don't want to. I want to see you."

"I'll tell him what you said about seven o'clock in the morning."

"Thanks."

After the conversation, McCall leaned back in his chair and put his feet on the desk. He was fairly certain that Celeste Grigg would meet him. Maybe she would even tell Winnow that he had invited her out for a drink. And maybe the lawyer would encourage her to meet him to see what she could learn.

What a cynic I am, he thought.

During the remainder of the morning and into the early afternoon, McCall worked on a story about the murder. He did sandwich in a lunch break with Ramirez, then, just before three o'clock, drove to the police station. He met Haloran and they went to Sprite's office.

The psychiatrist greeted both of them with a kind of cold disdain, as though they were interrupting something in his life that was much more important. McCall figured that it was good the man was a psychiatrist instead of a real doctor. A field rat would have a better bedside manner.

Sprite motioned for them to take chairs and said, "Let's get on with this. I've got a very busy schedule."

His manner angered McCall, but for the moment he was determined to maintain the peace.

"As I told you," Haloran began, "the reason I wanted

121

McCall here was because he questioned Dr. Barrington and Mary Murphy first. I figured that between the three of us, we might be able to come up with something that will help us with the case."

"I doubt it," Sprite replied. "My assessment of both Dr. Barrington and Ms. Murphy is that their emotional attachment to the dead woman has caused them to reach some illogical conclusions. There is nothing in what they said that could possibly be of value in solving this case."

The man's arrogance angered McCall. He attributed part of it to an overcompensation for shortness of height, but it was still inexcusable.

"Just like that," he injected, the sarcasm dripping in his voice, "you can dismiss what two people say as being unimportant in the case?"

"Yes, just like that," Sprite replied. "Whether you accept it or not, McCall, I am a trained expert in this area."

"It doesn't take much training to be an expert in bullshit."

"That's enough, you two," Haloran interceded. "Let's just stick to the facts."

McCall laughed. "That's hard to do, Bill, when you have someone giving psychiatric evaluations. Fact and psychiatry are worlds apart."

"I hardly think you're qualified to make such an evaluation," Sprite said.

"I'm an expert in bullshit, Lewis, which is why I can see right through you."

"I knew damn well we couldn't have a civilized conversation with you here," Sprite said. "I told Bill that before I agreed to this meeting."

"You're too sensitive, Lewis, or maybe you just need psychiatric help."

"Look," Haloran said, "if you guys will stop insulting each other, we can get on with this. Now Lewis, do you think there's any validity to Ms. Murphy's or Dr. Barrington's assumption that Roget is a homosexual?"

"Not that it makes any difference to the case," the psychiatrist answered, "but I doubt that either of them are capable of making such a judgment about the man's sexual preferences. In my opinion, their affection for the victim and dislike for her husband caused them to make such a judgment."

"Maybe their dislike for Roget is because they sense his homosexuality," McCall said.

"I hardly think so," Sprite said. "Do you think people instinctively know when someone is homosexual?"

"Beats the hell out of me," McCall answered. "I just wait until a guy tries to grab my dong in a restroom, then I know."

Haloran chuckled. "Do you have much trouble with that?"

"Only when I'm using the police restroom."

Even Sprite smiled at the remark.

"Look Lewis," McCall continued, "whether Roget is or is not a homosexual is merely conjecture at this point. But don't you consider his sexual activity with his wife a bit strange?"

Sprite leaned back in his chair and replied, "I don't know what strange sexual behavior is anymore. And we really don't know that the victim was telling the truth about her sex life."

"That's true," McCall agreed reluctantly, "but if she was, don't you think there is some basis to the gut reactions of Dr. Barrington and Ms. Murphy?"

"I'm really not trying to be argumentative," Sprite answered, "but I can't label someone a homosexual just because two people think he's queer. Maybe I'm just too cautious, but until a man comes out of the closet, I feel uncomfortable labeling him a homosexual. To tell the truth, I don't even feel comfortable then.

"Besides, I still don't see what difference it makes to this case as to whether Roget is homosexual or not. Doesn't he have a perfect alibi?"

"Maybe all this doesn't make a damn bit of difference," McCall argued, "but I learned a long time ago that you can't know enough about the players. And in this case, I think his sexual preference might have a lot to do with the murder. I just want to know everything there is to know about everyone connected with Laurie Roget."

Sprite said, "You make it seem like a personal thing."

"Every story I work on becomes personal."

"I thought you journalists were supposed to be objective, unemotional, uninvolved, just recorders of fact," the psychiatrist said.

"Screw objectivity and what everyone thinks a journalist should be," McCall answered. "I'm an advocacy journalist.

"And don't we get into this same damn discussion every time I talk to you, Lewis?"

Sprite grinned. "We always do, but I keep bringing it up in the hope that you'll change; that you'll someday accept what is considered the normal role of a journalist."

"Fat chance of that ever happening," Haloran said. "McCall is the original Lone Ranger, and I think he figures I'm Tonto most of the time."

McCall realized that Sprite was trying to be humorous, so he taunted with, "I can't understand a psychiatrist wanting anyone to play a normal role. If everyone did, you'd be out of a job.

"And that reminds me, have you come up with your normal bullshit psychological profile of the killer?"

"Not yet, but when I do I'll give it to Tonto. He can decide whether he wants to share it with you."

"Funny," McCall replied with a grin. "I'm sure you'll come up with something like you usually do, that the killer is suffering from chronic irregularity because he was not a breast-fed baby, which triggered his violence toward Mrs. Roget, who just happened to look like his aunt."

"I think you've got it, McCall. There's no point in me doing a profile when you have everything nailed down that well."

"If I have any ability in the area," McCall responded, "it comes from having read so many of your bullshit reports."

"What I'd really like to do, McCall, is to give you some

psychological tests."

"It wouldn't do much good. I was a breast-fed baby, still like tits, and I'm regular as clockwork. But I'd agree to the tests if you'd take the same ones, and if you'd agree to have them evaluated by an independent source."

Sprite laughed. "I think you'd be surprised."

"Maybe, but I doubt that you have any tests that I haven't already taken. Besides, there's nothing particularly virtuous about sanity, especially in today's world."

"Are you implying that the tests you took showed you were a tad off center?" Sprite asked.

"That's something else for you to worry about. If I'm not mistaken, the tests showed that I'm capable of a homicidal rampage against psychiatrists. In fact, I kicked the shit out of the guy who gave me the tests."

"That figures," Haloran said. "Sometimes I think you'd rather kick the shit out of somebody than write."

"Most of the time it's more satisfying," McCall agreed. "But I didn't come here for bullshit. I came for information. But I feel like I'm leaving with less than I came with."

"Maybe," said Sprite, "it can be equated with a patient going to the doctor and finding there's not as much wrong as he thinks."

"I can't buy that," McCall answered. "There's too much of a stench for that to be true."

Sprite shrugged his shoulders. "I've told you what I think. Your instincts are obviously telling you something else. And from what I know of you, you'll always go with your instincts."

McCall grinned, "I can't believe you said that, Lewis. Haven't you heard that everything is learned, that there's no such thing as instinct?"

"I have an open mind."

After McCall had left, Haloran said, "Lewis, I think that's the first time you and McCall have been halfway civil to each other."

"Don't count on it continuing. You know I don't like the

sonofabitch."

"But you have to admit he's good at what he does."

"I don't doubt it," the psychiatrist admitted. "He may be a great deal like the killer you're after, so he's already got a leg up on you."

"What do you mean?"

"I know that he's your friend, Bill, but McCall is a man capable of unbelievable violence. I don't think he has any trouble thinking like a killer. For that matter, I don't think he would have any problem killing."

Haloran argued, "Some of what you say is probably because you don't like him."

"No, I'm basing my opinion on all the conversations I've had with McCall. You know that he has a violent temper. And some of the things he says makes me know that he's capable of taking a life."

"McCall's liable to say anything," Haloran said in defense. "He bullshits all the time."

"Well, I'm just telling you what I think. He's your friend, not mine. He might someday cause you some embarrassment."

"You're right about him being my friend, and I'll take my chances on him embarrassing me. And I'm sure that he did do some killing in the war. A lot of people did."

"But I'll bet McCall enjoyed it," Sprite said.

CHAPTER ELEVEN

Back in his office, Haloran gave some thought to what Sprite had said. The psychiatrist was right in saying that McCall had a quick temper. Haloran had seen that often enough. And he did have that streak of righteous indignation when it came to dealing with criminals.

But hell, Haloran thought, I've got that, too.

There was no doubt that McCall was a bit different, but as to whether he was capable of premeditated and unjustified homicide, the detective doubted it. As for justifiable, maybe. It was a little easier to see McCall in the role of an avenging angel.

Haloran didn't tell Sprite, but he admired McCall for his intolerance; his absolute aversion to being forced to accept the status quo. He liked the fact that McCall didn't always play by what were regarded as accepted rules.

He wondered if he might not be the same way if he wasn't forced to accept the legalities of his profession.

Of course, all the speculation in the world didn't really answer that question. Nor could he understand why the doctor's comments had triggered such intense thought about his friend.

Haloran smiled, remembering a recent incident with McCall. He had asked the reporter to meet him at a country and western bar for a drink. While there, a drugstore cowboy had challenged McCall for looking at his girl. McCall responded by tearing every button off the guy's shirt, then offered to take him and all his friends on outside the place. The guy wasn't about to get sucked into that, nor were any of his friends. The cowboy and his pals had simply positioned themselves on the other side of the bar where they could give McCall hard looks.

And McCall taunted them.

In that way, McCall could be a danger to his career. If there had been a fight, he would have been duty-bound to help the reporter. And it wouldn't look too good for a police lieutenant to be involved in a brawl. The chief would frown on it.

He had tried to talk to McCall about the incident, but his response was, "This happens every time I go into one of these damn places. I don't know whether it's the longneck bottles of beer, or that every asshole who owns a pair of boots and jeans hates a guy who dresses well."

McCall's logic was always out of synch with the rest of the world's.

CHAPTER TWELVE

The Plum was not crowded when McCall arrived a few minutes after five. He knew that such a business lull was only momentary, that the place would soon be crawling with three-piece suits and a variety of secretaries in all shapes and sizes. The Plum had never been labeled a "meat market", but it wasn't a bad place to find someone if you wanted to get laid.

McCall hated the place, but it was one of the nicer bars in San Antonio.

He found a corner table that gave him a good view of the front door, ordered a scotch and water, made smalltalk with a skimpily-clad cocktail waitress and observed the clientele entering the bar. He liked playing mental games with himself, observing people and writing stories about them in his mind. He had tried to play the game with Cele, verbalizing the stories aloud. But she didn't like it, thinking that he was, in a sense, invading a person's privacy.

Hell, it was just a game.

There was no missing Celeste when she walked through the door. The three-piece suits all along the bar turned and stared. She saw him even before he got up from his chair. And as she made her way toward the table, most of the male eyes in the place were magnetized to her perfectly shaped buttocks.

McCall held a chair for her and said, "I'm glad you could come."

"I can't stay long."

He grinned. "Neither can I. You're not the only woman in my life."

His attempt at humor eased the minor tension prevalent in a meeting where neither person was sure of the other's intentions.

"You're married then?" she asked.

"No, not really."

"What's this 'not really' business? You're either married or you're not."

"Well, I do live with someone, but we're not legally married."

"Are you planning to make it legal?"

"I don't know."

"Who does?"

The waitress came on the scene, diverting the conversation to a more impersonal question from McCall. "What'll you have?"

"A glass of white wine," Celeste answered.

"I'll have another of the same," McCall said.

As soon as the waitress left, Celeste continued, "Well, Mr. McCall, you didn't answer my question."

"What's this third degree business? I'm the one who's supposed to be asking the questions."

"You're talking to someone who doesn't have any answers," she replied with a laugh.

"Or you won't give any. I'll bet you know more than you even realize."

"About what?"

"For one thing, you might tell me what your boss is like."

"Oh, if I'd known you were interested in him, I would've brought him along. But then, I thought you might be a little

130

interested in me. That was before I learned you were sort of married, though."

She was teasing, but McCall sensed a certain disdain in her voice. Maybe she was a bit interested in him, disappointed because he wasn't available.

He reacted with, "I'm sorry. My job involves so much questioning that it seems like every sentence I make requires an answer. But I really didn't invite you here to interrogate you. I asked you because I wanted to get to know you. And I'm probably not as tied down as you think."

If she realized what he said was in part a lie, she didn't show it. Instead, she smiled with a bit more acceptance than he had anticipated. Maybe, he thought, she's setting me up. He was not one to let his guard down, not for anyone.

"I'm glad," she said, "that you don't consider me a one drink stand. Or do you?"

He liked that. A woman with a sense of humor.

"No, I'd say you are definitely a several drink stand. Maybe several hundred."

The waitress arrived.

"I'll bet you say that to all the girls."

"Hardly. How about a toast to what may be?"

"Why not." The reply was not a question.

They touched glasses before drinking and after she had taken a sip she said, "Smooth. You and the wine. Do you practice your routine often, or is it some sort of natural gift?"

He laughed. "Cut me some slack. I'm the serious type."

"Sure you are," she retorted.

"I am."

"You don't have to bullshit me, McCall. You can romance the hell out of me, even pour a couple of bottles of wine down me, but you're still not going to get my pants off."

"My gosh," he responded, laughing at the challenge. "Can't you accept my intentions toward you as honorable?"

"Forget it. You undressed me with your eyes the first time you saw me."

"If you didn't like it, why are you here?"

"Curiosity, I suppose. It fascinates me that you were able to make Bob Winnow squirm. He's usually Mr. Cool."

"I'm sure your boss isn't afraid of me. He probably just had a bad case of indigestion or something."

"My glass is empty."

McCall motioned to the waitress and said, "You need to drink up, because it may take awhile to get two bottles of wine down you."

She laughed, then soberly said, "The little creep."

"Who?"

"Bob Winnow."

"What's the matter? Has the good Mr. Winnow been putting some moves on you?"

"Are you kidding? Baby, I'm strictly window dressing. So are the rest of the women in the office. For that matter, so's Mr. Winnow's wife."

"What do you mean?"

"You don't know?"

"If I did, I wouldn't ask. You see, I've really never had any contact with your boss."

"If I tell you, you're not going to say anything, are you?"

"Hell no. Confiding in me is like talking to a priest. I never betray my sources."

"I wouldn't trust a priest, and I sure don't want to be one of your sources."

Her glass was empty again. He motioned to the waitress for a refill. She drank wine like most men downed a shot of whiskey.

"I promised not to ask questions," he said, "so I won't."

"You didn't ask," she replied with resignation. "I was in the process of volunteering the information. I just thought you knew that Bob Winnow was queer as a three dollar bill."

"No, I didn't know. I've recently heard talk about Paul Roget, but I didn't know about Winnow."

"Paul Roget," she said with a false laugh. "What an asshole.

You may not believe this, Matt, but there's not a straight guy in the office."

"That's a little hard to believe."

"It's true, though."

"What about Winnow's pal, Clark Ramsey?"

"The district attorney?"

"Yeah."

"I don't know. He calls a lot, but he never comes by the office. I think they see each other quite a bit, though, and they sure talked a lot on the phone today after you came by the office."

"Did you hear any of the conversation?"

"No, but Bob was fidgity as an old woman. I thought he was going to hyperventilate."

"By the way, do you by any chance know where Paul Roget is?"

"I know this sounds ridiculous, but I think he's in Mexico."

"Are you serious?"

"I may be mistaken," she said, "but I'm pretty sure that I heard Mr. Winnow and Mr. Darden talking about Paul Roget and Francis Reynolds going to Mazatlan."

"Do you remember what day that was?"

"It was the day after Mrs. Roget was killed."

The sonofabitch, he thought. He couldn't wait to get out of town with his lover. I hope one of them chokes on the other's sperm.

"Did you know Mrs. Roget?"

"I met her a couple of times. She was nice."

He noticed that her glass was empty. "Do you want another?"

"No thanks. To tell you the truth, two's usually my limit."

"So, there was really no chance of me getting two bottles down you to see what would happen."

"Afraid not. But the truth is, I don't have any pants on, either."

"Now that's interesting, but I'm not sure I can believe you."

"You mean that I'm going to have to prove it?"

"It's the only way I'll ever be able to trust you again."

"Well, my car's in the shop, so I had a friend drop me here. I was counting on you giving me a ride home. If you'll do that, I suppose that I'm duty-bound to prove to you that I'm truthful."

"You have your ride, but I'm providing it only to allow you the opportunity to prove your truthfulness."

"Matt, I have some very good wine chilling in the refrigerator, an excellent stereo system, and a most comfortable bed. I'll show you some truthfulness that you won't forget."

McCall signaled for the check. He remembered that he had promised Lanelle that he would see her at nine. She would have to wait.

CHAPTER THIRTEEN

Bob Winnow showed up at the newspaper the next morning. McCall recognized him across the rows of VDTs that separated them, though the lawyer did look different in person than in his newspaper photos.

McCall watched as one of the editors at the city desk pointed in his direction. Then the smallish man advanced quickly toward him, or at least it looked as though he was moving rapidly. McCall had often observed that short people looked busier and faster than larger people, even when performing the same functions at a much slower pace. Short women were, in some situations, exceptions to his observation. It had been his experience that they were not as frantic in bed as some of the taller women he had encountered.

He rose from his chair to greet the man with the pasted-on smile, noting the rouge-like glow on his chubby cheeks.

"I'm Bob Winnow," the man said, sticking out his hand.

McCall gripped the hand and shook it. It was as he had anticipated. Clammy, soft.

"You obviously know who I am," the reporter replied. "Have a seat."

Winnow sat and in a too-apologetic tone began, "I'm sorry that I was unable to see you yesterday. My schedule was very tight."

"No problem. I understand tight schedules." If the man wanted to lie, it was fine with McCall. Celeste had told him Winnow hadn't had any pressing business the entire day.

"I'm here," Winnow explained, "because you indicated to my secretary that you had some new information on the old Webster lawsuit. Frankly, I thought the paper's interest in that was over and done with years ago."

While Winnow was talking, McCall was recalling Barbara Walker's description of the man she had seen in the neighborhood on the day of the murder. Winnow might fit the bill in terms of height. McCall guessed him to be five-feet six or seven-inches. But even with the three-piece pinstripe suit, the man couldn't hide that he was a bit on the chubby side. He was also in his fifties, the hair a pale orange in color and very thin.

"Dirt has a way of turning up," McCall responded, "especially if you try to bury the truth in it."

Now somber and unsmiling, Winnow said, "A very noble statement, Mr. McCall. Are you a noble man?"

"I suppose that would depend on your interpretation of noble, Mr. Winnow. I don't know. What do you think?"

"I think that from what I've read of your writing, and I've read a number of your stories, that you consider yourself some sort of crusader for right. A champion of the underdog."

"I assume from your sarcastic tone that you don't consider that very noble."

"I'm not implying that at all, and I certainly didn't intend to sound sarcastic. I just think that you, like a lot of other newspaper people, get carried away when you think you've uncovered some great wrong. But I'd hate to think that you'd let your zeal override common sense."

McCall couldn't help but smile. It was amusing, a lawyer talking about common sense.

"Well, I want you to know how much I appreciate your

willingness to evaluate my work and motivation," he said, "especially in light of the fact that I didn't pay you for counsel on either. But what I'd really like to know is what motivated you to come here this morning?"

"My motivation is simply that I don't want a client to suffer any additional embarrassment over a long put to rest lawsuit."

"Your client being Clark Ramsey."

"That's right. Clark is a friend and still retains me to handle many of his legal affairs, even though he's quite capable of handling them himself. I don't know what you think you've found out, but I can assure you that my client is legally blameless in regard to the situation with the Websters."

"What about morally?"

"I think we have to leave what is, or is not, moral to the Lord," Winnow piously replied.

McCall detested people who hid behind religion, especially people like Winnow. "Let's just say that the Lord didn't have time to deal with the morality in this case. He asked me to handle it."

Winnow's face flushed to a pale crimson. "I was told you would be a difficult man to deal with."

"Now who on earth would tell you something like that?"

"Everyone I talked to."

"I suppose that I should be flattered that you thought it necessary to check on my psyche. But I just can't believe anyone would consider a person as good-natured as I am difficult to deal with."

"I was told that you had not been assigned to look into the Webster case."

"That's right. But your source should have also told you that I'm rarely assigned anything. I operate pretty much as I choose."

"I was told that. And I admit to being curious as to why you would dig into something as old as the Webster matter. What prompted you to even think about it?"

"To tell the truth, I was checking up on you."

"You were what?"

"Just what I said. I was checking on you to try to find why the police haven't been more insistent about questioning Paul Roget. I figured it might be because he works for you."

"So, you assumed the reason was the client-lawyer relationship I had with Clark Ramsey?"

"Not had, have," McCall corrected. "You're still Ramsey's lawyer."

"That's true," Winnow admitted, "and as I said earlier, we're also good friends. But Clark would never let that interfere with his duty."

"For some reason, I find that a little hard to believe."

"I don't care if you do doubt it, Mr. McCall. Clark Ramsey's one of the most decent men I've ever met."

McCall laughed. "Maybe you should start meeting more people."

"Some of the people I happen to meet, and who happen to be friends of mine, are among the top management of this newspaper," Winnow warned.

"Like I said," McCall reiterated, "you ought to start meeting more people. And you certainly ought to try to meet some people who are interesting."

"You wouldn't say that to them."

"Wanna bet?"

Winnow reminded McCall of a little old lady. Maybe he was. Maybe through some biological screw up, this thing before him had been doled out an overabundance of female genes. And McCall didn't care whether Winnow could help it or not. He still hated queers. And for someone to be queer and a lawyer, that was just too much.

But in spite of his feminine mannerisms, he sensed that Winnow was a dangerous adversary.

"I suppose that I should envy you, Mr. McCall, your bravado and obvious disregard for authority."

"I don't give a rat's ass whether you envy me or not. And as for these people allegedly in authority at the newspaper, don't kid youself about their friendship. If I turn up something on you and Ramsey, they'll be on both of you like a pack of dogs. They'll deny ever having known you.

"And if you think you can convince any of your newspaper friends to order me off this case, be my guest. You'll find that none of them have the balls to try. And you can quote me."

"I will," Winnow promised. "But Clark has nothing to hide. If you want to waste your time, go ahead. However, if you print anything derogatory about me or my client, I'll take legal action against you and the newspaper."

"If you take legal action against me, it will be for writing the truth."

"You newspaper types have a knack for twisting the truth."

"I can't believe a lawyer has the audacity to talk about anyone twisting the truth."

Winnow shrugged his shoulders. "We're not getting anywhere, are we?"

"We don't seem to be."

"What do you really want from me?"

"Just the truth. You can start by telling me where you have Paul Roget hidden."

"And if I do, you'll drop this Webster thing?"

"You have to be kidding."

"What do you want?"

"I want an exclusive interview with Roget."

"That's not possible."

"Why not? Isn't he in town?"

Winnow reacted too quickly. "Why would you think he's not in town? I can assure you that he's here."

"It was just a hunch on my part. If he's here, I don't know why you'd be afraid for me to talk to him."

"I'm not afraid to let you talk to him, but the police haven't even talked to him yet."

"I want to talk to him before the police do."

"That's impossible."

"No, it's not."

"Well, what Paul Roget does is strictly his decision."

"I doubt that," McCall countered. "My guess is that you're in command of this whole situation. I'd bet that you're advising him on everything he should do."

"I won't deny that I give him advice."

"Then you should advise him to talk to me."

"My advice would be to the contrary."

"If the man's innocent, I could probably help him."

"Because he is innocent," Winnow said, "he can do without your help."

"We'll see. Listen, Bob, I hate to break up this party, but there are some other things that I have to do." McCall liked to be the one to end a conversation, feeling it gave him an advantage over an adversary.

"I suppose that you're going to continue this Webster thing?"

"You suppose right."

"Well, I'm certainly not worried about it. If you want to waste your time, that's fine. I know that the only reason you're doing it is to try to get to Paul Roget through me. It won't work, and you're being very small and vindictive."

McCall laughed. "That's a queer thing to say, Bob."

CHAPTER FOURTEEN

Laurie Roget's funeral was conducted under gray skies and amid intermittant showers. It was a simple graveside service, directed by a tall, gawky-looking minister who was seemingly oblivious to raindrops.

McCall was moved by the simplicity of the setting and by the caring tone of the minister. The whole of the scenario was so much more appropriate than many funerals he had attended. With those funerals, pomp and ceremony seemed more important than the one being buried.

The fact that a person was glorified in death, but nothing more than a Social Security number in life, bothered McCall. He thought the final salute to a person should be a reflection of the way he or she lived their life. That's why he thought the simplicity of the occasion was a fitting tribute to Laurie.

But while he was contemplating the mood of the moment, McCall did not forget his primary purpose. He was looking for a murderer.

And there were some very good prospects attending the funeral.

First and foremost, of course, was Paul Roget. It was

McCall's first time to see Roget in person. He fit Barbara Walker's description. But then, so did Roget's friend, Francis Reynolds. Reynolds was standing by Roget's side and there was a striking resemblance in the two men.

Bob Winnow was also at Roget's side, glaring at McCall. When he was sure no one was looking, McCall gave Winnow a wink and a smile.

From a discreet distance, one of the newspaper's photographers was taking pictures of the funeral's participants. McCall wanted to know the faces as wel[1] as the names of the players.

The reporter had stationed himself between Mary Murphy and Dr. Barrington, enabling the nurse to point out Laurie's parents and three sisters. Two of the sisters were married and accompanied by their husbands.

The entire ceremony lasted no more than fifteen minutes. The traditional shaking hands with the bereaved and offering words of comfort was not observed. As soon as the casket was lowered into the ground, family members and close friends were whisked away in long black Cadillacs.

McCall noted that Roget was accompanied in one of the cars by Winnow and Reynolds.

"Well, Mary," McCall said to the tearful nurse, "now that Laurie's laid to rest, maybe I can get some answers as to who killed her and why."

Mary didn't speak, just nodded agreement. It was not, McCall decided, a good time to talk.

CHAPTER FIFTEEN

It was three days after the funeral before Paul Roget finally talked to police. He was not, however, alone when questioned. Roget was accompanied by Bob Winnow and Jetton Mitchell, the top defense attorney in the state.

Jet Mitchell had, in fact, earned a national reputation for getting obviously guilty clients off the hook. He was shrewd and expensive. Too expensive, really, even for a well-paid corporate attorney like Paul Roget.

"You know what I thought when Roget walked in with Mitchell," Haloran told McCall over a breakfast of ham and eggs. "I decided right then and there that the sonofabitch was guilty. Nobody hires Mitchell unless they're guilty."

"What about Roget's alibi?"

"That's what makes this whole thing so crazy. I'm pretty sure Roget's alibi will stand up, so why in the hell would he get Mitchell mixed up in this thing? And why would Mitchell want to?"

"Well, the man does like headlines," McCall reasoned, "and he's been out of the limelight for awhile. After all, not too many people can afford his fees."

"Do you think Roget can?"

"Maybe, but my guess is that someone else is picking up the tab. Or that Mitchell is handling the case as a favor to someone."

"But not as a favor to Roget?"

"I doubt that he had even met Roget until he agreed to handle the case. Jet's more reclusive than most, and he sure wouldn't cotton to a wimp like Roget."

"It still doesn't make sense. With his alibi, why in the hell does Roget need Mitchell?"

"Maybe Roget had his wife killed."

"I can't buy that."

"I'm not trying to sell it. You asked why, so I'm just suggesting a possibility."

"You're unusually calm this morning," Haloran observed. Doesn't the fact that Roget has a high-powered defense attorney piss you off?"

"Not at all."

"Why not? Usually, everything pisses you off. And you've been pissed about Roget from the beginning."

McCall laughed. "You misread me, Bill. I have no quarrel with anyone about the way things are going."

"Bullshit."

"The truth is, I'm glad Jet is Roget's attorney. He's good copy. I sure won't have any trouble getting him to talk. I've covered some of his trials in the past and we get along fine."

"Yeah, I remember. So, do you think he'll tell you what you need to know?"

"Of course not. But the old bastard will at least talk to me. He'll do everything he can to sell me on the idea that his client is the real victim. I'd almost bet that he's waiting for me to call, because he knows that I'm covering the case."

"I hate the old sonofabitch because he's always getting some guilty bastard off," Haloran reiterated.

"Don't forget the guilty bitches," McCall reminded. "He gets them off, too."

"By the way, did you learn anything from your conversation with Roget?"

"Not much," Haloran admitted. "He claims that he left the house about seven in the morning on the day of the murder. He also gave me a slew of witnesses who saw him from about eight o'clock on.

"And he'd written down a list of people who had been to the house during the past couple of months. Repairmen and such."

McCall nodded. "That's Mitchell's work. He anticipated that you'd want that kind of information."

"I did want it," Haloran said, "but I kind of like to ask. I don't like to be anticipated."

"Then don't be so damn predictable."

"Certain facets of police work are predictable."

"Tell me about it," McCall lamented.

"Goddamit, McCall, I'm not allowed to operate like some off-the-wall newspaper type."

"That's too bad. If you did, you'd probably solve more cases."

The detective grumbled. "Do you want me to tell you the rest of this shit or not?"

"I'm all ears."

"Well, according to Roget everything was peaches and cream between him and his wife. That's enough to make you suspicious right there, because I don't know of a couple that has as good a relationship as he painted. Of course, I'm sure I had in the back of my mind what Mary Murphy and Dr. Barrington had told me. And I couldn't help but remember the few clothes that Mrs. Roget had."

"Did he say why he delayed talking to you?"

"Just that he was so grief-stricken that he couldn't talk about it."

"Did he say where he'd been staying?"

"Winnow said Roget had been staying with him. To tell the truth, Roget didn't do much talking. Mitchell and Winnow did it for him."

"Pardon me for saying so," McCall responded with a chuckle, "but I anticipated that."

Haloran laughed. "Asshole."

"Did Roget have anything to say about the lipstick message on the mirror?"

"Only that he has no enemies. At least, none that he knows about."

"And what about the delay in calling the police after he found the body?"

"Mitchell said the delay was because Roget was in shock. And still is."

"But Roget didn't personally respond to your question about the delay?"

"Like I said," Haloran reiterated, "Winnow and Mitchell did most of the talking."

"Did you mention the bedroom being overly neat, to the point where it didn't even look lived in?"

"Naw, I thought I'd save some of that stuff for later, if the need arises."

"You know what bothers me?"

"What?"

"The fact that someone did a cleaning job on the bedroom and left the kitchen as it was."

"Wasn't it you who said the bedroom was cleaned because Roget moved out all his porno stuff?"

"Did I say that? Hell, I say so much profound stuff that I can't remember it all. If I said it, though, it must be right."

Haloran had been eyeing a piece of ham on McCall's plate. "Are you going to eat that ham?"

"No, and I'm not going to eat the toast, either. So be my guest."

Haloran speared the ham with his fork and pulled the side plate of toast toward him.

"Did you give Roget a lie detector test?" McCall asked.

"We wanted to, but Mitchell wouldn't let him take it. He claims Roget's already passed a privately administered test."

"I'm sure he has. Old Jet doesn't miss a trick."

McCall left Haloran nursing a cup of coffee and headed for the *Tribune*. Enroute, though, he decided to pay a surprise visit on Jet Mitchell. From past experience, he knew the lawyer usually got to his office early in the morning. He also knew that Mitchell would be expecting him to telephone instead of just drop in. He figured an unscheduled, surprise visit might just work in his favor, though he really doubted it. Mitchell was too shrewd to be taken by surprise.

Still, it was worth a try.

One of the things McCall appreciated about Mitchell was that, even with all his affluence, he continued to office at the same building where he had first begun his law practice. And Mitchell had never expanded the size of his office, remodeled it in any way, or replaced any of the original furniture.

After his very first meeting with Mitchell, McCall had surmised that the lawyer enjoyed playing the role of an eccentric. That had been reinforced with every subsequent meeting.

McCall took one of the building's tired elevators up to the floor where Mitchell officed. The slow, creaky ride was not one for an impatient man.

He had been to the office on a number of occasions. The journey was not strange. The only thing he dreaded about the visit was having to deal with Mitchell's dowdy secretary. McCall wasn't sure, but he guessed she had come with the furniture.

That's why he was surprised when, on opening the door, he was confronted by a beautiful young woman. She was shapely, maybe twenty-five, with flowing auburn hair that surrounded a pixie-like face. The hair stopped halfway between her waist and shoulders.

"May I help you?" she asked.

"I'm here to see Mr. Mitchell."

"Do you have an appointment?"

Before he could answer, a voice roared from the inner office,

"Who is it?"

"It's Matt McCall," he yelled back.

There was the sound of shuffled paper, heavy feet on the floor, and then Jet Mitchell was standing in the doorway. "My god, Matt, it's been awhile. What have you been up to, boy?"

"Can the bullshit, Jet. You know damn well what I've been up to. It's what you've been up to that I'm here to talk about."

Mitchell laughed. "Now what in the world does that mean?"

The lawyer was pushing sixty, though a full head of hair and a face devoid of wrinkles belied the fact. Other than an excess thirty or so pounds on his six-feet two-inch frame, Mitchell looked a picture of health.

"Matt, you'll have to forgive my manners," he said. "This is my secretary, Sally. Sally, meet my good friend, Matt McCall."

McCall and Sally each acknowledged the introduction, but Mitchell wasn't through talking. "Sally's my new squeeze. I don't think there's anything wrong with an older man and younger woman, do you? Of course, you don't."

The girl blushed and McCall replied, "Domestic tranquility is not my specialty."

"Loosen up, Matt. Sally's my daughter. From my third or fourth wife, I can't remember which. But she's damn pretty, isn't she?"

McCall agreed that Sally was indeed pretty. And he figured Mitchell was being truthful in not knowing whether Sally was a daughter from his third or fourth wife. The man might be reluctant to change his offices or his furniture, but he had been married seven times.

"Are you married, Matt?"

"Not exactly."

"Good answer. Hell, you ought to take Sally out. If she's anything like her mother, she'll show you a damn good time."

Sally had turned her back to them, busying herself with something that didn't need to be done. McCall decided it was time to rescue her.

148

"Jet, I need to talk to you a few minutes. Do you have the time?"

"I always have time for you, Matt. Come on in my office."

McCall followed Mitchell into an office that was strewn with papers and books. He had to remove a stack of papers from a chair in front of the desk to sit down.

"Excuse the mess," Mitchell apologized, "but I'm working on my memoirs. There's probably going to be a chapter about you, Matt."

McCall laughed. "Don't do me any favors. By the way, what happened to your old secretary?"

"The old bitch up and died on me."

"That was damn inconsiderate of her."

"Well, it was," he said with a laugh. "I'm still having trouble finding shit around here."

"Speaking of shit, Jet, why in the hell did you get involved in this Roget murder case?"

"Now, what's that suppose to mean?"

"Hell, I don't think there's any hidden meaning to my question. But a lot of people have to wonder why a supposedly innocent man...one, I might add, who hasn't been charged with anything...saw the need to hire the best defense attorney in the state. And not only do I wonder about him hiring you, I wonder if he has the kind of money it takes to pay you."

"My gosh, Matt, to hear you talk you'd think that my only motivation in life is money."

"No, I don't think that. In fact, I've always thought your fees were an ego thing. And I can identify with that."

Mitchell chuckled. "You're alright, Matt."

"You still haven't answered my question. Why did Roget think it necessary to hire a criminal lawyer? Any lawyer for that matter?"

"I see nothing unusual about it. Besides, I'm really just acting as a consultant. Being a corporate attorney as he is, Paul is totally unfamiliar with the various procedures involved in a criminal investigation concerning a murder.

"I've known Bob Winnow for more than twenty years, and it was Bob who initially called and asked me some questions. Then, because Paul was so emotionally upset, we just put things on a more formal basis."

"I'll try to refrain from commenting on how little Roget must have learned at school," McCall said. "There's still the question as to why he was unavailable to police for several days after the murder?"

"I've already told you how distraught he was," Mitchell answered. "I'm sure you can understand that. It's not everyday that a man's wife is murdered."

"That's true. But I can't understand a man not doing everything in his power to help find his wife's killer. And that would involve talking to the police. Immediately."

"Everyone doesn't handle grief the same way," Mitchell reasoned.

"Seems I've heard that before."

"Besides, Paul did talk to police on a limited basis."

"That's news to me. And I'll bet it's also news to Bill Haloran."

"Well, I'll admit that he didn't talk directly to police, but Bob Winnow got questions answered and reported back to authorities."

"Obviously," McCall said, "Bill Haloran was not one of those authorities."

"No, I think Bob reported directly to Clark Ramsey. And I'm sure that Clark got word to Detective Haloran that everything was under control."

"Through the chief, you mean?"

"Yes."

"I'm sure you'll understand my curiosity, Jet, in wondering why Winnow did not talk to the detective in charge of the investigation?"

"I think it was a matter of Bob just feeling more comfortable talking to Clark. They go back a long way together."

"Yeah, I know. But the district attorney's office doesn't normally handle a murder investigation."

"But they do have jurisdiction to do so."

"That's true. But aside from the ethics of the situation, when did you first talk to Roget?"

"I talked to him the day before the funeral. And frankly, I realized right then that he wasn't in the right emotional state to aid in an in-depth investigation."

McCall laughed. "Damn, Jet, are you practicing psychiatry without a license?"

"For God sakes, Matt, you don't have to be a doctor to know when someone's hurting inside. The man couldn't answer a lot of my questions because he would just break down and cry."

"Don't they teach crying in law school? I've seen you put a few tears on a jury."

Mitchell grinned. "You're cold. Really cold."

"Just save your dramatics for the courtroom, Jet. You should know by now that I want facts, not bullshit."

"So, I guess you're not going to put anything about a grieving husband in your story?"

"I'm going to put what you say, so you might want to start sounding believable."

They laughed together. Both enjoyed bantering.

"Actually, Paul was available for questioning the day after the funeral, but Bill Haloran was in court. So the delay wasn't all our fault."

"You're unbelievable. Your client evades the police for a week, and now you're trying to sell the idea that the police wouldn't talk to him when he was ready."

"Maybe that won't float," Mitchell said, "but the real issue is the time of death. My information puts the time at about nine or ten o'clock in the morning, which means my client was already at the courthouse when the murder occurred."

"Your information on the time of death, I presume, is based on an examination of the stomach contents of the victim?"

151

"Partially," Mitchell replied. "Paul left his house at about seven o'clock on the day of the murder. He went to the office, worked thirty minutes or so, then took a bus to the courthouse. He got there shortly before eight-thirty.

"As you know, he was on jury duty, so he was around a lot of people there until about twelve-thirty. I've talked to some of those people and received verification.

"At about twelve-thirty he went to eat at Lupita's, had a hamburger, french fries and cold drink and came back to the courthouse," Mitchell continued. "He read a book on parenting until . . ."

"Whoa," McCall interrupted. "It's really getting deep in here, Jet. Roget has the All-American lunch of common folk, does his civic duty by showing up for jury duty and carries around a book on parenting to read in his spare time. C'mon now."

"A little much, huh?"

"More than a little much."

"I swear to God, Matt, that's what the man told me."

"Oh, I believe that. He probably even got a little help from his friends in concocting the bit about the book on parenting."

"Who do you mean?"

"Winnow and crew."

Mitchell ignored the reference to Winnow and said, "After *allegedly* reading the book on parenting, Paul went back to the central jury room at about one-twenty and was there until three-thirty. The only time he wasn't around people who could verify his whereabouts was during the time he was eating lunch and reading. I'm sure, however, we can find people who saw him during this period."

"I'm sure you can," McCall agreed. "And I'm sure you drove from the courthouse to the Roget house and back to make sure such a trip was impossible in fifty minutes."

Mitchell laughed. "I did."

"So did I. I made the trip in thirty-five minutes."

"Did you begin your drive at twelve-thirty?"

152

"No, I walked out of the jury room at twelve-thirty," McCall said. "I got in my car, which was parked in the courthouse parking garage, and drove to the Roget house. When I came back, I parked in the garage again and walked to the central jury room. I did all that in thirty-five minutes."

"You must have driven like a bat out of hell," Mitchell said, "because it took me forty-eight minutes from the front of the courthouse."

"There are those who say I drive rather quickly," McCall admitted.

"It doesn't matter, anyway," Mitchell said, "because Paul didn't have a car in the courthouse garage or parked out front. He rode the bus from his office."

"So he says," McCall challenged. "The courthouse garage is self-park, so no one could testify that he didn't park there. Or that he did. And his office parking is also self-park. Do you have any witnesses who saw him on the bus?"

"No, but I'm sure we could get some."

"You probably won't have any trouble. I'm sure some of Winnow's lawyer friends will suddenly remember that they were on the same bus with Roget."

"Damn it, Matt, what are you trying to imply?"

"I'm not *trying* to imply anything. I'm doing it."

"Anyway, there are plenty of witnesses to collaborate Paul's story."

"Wonderful. Then he and Winnow over-reacted in hiring a defense lawyer of your stature. Of any stature for that matter."

"Is that a question?"

"No, I think it's a fact."

"No, I don't think they over-reacted at all. As I explained earlier, Paul has very little knowledge of criminal law."

"He would need very little with his alibi."

"I don't think Paul has ever been a serious suspect," Mitchell said. "I think the only concern the police had in questioning him was that, other than the killer, he was the last person to see his wife alive."

"I'm sure you've heard rumors about how demanding Roget was on his wife."

"You mean how he expected everything to be scrubbed and spotless?"

"Among other things."

"You of all people ought to know that you get that kind of stuff after something like this happens. People love to talk, even if they don't have any facts."

"Some may have more facts than you know."

"You're bound and determined to tie Paul to this murder, aren't you?"

"Only if he's guilty."

"The evidence says he isn't."

"The jury's still out on that, Jet. Even if he didn't personally commit the murder, there's another possibility."

"You're barking up the wrong tree, Matt."

"Maybe so, But I'll bet you've wondered yourself how a killer got in the house, Mrs. Roget being so afraid of strangers and all. Unless, of course, she knew the killer. Or unless Roget gave him a key."

"Are you suggesting a professional hit?"

"No, this was an amateur. A pro would have made it look like a burglary, and a pro wouldn't have stripped a woman and strangled her. This was more like a ritual murder."

"You're getting on some mighty shaky ground, Matt. But I don't care what direction your story goes, just as long as you don't engage in some sort of personal vendetta against my client."

"You know me better than that."

"You're right. I do know you. I know that you like the smell of blood. Just be sure you're right."

After the warning, they exchanged a few pleasantries and McCall left Mitchell's office. Sally looked up from her typewriter as he was leaving. On impulse he said, "In spite of your old man, I'd be pleased to buy you a drink this afternoon."

"Five-thirty," she replied. "You can pick me up here."
Her immediate acceptance surprised him.
"I'll be here," he said.

CHAPTER SIXTEEN

When McCall returned to his office, Ramirez told him the double-o-seven guy had called again. There were also "phone me" messages from Cele, Lanelle and Celeste.

"Damn, you're a busy man," Ramirez said with a laugh.

McCall got on the horn with Arnold first, and discovered that the agent was anxious to share some information.

"I don't know how you can dig up so much shit, Matt, but this Webster thing is a real can of worms."

"Spare me the accolades, Arnold, and give me what you've got."

"You'll remember that I told you the Army had written Webster off as just another drunk soldier who couldn't keep his car on the road."

"I remember."

"Well, in thoroughly checking Sergeant Webster's background," Arnold continued, "I found that he was a teetotaler."

"There's always a first time."

"Maybe so," Arnold agreed, "but there's more. The car Webster crashed and burned was a rental, but he didn't rent it."

"Who did?"

"Webster's name was on the agreement, but it wasn't his signature. It was a forgery."

"Where in the hell did you get the rental agreement?" McCall asked.

"The Army had it in Webster's file. They got it from the car agency when they were investigating the accident, but it never occurred to any of the bozos to check the signature."

McCall knew that it wouldn't have occurred to many people. Arnold was damn good.

"That's a good piece of work, Arnold. I'd like a copy of the rental agreement."

"You've got it, but there's more."

"Hit me with it."

"Webster's GI insurance ended up in your hometown, but the mother only got half of it."

"I think I know who got the other half, but go ahead and tell me anyway."

"A lawyer named David Darden got five thousand."

Poor dumb Harold Webster, McCall thought. Why couldn't they have left the poor bastard alone? He wouldn't have bothered them, but they were obviously leaving nothing to chance. Darden had even cut himself in on the insurance to pay his exorbitant fee.

"It's obviously murder," Arnold continued. "Do you want me to stay on it?"

"Not for the time being. I know who killed him."

"I figured you did. Call if you need me."

"I will, Arnold. And thanks."

After McCall had hung up the phone, he sat glaring at the VDT. There was really no reason for Laurie's and Webster's deaths to be tied together. The Webster murder had no connection. It was just something he had stumbled on by chance.

Turner Sipe interrupted his thought processes with, "Are you going to have a story today?"

He turned in his chair to face the city editor, who looked shorter standing than when sitting down.

"Yeah, Turnip, I'll have a story. Roget went out and got himself a high-priced lawyer, Jet Mitchell. But I'll bet you already knew that. I'll bet your old pal Bob Winnow told you."

Sipe's face colored. "I didn't know. When will you have the story?"

"When it's ready, you'll be the first to know. And Turnip, don't screw it up. If one word's changed, I'm going to kick your ass nine ways from Sunday."

"Quit trying to threaten me, McCall."

"Listen, you bottle-butt bastard. I'm not trying to threaten you. I am threatening you. Just don't screw with my copy."

Sipe muttered something under his breath while making his way back to the city desk. But McCall knew that his copy wouldn't be changed.

"You sure do bully that man," Ramirez said. "How about some coffee?"

"I could use some."

"I'll get it," Ramirez volunteered.

While Ramirez was gone, he called Cele. She answered after only four rings.

"Hi, baby," he said.

"Matt?"

"You'd better hope to hell it is," he teased. "I'd better not find out that anyone else talks to you the way I do."

She laughed. "Oh, I wouldn't let you find out."

"Have you had a good day?" He thought he remembered her telling him that she was going shopping and to exercise class.

"I certainly have. You're going to love the new dress that I bought. And the new nighty."

"Yeah. Well, I can already tell you that I'm partial to the nighty. I guess it's 'cause I'm horny. Just for you, of course."

"Ha! I'm always surprised when you remember my name."

"Louise," he teased, "how can you say something like that?"

"It's a good thing I have a sense of humor," she said.

158

"You have one of the best," he agreed, "but I am horny for you."

"So, what else is new? You're always horny."

"Having you takes the edge off quite a bit," he said. "And I'm anxious to see the new nighty. I'll bet it's something you'll look good out of."

"Meaning I won't have it on long if you have your way."

"Gosh, it's getting to where you can read my mind. That's scary."

"Anyway," she sighed with resignation, "what time are you coming home?"

"I should be home by nine."

"Good. We can have a late candlelight dinner."

"Sounds good."

"I'm making a tuna casserole and a nice salad," she said, "so don't be late."

He was mentally bemoaning Cele's dinner menu when Ramirez brought the coffee. He took a swallow of it and grimaced.

"Something wrong with the coffee?" Ramirez asked.

"No. Why do you ask?"

"You looked like you'd just tasted a mouthful of shit."

"I won't have that until tonight," he answered without explanation.

Before writing his story, he decided to call Lanelle and Celeste.

"If you're interested," Lanelle said following a customary greeting, "he's leaving for a few days."

"I'm interested," McCall replied. "Let's make it about eight o'clock."

She laughed. "We can *make it* anytime you like."

When he talked to Celeste, she invited him to a wine-tasting at her apartment.

"I don't know," he crawfished. "I don't like to be around a lot of people."

"Don't worry," she assured. "You're the only one invited.

159

And you're in charge of bringing the wine."

"In that case, count me in. When is this taking place?"

"Saturday night."

It was perfect. Cele was spending the weekend with her parents. Because she was living with him, the visits to her parents were an attempt to ease the tension created by the situation. McCall knew that before the weekend was over, she would have an argument with her mother and return home frustrated and dejected. It was always the same.

He often thought Cele's parents could do everyone a favor by getting themselves killed in a car wreck. Just a one-car collision, though. No point in taking anyone else.

"Anything in particular that you want me to do?" Ramirez asked.

"No, go home and get some rest. I'm going to bang out this story and then I'm going to leave."

"Want me to get you another cup?"

"Naw, I'll get it. I need the exercise."

McCall finished the story about five-fifteen. His timing was perfect, because it would take no more than fifteen minutes to get to Jet Mitchell's office and Sally.

She was filing when he walked in. "Busy, I see."

"Not really. Bored would be more like it. There's not much to do around here."

"That's surprising. I figured Jet would have you typing his memoirs."

"I can't read his writing. The only one I knew who could was Mrs. Gray."

"His old secretary?"

"One in the same. It's a shame she died, but it was probably preferable to working for daddy."

McCall laughed. "Jet doesn't seem all that bad."

"You don't know. He can be a real asshole."

"That seems to be common in all lawyers. But let's not get into that. What about you?"

"What about me, what?"

"Well, for one thing, why are you working here as Jet's secretary?"

"Where else could a girl with a degree in elementary education make fifty thousand a year?"

"If nothing else, it sounds as if your father is generous."

"He just feels guilty. I never saw him when I was growing up, even though I'm the only child from all his marriages."

"I know he was just kidding when I was here earlier, but which wife was your mother? The third or fourth?"

"She was his third, and I doubt that he was kidding. He wasn't all that wealthy when they were married, either."

"Did your mother remarry?"

"Yes, and my stepfather is everything that my real father isn't."

"What does he do?"

"He's an airline executive. But listen, I didn't know I was going to get the third degree. I thought we were just going to have a drink."

"Sorry. I guess I tend to interview everyone I meet. Where do you want to go for that drink?"

"Why go anywhere? My father has some of the world's best liquor in his office."

"But that would be you buying me a drink," McCall protested.

"No it wouldn't. It would be Jet Mitchell buying both of us a drink. And believe me, he can afford it. Besides, what would be wrong with me buying you a drink? You're not one of those male chauvenists, are you?"

"I thought it was obvious."

"Good," she responded. "I'm not all that interested in being liberated."

She led him into Jet's office and instructed him to take a seat on the couch. Then she opened the double doors at one end of the room to expose an elaborate bar.

"What will you have?"

"Scotch and water will be fine. You know, as many times as

I've been here, I didn't know what was behind those doors."

"I'm not surprised. Daddy never asks anyone to have a drink with him."

"That's a bit strange, isn't it?"

"Well, he's a whole lot strange, but the reason he doesn't drink with other people is because he doesn't want anyone to know he's an alcoholic."

"That's hard to believe."

"I should know," she said.

"If he's trying to keep it a secret, why did you tell me?"

"He's the one who's trying to keep it a secret, not me. Besides, you can't do anything with the information. You're certainly not going to print it."

"That's true."

She handed him his drink and sat down beside him. "Don't you think this is better than a noisy bar?" She had a glass of wine.

"It is," he agreed. He liked her perfume, and the fact that she was showing a considerable portion of her shapely legs. "Did Jet know you were going to have a drink with me?"

"Of course. He told me all about you and suggested that I pump you for information."

McCall laughed. "The old bastard. So, I've been forewarned."

"Sure, but I'm not interested in pumping you for information, especially if it's going to help Bob Winnow or any of his flunky legal associates."

"I take it you don't like Mr. Winnow?"

"The man gives me the creeps," she said.

"Well, he sure doesn't seem to be your father's type, which is why I was surprised to learn about their long association."

"What association?" she questioned. "Did daddy tell you that Bob Winnow is a friend of his?"

"He implied that, yes."

"He thinks about as much of Bob Winnow as I do," she said. "They've rarely ever spoken to each other over the years."

"He told me he was representing Roget because of his long association with Winnow."

"He's acting as a consultant to Mr. Roget for one hundred thousand dollars and whatever publicity he can get you to give him. And I think the publicity is more important to him than the money."

"A hundred thousand is an awful lot of money for an innocent man to cough up."

"It's Bob Winnow who's paying the money," she said. "He gave my father an initial payment of fifty thousand. It was his personal check and I have a copy of it on file. I also have the signed contract made between my father and Bob Winnow."

"So Winnow's the one who's paying the bill."

"That's right. If you like, I'll make you a copy of the check and the contract."

"Sure, I'd like that."

"First, though, I want you to kiss me."

"That'll be great, too," he said, pulling her close and crushing her lips with his. She struggled to get into a position where her body would be pressed against his, then whimpered softly as their tongues passionately caressed.

There was no resistance when he pulled the panty hose over her hips and down the length of her legs. Nor was there any combat, physical or mental, when he put his hand inside her panties. The discoveries his fingers made caused her to groan with pleasure.

Then the panties were on the floor and he was on top of her, moving rhythmically inside her while her fingernails dug into his back. After a few moments she came. Then moments later a second time. She had a third orgasm before he came.

There was a moment of quiet exhaustion, then her evaluation, "That was wonderful. Did you enjoy it?"

"I was hoping it showed."

"It did. I could go another round when you're rested."

"I'm all for it," he said, "but while we're waiting, get me the copies of that check and contract."

CHAPTER SEVENTEEN

McCall was not sure what, if anything, he could do with the material Sally had provided. He did think the newspaper's readers had a right to know that such a contract existed. And they certainly should be made aware of the fact that a supposedly innocent man was paying a hundred thousand dollars for counsel from Jet Mitchell.

Of course, it had been Winnow, not Roget, who had negotiated the contract. And it was Winnow who had made the initial payment of fifty thousand.

It all added up to something strange in the woodpile. If Roget was not guilty, it just didn't make sense to give Mitchell that much money. Or to retain him at all. Someone was trying to cover up something. What the something was, McCall was determined to find out.

And since Mitchell had mentioned his longtime friendship with Winnow, McCall looked forward to asking Jet why he thought it necessary to draw up a contract with so good a friend. It amused him to think about Jet trying to come up with a logical answer, though he was certain the man's legal mind would be equal to the task.

As for asking Winnow why he negotiated the contract, that probably wouldn't do much good. Nor would it do any good to question him about writing the check for fifty thousand. He could always say that it was simply a personal loan.

In any confrontation, in fact, Winnow would probably come out a hero for being so generous and supportive of the young lawyer.

For the moment, anyway, McCall decided to do nothing with the contract information. To write about it, or to confront Winnow, would expose Sally. And he was reluctant to do that.

He had shared the information with Bill Haloran, causing the needle in the detective's suspicion level to climb into the red zone.

As for Sally, she was a strange one. It was fairly obvious that she wanted to punish her father for his past transgressions toward her, whether real or imagined. Or she was, perhaps, just trying to get Jet's attention.

From McCall's evaluation of the man, he figured Sally was pissing into the wind in any kind of one-on-one confrontation with her father. Jet was pretty much oblivious to everything except the law and nurturing his ego.

And in spite of what McCall considered Jet's "asshole ways," he couldn't help but like the man. Jet was what he was, pure and simple. Nothing more, nothing less. That in itself was a rarity.

He knew that Jet would lie to him and mislead him in every possible way. But Jet knew that he knew, which made the chemistry between them all the more unique.

CHAPTER EIGHTEEN

McCall was moving a portion of some unidentifiable seafood casserole around on his plate when the call about the arrest came. He considered the call a godsend, since there was no way that he was going to be able to convince Cele that he liked or had eaten any of the concoction that she had prepared especially for him.

"I have to go, baby," he said. "There's been an arrest in the Roget case."

"Don't you have time to finish eating?"

She looked beautiful by candlelight. He didn't regret leaving the meal, but he had wanted to spend the evening with her.

"I'm afraid not," he replied. "I'll grab something when I can."

"Don't," she admonished, "eat any junk food. I'll fix you something when you get home."

He grinned. "I'm going to want something besides food when I get home."

"You can have that, too."

They kissed and he was off and running.

McCall had learned from the phone conversation with one

of the paper's editors that a repairman had been arrested for Laurie Roget's murder. He wondered why Haloran hadn't called him.

He made the trip to the police station in record time, then weaved his way through the maze of desks to Haloran's office. When the detective saw him, he immediately went on the defensive.

"Hell, I didn't know, McCall," he apologized. "If I had known, I would have called you."

"What do you mean, you didn't know, asshole. You're the detective in charge of this case, aren't you?"

"That's kind of debatable, since it seems I'm the last one to know anything around here."

"You didn't know that an arrest was going to be made?"

Haloran nodded in the affirmative, then said with a kind of beaten resignation, "I didn't have a clue. Look, I need to get out of this fuckin' place. Let's go down to the diner and have some coffee. I'll even buy."

McCall laughed. "Hell, nothing could be that bad, Bill."

"Yes, it can,"Haloran said somberly.

After they had occupied a booth and after the waitress had brought two cups of coffee, Haloran began with, "You knew that I was off today, didn't you?"

"How in the world would I know that? It may come as a shock to you, but I don't keep a record of your work schedule. It seems to me, though, that you're always on duty. But then, I don't frequent the police station that often on a Saturday."

"The whole thing's screwy," Haloran said, "but from all indications, they have the killer."

"What do you mean, 'they'?"

"Well, I sure as hell didn't have a clue as to what was going on. I would have called you if I had been making the arrest, because I told you I would."

"I still want to know who 'they' are."

"Clark Ramsey, the district attorney's office."

"C'mon, don't bullshit me."

167

"I'm not. According to Ramsey, he's been on the case from the beginning. And he's crediting Roget with being a big help in solving it."

"Pardon me while I puke, but this whole thing smells."

"Maybe so, but after looking at the paperwork I'd say they have a damn good case."

"And even though this was your case, they didn't involve you in the arrest? And what the hell is going on? The district attorney's office usually leaves the homicides to the police."

"But they don't have to," Haloran said. "And Ramsey says he decided to get on this one as a favor to his good friend, Bob Winnow."

"How cozy."

"Ramsey claims his office tried to reach me several times during the day and got no answer. He said they decided I was out of town."

"And?"

"My wife and I were home all day. And at least one of us was in the house all the time."

"And did you make that salient point to Mr. Ramsey?" McCall asked, the disdain in his voice very pronounced.

"I did."

"To which he replied?"

"He said there must have been something wrong with my phone."

"Well, you sure can't argue with that kind of logic. When did you find out about the arrest?"

"On the six o'clock news. I don't guess you were watching TV, huh?"

"If I was, I wasn't watching one of those so-called newscasts."

"When I heard it on TV," Haloran said, "I figured you already knew about the arrest. It wasn't until I got to the station that I found out that Ramsey had alerted all the media except your paper."

"Who told you that?"

"Never mind. I have sources, too, McCall."

"Knowing what a grandstander he is, you'd have to figure Ramsey would have all the TV people handy for the arrest," McCall said. "But I'd say he made a serious boo-boo in ignoring my paper and me."

Haloran laughed. "I'd say that he probably did. But you know what it is, McCall. The man's trying to punish you for stepping on his toes, and on the toes of his friends. And he cut me out because of my association with you."

McCall shrugged his shoulders. "He can play games with me all he likes, but you have a career to think of. Maybe you ought to stop associating with me."

"Are you kidding? Lose all those free meals and tickets to the ball games? To hell with him."

"It's good to know," McCall said with a chuckle, "that our friendship is based on such a firm foundation."

"I thought you'd be pleased. Seriously, though, if I can help you get the sonofabitch, I'll do it."

"I may just give you the opportunity. But, you know, we haven't talked about the guy who was arrested. Fill me in on him."

Haloran took some papers from his inside coat pocket. "Here's a copy of the arrest report and everything else I could put together for you."

"My gosh, Bill, you must really be feeling guilty. I didn't even have to ask."

"It's not guilt. I'm just pissed. They really screwed me on this one."

"Well, don't take it so hard. Assholes have asshole ways, and Clark Ramsey is the true personification of an asshole."

"No argument from me," Haloran responded.

"So, what about this Paul Broadus? Is he a prime suspect?"

"I'll say. He's a real screwball, been in and out of jail since he was a kid. Pervert, too. Liked to go around exposing himself."

"That doesn't mean he's capable of murder."

"Doesn't mean he isn't, either."

169

"Granted," McCall agreed, "but what was the basis for the arrest?"

"It's all in the material I gave you. I included a copy of the affidavit seeking a warrant for his arrest."

"I know it's all here, but I don't want to read all this crap right now. Just give me the basics."

"Well, one of the handwriting experts in the forensic lab said Broadus wrote the lipstick message at the murder scene. He compared the lipstick message with some handwriting samples from Broadus' employer and said they match. At least, that's what the affidavit says."

"That's it?"

"Not all of it, of course."

"Where did Broadus work?"

"Nichol's Department Store."

"How convenient," McCall said. "But I'm sure he wasn't friends with Roget's lover."

"I knew you'd start in on that shit when I told you where he worked. I don't guess you'd buy coincidence?"

"No way. I'm too much of a cynic for that. And what, pray tell, did Broadus do for Nichol's?"

"He was a repairman."

"And I'll bet he made some service calls to the Roget home?"

Haloran laughed. "Your perception amazes me."

McCall smiled. "Not what I'd call great detective work on my part. But then, if great detective work had been involved, Clark Ramsey's boys couldn't have handled it."

"The little girl also identified Broadus as the man she saw walking in the neighborhood," Haloran said.

"And I'll bet she made that identification from mug shots Clark's boys just happened to have in hand."

"Bingo, you're batting a thousand."

"Bill, I talked to that kid myself, and from what she told me, I don't think she could positively identify the man she saw that day."

"I'm just reporting what's in the affidavit."

"I'm not being argumentative, but this smells. Maybe I just feel that way because Ramsey's involved. I admit to being prejudiced where that sonofabitch is concerned."

"Hell, you're prejudiced where everybody's concerned," Haloran said, "but it looks to me like they've got a good case."

"They don't have shit."

"You just want to nail someone else for the murder, McCall. Can't you accept the fact that an ordinary repairman might be the murderer?"

"I'll accept the 'might' part of your statement, but I still say there's more here than meets the eye. It sure is convenient, too, that the repairman works for the same company where Francis Reynolds works."

"Reynolds works in the company's corporate office. I doubt that he knew Broadus existed before tonight."

"I don't. Working in the corporate office, he'd have access to the company's personnel files. He'd know that Broadus had a criminal record."

"Why do you do this?" Haloran said with resignation. "Why can't you accept this as just a simple open and shut case?"

"If I did that, you might get lazy."

"Have it your own way, you silly bastard, but it's all over."

"We'll see."

After leaving the diner, McCall went to the newspaper and cranked out a story on the arrest.

Afterward, he decided to check out some things in the affidavit. Harvey Faulkner was the handwriting expert identified in the document. McCall knew him, knew that he was a straight shooter. But he also knew that he wouldn't be able to get any information from Harvey.

That's why he decided to call Marie Cox. Marie was a divorcee who worked in the forensic lab, one he had dated casually before meeting Cele. He doubted that she would be home on a Saturday night, but on the chance that she was . . .

She answered after the second ring.

"Guess who?" he said.

"I'd know that voice anywhere. What in the hell do you want, McCall?"

"Damn, is that any way to greet an old friend?"

"I wouldn't know. But you can cut the bullshit and tell me what you want. I want you off the line because I'm expecting a call."

"Boyfriend?"

"Is everything still a question with you?"

"Damn, Marie, why are you being so difficult?"

"Because I don't want to mess with you anymore, McCall. You're not at the top of my list of favorite people, so state your business."

"I want to know about Faulkner's findings in the Roget case."

"I should have known. Sorry, McCall, but I don't know anything."

"You're bound to have heard some talk."

"Maybe, but why should I tell you?"

"Now you're asking questions. How about for old time's sake?"

"You have to be kidding. You dumped my ass for that kid you're living with and you want to talk about old time's sake. Screw old time's sake."

"So, forget old time's sake. What if I get you that stereo you wanted?"

"Oh, the one you promised me before you met your child bride?"

"We're not married."

"It's just a matter of time, McCall. Just a matter of time."

"Damn it, Marie, do we have a deal or not?"

"Don't be so overly sensitive, McCall. A man of your years could go just like that. We've got a deal, though. One thing, though. Am I going to have to take my clothes off to get the stereo?"

"Not for me, you're not. The paper's going to pay for it, not me."

"So, what do you want to know?" she asked.

"Anything and everything you heard regarding Harvey's findings."

"Well, I can tell you this much. Harvey was pretty pissed that his findings were used in the affidavit to arrest the guy they nailed tonight. He told'em his findings were inconclusive and that he hadn't finished his analysis. He only said that he noted similarities between the suspect's handwriting and the death-scene message.

"And I guess you know it was Clark Ramsey's people who brought Harvey the handwriting samples. They got them from Nichol's Department Store."

"Yeah," McCall said, "I know that. Anything else?"

"That's all I know."

"You've been a big help, Marie."

"Matt."

He knew her mood had changed when she called him by his first name. "Yeah, Marie."

"If you bring the stereo over, I'll take my clothes off for you."

"That's very tempting." He made a mental note to stay away from Marie.

Since the handwriting analysis was inconclusive, chances were that eleven-year-old Barbara Walker's identification of Broadus might also be a bit shaky. He figured that Ramsey, for some reason, had moved faster than the evidence merited.

Of course, the affidavit referred to Broadus' work records, which showed that he had been at the Roget home on four occasions to do repair work. And there was mention of ten-year-old Ronnie Hollis seeing a van in the area on the day of the murder. But McCall remembered that Ronnie wasn't all that sure about when he had seen the van.

To McCall, it looked as though Ramsey's troops had put together a hodgepodge of circumstantial evidence, but nothing of substance. Why had they moved so quickly? Why hadn't they waited until they had a solid case?

He decided to call Lanelle. When she answered and heard his voice, she said, "I thought you were coming over tonight."

"I was," he said, "but they arrested a guy in the Roget murder."

"I know. I saw it on the news."

"You shouldn't be watching that trash."

She laughed. "When I read the paper, I get ink all over my hands. Besides, if I had waited to read about it in the paper, I wouldn't have known until morning."

"You'd at least know a helluva lot more about it, though."

"I'm not all that concerned about it. Hubby and the kid are gone, I have some excellent wine chilling, and the hot tub awaits. Now, how soon can you get here?"

"Whoa, Lanelle. Your offer is tempting as all get out, but I've got to put a story together."

"That's not going to take you all night."

"No, but it's going to take me a couple of hours."

"I can wait."

"Fine," he concluded. "Then I'll be there when I finish."

"I'll be waiting."

"Listen, Lanelle, did Mrs. Walker say anything to you about the police questioning her daughter?"

"We talked about it."

"Well, I was a bit surprised that the kid was able to identify the suspect as the killer."

"If you're talking about the guy who was arrested, she didn't."

"What do you mean?"

"They showed Barbara some pictures and she told them that the man in the pictures could have been the man. But she wasn't positive."

"That's interesting."

"They must have some other evidence," Lanelle said, "because I don't think they could have arrested him on Barbara's say so. At least that's what Barbara's mother told me."

"I'm sure you have the straight story."

"So, damn it, get your work done and get on over here."

"I'm coming. I'm coming."

She laughed. "Save that part."

The woman is unbelievable, he thought.

He called Celeste.

"I thought you were coming over tonight," she said immediately after he greeted her.

My God, did I promise every broad in town that I'd be over tonight? he wondered. Then he remembered that he had promised to have a wine-tasting with Celeste. His plans had changed because Cele had decided not to visit her parents. But he had forgotten to call Celeste.

"There's been an arrest in the Roget case," he explained. "I had to work."

"I saw it on the news. How late do you have to work?"

"I don't know. You never know in a situation like this."

"I don't care how late it is, I want to see you."

"I'll get over there if it's humanly possible," he promised.

"Make it humanly possible," she commanded.

My God, he thought. How am I going to manage this?

"OK, I'll be there, but I do have a question for you? Does Paul Roget use Sweet'n Low?"

She laughed. "That's a strange question. But yes, he does use it. Mr. Winnow and Mr. Darden use it, too. Does that help?"

"Maybe. Do you know if Francis Reynolds uses it?"

"He does. I've seen him when he visits. I use it, too."

"You're not a suspect."

"Knowing you, I'm a bit surprised. I figured everyone was on your list."

"C'mon, Celeste. Am I really that bad?"

"When it comes to being suspicious of people, no one holds a candle to you."

"Well, maybe I overdo it a bit, but I'm still pretty lovable."

"I'll give you an opinion on that after you get over here."

CHAPTER NINETEEN

McCall felt wiped out the next morning.

Lanelle had been demanding.

So had Celeste.

And Cele had been in a playful mood when he got home.

While drinking a steaming cup of coffee, he determined to revamp his personal life, something he had determined to do on many previous occasions. After two cups of coffee, the cobwebs started clearing and he called Bill Haloran.

He first called the police station, but the detective wasn't in. Well, it was early. So, he called Haloran at home.

He asked the half-asleep voice who answered the phone to find out if Broadus used Sweet'n Low.

"Damn it, McCall," Haloran mumbled, "don't you know it's Sunday? Why don't you give up?"

"Never."

Haloran called back about thirty minutes later. He had talked to a jailor about Broadus' coffee drinking habits.

"He said Broadus used two packages of sugar in each cup of coffee he was served. Of course, sugar is all they offered him."

"Damn."

"Sorry, McCall."

"Don't worry about it, asshole. I'll find out what I need to know from a reliable source."

Haloran laughed. "You can always find one of your so-called reliable sources, but I think you're pissin' into the wind on this deal."

"It won't be the first time. But damn it, something smells here and I'm going to find out what it is. But it doesn't look like I'm going to get any help doing it."

"Whoa, pardner," the detective cautioned. "I may think this Broadus bastard is as guilty as hell, but you can sure the hell count on my help in making sure we have the right man."

"Thanks, Bill, I wasn't implying anything about you. I know that I can count on you."

"Damn right, buddy."

"I'll call you if I turn up anything."

"Do that. And, McCall..."

"Yeah?"

"I don't think you're right, but just in case...well, be careful."

"I will."

McCall then telephoned Ramirez. "Meet me at the office in twenty minutes."

"Damn, McCall, it's Sunday," he protested.

"So, what does that mean?"

"It's my day off."

"Day off, hell. When you're working on a major story, you don't have a day off."

"I thought the killer had been arrested."

"A man's been arrested, but we're still operating on the premise that a man's innocent until proven guilty."

"Enough said," Ramirez replied with resignation. "I'm on my way."

After hanging up, McCall went to the bedroom and kissed Cele lightly on the cheek. She was still sleeping soundly. He then headed his car to the *Tribune* Building and was ten

177

minutes into the Roget file when Ramirez arrived.

"Want some coffee?" Ramirez asked.

"Thanks," he replied, still engrossed in the police report he was reading. When Ramirez returned with the coffee, he looked up and said, "Let's go over what we've got here."

Ramirez nodded agreement.

"First," McCall began, "we have a rather bizarre murder and a problem in establishing an exact time of death. Of course, that's not all that unusual. Only the TV coroners can pinpoint exact times. But if we can establish that death occurred during certain hours, the husband is off the hook. At least in terms of having committed the murder himself.

"We have a case here where the husband took his own sweet time in talking to police, and then only after his boss employed one of the highest priced defense attorneys in the state. And we're supposed to believe that this hotshot attorney was hired simply because innocent husband is unfamiliar with criminal law, an unfamiliarity that should have the dean of his law school spending sleepless nights.

"Innocent husband's boss says the high priced criminal lawyer is acting only as a consultant, a fact verified by the hotshot lawyer, he being one Jet Mitchell.

"But being newspaper types, familiar with abject poverty, we find that a hundred thousand dollar fee for doing a little consulting is, to say the least, extreme overkill. And we have a problem understanding why an innocent man is willing to cough up that kind of bread.

"But then we also discover that it isn't innocent husband who's coughing up the cash. It's his boss, which makes even less sense.

"Of course, in the process of discovering this, we also find that innocent husband may well be as queer as a three dollar bill. In fact, all the evidence points in that direction. We even find that right after his wife's death, and prior to speaking with police, innocent husband may have been doing a tango in Mexico with tennis partner and lover, Francis Reynolds.

"And by another strange twist of fate, we find that Reynolds is a corporate attorney for the company that employed our recently arrested and alleged killer, Paul Broadus.

"Oh, I should not forget to mention that there are allegations that all the attorneys working with and for Mr. Bob Winnow are homosexuals, including old Bob himself.

"Nor should we fail to mention that during the course of this investigation, we pick up some strong circumstantial evidence linking District Attorney Clark Ramsey to a real estate swindle and murder.

"How am I doing so far?"

"It sounds like fiction," Ramirez concluded.

"I guess everything out of what we consider ordinary sounds like fiction," McCall acknowledged. "But we're talking about real people here. And we're talking about dangerous people."

"What about the guy who was arrested?"

"My theory?"

"Yeah."

"A patsy. A poor, dumb sonofabitch who was set up beautifully."

"Why wouldn't the police see that?"

"We're not talking police here. We're talking Clark Ramsey and a cadre of homosexual lawyers. For instance, when was the last time the district attorney's office got involved in a murder investigation?"

"That's something I wouldn't know about."

"The way things normally operate is that once the police have developed information on a case, the D.A.'s office will track down and subpoena witnesses. Sometimes they'll even make the scene, but they normally confine their efforts to narcotics and gambling. The D.A.'s office does have jurisdiction, of course, but I can't recall a D.A. investigating a murder since I've worked at the paper.

"What we have here is some sort of conspiracy that involves Clark Ramsey."

"If you're right," Ramirez said, "it's one that involves a lot of people."

"Right, and one that began several years ago. Laurie Roget's murder simply brought some previous crimes to light."

"But you really don't have any proof about any of this, McCall."

"The evidence is available, though. We're just going to have to dig it up. When a lot of people are involved, the evidence is usually easier to find. Some of these clowns have made mistakes. Now, are you ready to really get your hands dirty?"

"Sure," Ramirez answered, "but I'm guessing that since an arrest has been made, they'll pull me off working with you and put me on something else."

"I'll take care of that."

"Are you going to talk to Turner?"

"I'm going to talk to the whole crew...Turnip, Katie and Parkham. And I'm going to do it today."

"And you think they're going to give you a go-ahead to pursue this theory of yours?"

"I can't predict what they'll do, but I'm going ahead anyway. With or without their blessing."

"Unfortunately, I don't have the kind of leverage you have."

"You will in time. For now, I'll be the leverage for both of us."

"McCall, I've been meaning to tell you how much I appreciate you putting my name on the stories along with yours."

He laughed. "Don't patronize me, you little asshole. Get us some more coffee and we'll get to work."

While Ramirez was getting the coffee, McCall asked the switchboard operator and told her to call Parkham, Sipe and Katie.

"Ask them to meet me here in an hour," he said.

"McCall, it's awfully early and it's Sunday," she protested.

"What's all this early and Sunday shit? Just call'em. If they get pissed, it'll be at me, not at you. And another thing, remind Turnip to take a shower before coming down here."

"That I won't do," she said.

When Ramirez returned, McCall said, "To continue with our scenario, innocent husband has supposedly been supplying information to the police all along through our trusted district attorney, Clark Ramsey. This tidbit comes from Jet Mitchell, who I'm sure doesn't know about Winnow's and crew's homosexuality.

"But when it comes to misleading the general public or a jury, you don't want to sell ol' Jet short. He's a master of deceit, which is important to remember when dealing with him. You don't get in a pissin' contest with Jet until you have a full bladder. So, we have to come up with some solid stuff or we'll be up that well-known creek."

"Do you think the husband is guilty?" Ramirez asked.

"Not really. I don't think he committed the actual crime, but I think he may know who did. That's why we have this elaborate coverup."

"But what if the repairman is guilty?"

"If he is, he is. That's something we have to find out for ourselves, though. And I still want to know why the powers that be put such an elaborate wall of protection around Paul Roget.

"I want to know why the district attorney's office got involved in what would normally be considered a police investigation. And I want to know why the detective in charge of the investigation was kept in the dark by Clark Ramsey and his boys."

"Do you mean Bill Haloran didn't have any information on the repairman?"

"He knew Broadus had been to the Roget house, but didn't know an arrest was planned."

"Damn," Ramirez said, "I'll bet he's pissed."

"I don't think he's as pissed as I am. Ramsey got in touch with all the media except the *Tribune*. And he did that because he knows I've been checking on his dirty ass."

"So, where do we go from here?"

"In regard to the repairman, back to square one. We have a little information on him, but I want everything from the cradle until now. I want to know all his habits, even to how many times he goes to the john every day. We want to develop a profile on him that's as easy to read as a Dick and Jane book.

"And most important, we want to account for every minute of his time on the day of the murder."

"That may not be easy."

"And it may not be hard."

"What do you mean?"

"Most people are pretty predictable. They get into habits that aren't that easy to break. And that means they see the same people every day."

"I hadn't thought of it," Ramirez said, "but I guess you're right."

"Believe me. And human behavior isn't a matter of IQ, either. The smartest men are often the most predictable."

"But what about the crazies? The guy who killed Mrs. Roget may have been off his rocker."

"I doubt that he was, unless you want to say that all killers are crazy. But it's been my experience that the crazies are just as predictable as so-called sane folks. We just consider their patterns of behavior as abnormal."

"Where did you come up with all this shit?"

"Experience. I've observed the species a long time, so my hunches aren't always intuition. Of course, I'm not always right, but what the hell. It makes life a bit more interesting."

Ramirez laughed. "OK, so how are we going to approach this? Discovering all that we can about Broadus, I mean?"

"I'd say that a good starting point would be his wife."

"A lawyer usually tells the wife of a suspect to keep her mouth shut."

"True. Which means that we come in the back door."

"Meaning?"

"We talk to her parents, friends, relatives, anyone who'll listen. We convince them that we're trying to help the guy, not

182

hurt him. We even tell them we think he's innocent, because that's what they all want to believe. They'll get word back to the wife, and sometimes even the lawyer comes around.

"Let's face it, lawyers play all kinds of ethics games, but most of them have egos that love publicity. A case like this one can mean a lot to a defense attorney, because if he gets the client off and gets some good ink, then he's going to have a bevy of clients knocking down his door. And for most of them, the game isn't justice. It's money.

"We sure won't have any trouble getting people to talk to us, because they love to talk about the bizarre. And the fact that they know either the victim or suspect makes it all the better. For some of them, knowing the victim or suspect in a murder will be the biggest event in their lives."

Looking at the police report, Ramirez said, "I see that the Broaduses live in an apartment. You don't expect Mrs. Broadus to be there, do you?"

"No, but we won't have any trouble finding her. I've checked and found that her parents live here. I'm pretty sure that she'll be with them. Or they'll know where she is."

"Logical."

"In this case, yes. But things aren't always that easy. Now, before our illustrious editors get here, I need to make a couple of phone calls."

McCall had a note on his desk that Mary Murphy had called on Saturday night. She had called while he was with Lanelle.

When she answered, he said, "Mary, this is Matt. I'm sorry I didn't get back with you last night, but it was awfully late when I got your message."

"He's not guilty, Matt. I don't care what they say."

"You mean the repairman?"

"Yes."

"I tend to agree with you, Mary, but what are you basing that on?"

"I just know that Paul Roget had something to do with it."

"I agree with you on that, too, Mary, but without evidence

183

we're up the creek."

"It's going to be just like it was with Francis Reynolds' wife," she said. "Laurie's going to be forgotten, too."

"Whoa," McCall replied. "What's this about Francis Reynolds' wife? I thought Dr. Barrington told me he wasn't married."

"I just assumed that you knew. She died mysteriously last year. Suffocated, they said."

"I sure as hell didn't know a thing about it. Was it murder?"

"Not according to the sheriff's office in Jones County. They just figured it was an asthma attack or something."

"What did the autopsy show?"

"I wouldn't know about that."

"What was she doing in Jones County?"

"The way Laurie explained it to me, the Reynolds have a cabin on Jones County Lake. Annie Reynolds was up there painting the inside during the week and he was supposed to join her on the weekend."

"So, he wasn't there. And I'll bet he had a dandy alibi for the time period in which his wife died."

"I don't know much about it. I just know that Laurie liked Annie and was really upset about her dying."

"Laurie's going to be avenged, Mary. You have my word on that. It's going to be a priority item."

"I hope so."

After telling Mary goodbye, McCall dialed Haloran's home number. His wife answered and called him to the phone.

"Bill, did you know that Francis Reynolds' wife died rather mysteriously last year?"

"No, I didn't. Damn it, McCall, don't you ever quit? Talk about me working all the time."

"Let's not discuss my work habits. Are you interested, or not?"

"You know damn well I'm interested. How did she die?"

"Suffocation. Up in Jones County."

"Oh, shit," the detective said with resignation. "I'm not

talking about the suffocation. I'm talking about Jones County. There's more crap goes on up there."

"Well, I was going to ask you to check on the circumstances surrounding the death."

"I'll sure as hell try, but don't expect any miracles."

"When do you think you'll have some information?"

"How about tomorrow?"

"I was hoping to get something today."

"You asshole. Don't you know it's Sunday?"

"All of a sudden, everybody's got all this damn reverence for Sunday."

"OK, McCall, I'll drag my ass down to the station and make a few phone calls for you."

"Thanks, Bill."

He noticed, after hanging up the phone, that Ramirez had placed a fresh cup of coffee on his desk. He interrupted the young reporter, who was going through the Roget file, and told him about Reynolds' wife. Then he sipped the coffee and stared out the window, thinking that, with all its tentacles, there was no telling what direction the Roget case might lead. It was hard to get a handle on anything.

Parkham, Sipe and Katie finally arrived. They met in Parkham's office.

"What I'm about to tell you," McCall said, "may sound a bit unbelievable. But bear with me, because this has to be taken as a whole."

McCall then laid out all that he had learned while working on the Roget case, including the latest information on Reynolds' wife. He told them he suspected a conspiracy, and that he thought Broadus had been set up to take the fall for a murder that he didn't commit.

He could see that all three editors were shocked by his revelations, especially those concerning Clark Ramsey, Bob Winnow and his nest of homosexual lawyers.

After he had finished, McCall directed a question to Parkham. "Ed, what do you suggest that I do?" He already knew that he couldn't let go of the story, but he wanted to put Parkham on the spot.

But before Parkham could answer, Sipe said, "It looks to me like everything you have here is pure speculation, McCall."

"I agree," Katie said.

Parkham surprised McCall by saying, "I think you should go for it."

His response obviously shocked Sipe and Katie.

"Maybe some of it is speculation," Parkham continued, "but damn, if just part of it's true we have a great story. I hope to hell all of it's true, because the paper will get national recognition. And so will you, McCall."

McCall realized, of course, that Parkham's primary concern was his own career. A story of this nature would win awards, and it would enhance Parkham's reputation nationwide as a good managing editor.

The sonofabitch is smarter than I gave him credit for being, McCall thought.

"I appreciate your support, Ed," McCall lied, "but the only way I'm going to be able to tie this down is to be sure that we don't have any leaks. It's going to be tough enough without having an enemy in the camp."

"As far as I'm concerned," Parkham replied, "only the five of us will know about this."

"Unfortunately, that may be one too many."

"What do you mean?"

McCall answered, "Why don't you tell him, Turnip?"

"Tell me what?" Parkham asked.

Sipe fidgeted nervously and asked, "What am I supposed to tell?"

"About your friendship with Bob Winnow and Clark Ramsey. If either of them asks, you'll spill your guts."

"That's not true," Sipe protested.

Parkham was taking it all in, displeasure showing on his face.

"C'mon, Turnip, Winnow's been questioning you about my

activities and you've been filling him in on everything you knew. I just knew better than to trust you with some information."

"Is what McCall's saying true?" Parkham asked angrily.

"No, no it's not," Sipe pleaded. "I've talked to Bob Winnow on the phone, but I've never told him anything."

McCall knew that Sipe hadn't had anything to tell, but he wanted to plug all the holes, even the possibility of one. And Sipe's fear of Parkham would assure that.

"By God, there better not be any leaks," Parkham warned. "Do you understand that, Turner?"

Sipe nodded affirmatively. McCall enjoyed watching him squirm.

"OK, so we're backing you all the way, McCall," Parkham continued. "Do you need any more help?"

"Ramirez and I can handle it. Just make sure we get page one play on anything we turn up."

Parkham showed one of his rare smiles. "You got it. Just try to keep us out of a lawsuit. And try not to crack anyone over the head. We're still going through some legal hassles from the last time you decided to enforce the law."

"Don't worry," McCall said. "I don't want to dirty my hands on these clowns."

"And there's one other thing," Parkham said.

"What?"

"The next time you want to call one of these meetings, make it a day other than Sunday."

Everybody's a damn comedian, McCall thought.

CHAPTER TWENTY

Parkham, Sipe and Katie had been gone a couple of hours when Haloran called.

"I've got the information you wanted," he said. "Why don't we meet at the diner?"

"Good idea. I'm a bit on the hungry side."

Minutes later, McCall and Ramirez entered the diner and found Haloran occupying a booth near the rear.

"You want to flip," McCall asked, "to see who has to sit by the Mexican?"

"How in the hell do you put up with this guy?" Haloran asked Ramirez.

The young reporter grinned. "He kinda grows on you. And I take into consideration that he's close to being committed to an institution for the insane."

"I can believe that," Haloran said.

"What can I say?" McCall mock-questioned, then slid into the booth beside Ramirez. "So, what do you have, Bill?"

"Not so fast," the detective replied. "The extent of my information depends on the quality of lunch you buy me."

"Oh, brother. Your idea of quality is junk food. Well, go

ahead and order anything you like and I'll promise not to comment on it."

"That'll be a first," Haloran said.

The waitress had arrived, and was ready to take their order.

"Give me a couple of chili dogs," McCall said, "and go heavy on the mustard. I'll have a large milk to drink."

"Milk?" Haloran was surprised.

"Yeah, milk. You're giving me ulcers. Order clown, the woman doesn't have all day."

"OK, I'll take a couple of those chili dogs, too, and an order of fries. But give me a big coke instead of milk."

"Double that order," Ramirez said.

After the waitress had departed, McCall said, "Now, Bill, lay it all out. Nice and slow."

"Well, it's like you said," Haloran began, "the circumstances surrounding Mrs. Reynolds' death were a bit suspicious. But over in Jones County, law enforcement doesn't look at things the same way we do."

McCall questioned, "You're telling me they didn't see anything unusual about her death?"

"Right."

"What did the autopsy show?"

"There wasn't one."

"You're kidding."

"Unfortunately, I'm not. They're not real big on autopsies in Jones County. They just decided Mrs. Reynolds died of natural causes."

"Who found the body?" McCall asked.

"A deputy. Reynolds couldn't reach his wife on the telephone, so he called the sheriff's office and asked them to check on her. He told them he was worried because she had been ill."

"Oh, that's good," McCall said. "That's real good. And I'm sure Reynolds had a perfect alibi from the time he last saw his wife until the body was found?"

"That's about the size of it."

"And I'll bet the doors of the lake house were left open so the deputy could walk right in?"

Haloran grunted. "Why should I waste my breath telling you this, McCall? You already know the story."

"Didn't it seem strange to the deputy that a woman alone in a lake house would leave the door open?"

"He figured the reason was that she got sick and forgot to close it," Haloran replied.

"Did they even bother to find out what type of alleged illness she had?"

"She had a history of asthma."

"Can that kill you?"

"I dunno. I guess damn near anything can kill you. Anyway, the doctor who examined the body said she suffocated."

The waitress brought the food and they all dug into the chili dogs.

Between bites McCall said, "I thought you said there wasn't an autopsy?"

"There wasn't," Haloran reaffirmed. "One of the local doctors looked at the body and signed the death certificate. He's the one who decided the cause of death was suffocation. But my contact at the sheriff's department said they found no evidence of foul play."

"This really smells to me," McCall said.

"It is a bit putrid," Haloran admitted. "But you might as well give up on getting anything out of Jones County. They don't have a coroner, and the sheriff's office doesn't like to open the book on a closed case."

"I really can't believe all this," McCall said. "Am I just being paranoid, or is there a conspiracy here?"

"When you're on a story, you're always paranoid," the detective replied. "But I'd be the first to admit that there are a lot of unanswered questions on this one. And you just keep turning up bodies. I'm not sure there's any connection between Laurie Roget's murder and the deaths of Harold Webster and Mrs. Reynolds, but you do give an old cop a lot to think about."

"The fact that you think sets you apart from most of the police department."

Haloran laughed. "Let's not get nasty."

"If you're worried about nasty, wipe that chili off your chin."

Ramirez laughed as Haloran ran a napkin across his chin.

"You know what I'm thinking?" McCall asked.

"I'd never admit to that," Haloran said. "If I did, they might put me away."

"I'm thinking it would be good to know where Roget was when Mrs. Reynolds died. And I'm thinking it would be good to know where Reynolds was when Laurie Roget was killed."

"What are you implying?" Ramirez asked.

"He's saying," Haloran interpreted, "that we may have had swap-out murders."

"That's right," McCall agreed. "It would even explain the lipstick message on the mirror."

"Not a bad theory," Haloran admitted. "But we don't know for sure that Mrs. Reynolds was murdered."

"I don't think there's any doubt."

"Damn it, McCall, there is doubt. You're always going off half-cocked. You can't make any statements like that."

"Bill, I can make any statement I damn well please. And when have I ever been wrong on something like this?"

"Not often."

"When?"

"Hell, I don't know. I don't keep records of your half-assed statements."

"You can't think of a time, can you?"

"Not right off-hand."

"See."

Haloran mumbled, "Just because my memory isn't functioning doesn't mcan you've been right all the time."

"Hey, I don't want to butt into this argument," Ramirez said, "but let's not forget that there's a guy in jail for Mrs. Roget's murder."

"I hadn't forgotten Roget's patsy," McCall replied.

"Now, that's something else you don't know for a fact," Haloran said.

McCall challenged with, "Are you playing the devil's advocate, Bill?"

The detective came back with, "Someone has to."

"I'll bet," McCall said, "that within one week I'll have all the evidence necessary to prove that Broadus was framed."

"Are you going to manufacture the evidence?"

"That won't be necessary."

"Hell, I know better than to bet with you," Haloran said. "But what about the case Clark Ramsey and his boys have put together? Don't you think Ramsey's people checked out Broadus' alibi."

"Ramsey and his people can't find shit in an outhouse," McCall answered with disgust. "And they sure as hell weren't objective in their investigation. They set out to make Broadus guilty. And besides, I doubt if they talked to Broadus before the arrest. They probably don't know if he has an alibi or not."

"You're probably right," Haloran agreed. "But do you think you can be objective in investigating the situation? C'mon, McCall, I know you."

"I didn't say I was going to be objective. I'm going to nail these assholes, and that includes Ramsey. It's time someone put the silly sonofabitch away."

"Hey, don't get overwrought with me," Haloran said. "I wish you the best of luck, but this time you may really be pissin' into the wind. Taking on the district attorney isn't what I'd call a sure bet.

"And you'd best be sure you're going after the truth, not just trying to prove one of your theories."

"Don't worry about me, Bill. In this case, my theory is the truth."

CHAPTER TWENTY-ONE

"What now?" Ramirez wanted to know as they were leaving the diner.

"We talk to Broadus' neighbors, friends and, hopefully, his wife."

"Ramsey's people talked to Broadus' neighbors," Ramirez said. "According to our competition, Broadus was abusive, hollered at kids and so on."

McCall laughed. "And that's the stuff murderers are made of, huh? If everyone who hollered at kids was convicted of murder, there wouldn't be many parents left."

"Good point."

They got in McCall's car.

"Besides," McCall continued, "since when do we accept anything the competition prints. You know those dips got all their information right from Ramsey's mouth. They never check anything for themselves. Eddie, if you're going to be a good investigative reporter, never accept the party line on anything."

It was only a twenty-minute drive to the apartment complex where the Broaduses lived.

"Where do we start?" Ramirez asked while exiting the car.

"We start with anyone who'll talk to us. But I guess the manager's office should be the first stop."

But as they were walking toward the manager's office, McCall saw a woman working in the yard and said, "Let's talk to her."

They identified themselves to the woman, who told them her name was Chris Darling. She said she was the yard person for the complex, also lived there.

"You obviously know why we're here," McCall said. "We want to know anything you can tell us about Paul Broadus."

He made note of the fact that the robust-looking woman had big, well-shaped tits. She was fairly attractive, probably in her early thirties. The tits looked firm enough, but her ass was, perhaps, a little flabby.

"Well, I can tell you this," she said, "the man's getting a raw deal. It's unfair the way the papers have treated him."

"Don't blame me," McCall replied. "We haven't printed anything negative about him."

"You printed that stuff about his prison record."

"Well, yeah, we printed that. But that's public record stuff. We haven't tried and convicted him."

She argued, "I hear he has an alibi, so I don't see what purpose could be served by printing all that stuff about him exposing himself. You sure didn't make a big deal about that football player who exposed himself to those kids last year."

"We reported it, though. And you have to remember, he wasn't accused of murder."

"He should have his cock cut off."

McCall and Ramirez laughed.

"Well, he should have it whacked off," she reiterated with a smile. "Kids look up to those guys."

"I won't argue with you on that," McCall said. "I'm a proponent of capital punishment and, brother, that's capital. But we're not here to argue the pros and cons of castration. We just need some information on Paul Broadus, and not so we can hang him. We just want to get the truth."

"The truth is," she said, "that I like Paul. He's always been very nice to me. In fact, either the day before or the day of the murder, we had a conversation about his and Annie's Siamese cat. She's gorgeous."

Broadus' wife's first name, Reynolds' wife's first name. The same. Another coincidence, McCall thought. There were just too many of them.

"You just can't tell me that man is guilty," Chris continued. "Sure, he hollers at kids. I do, too."

"Since you call the Broaduses by their first names, I suppose you know them pretty well."

"It's a small complex. You get to know a lot of the people who live here. But Paul and Annie have been very nice to me. I've had coffee with them a few times."

"Do you recall whether Paul used Sweet'n Low in his coffee?"

"That's a strange question."

"Maybe. But it's important. Do you remember?"

"Neither of them uses it," she replied. "I know because I wondered why Annie didn't. She's a bit heavy anyway, and now, with the baby coming on, she needs to watch her weight."

"So, she's pregnant?"

"Very."

"And you think Paul's gotten the short end of the stick in regard to this murder investigation?"

"He's a nice man," she said. "I don't care what anyone else says. But with the newspapers and television crucifying him, what are people to think? Look at the husband. He's the logical one. There's some weird stuff going on. I mean, c'mon, he wouldn't even talk to the police for a week.

"And Paul, he's had ample opportunity to rape and kill me. This whole thing just breaks my heart, because even if he's acquitted he can never hold his head up again.

"I'm not the only one here who believes he's innocent. If you knew the man, you'd understand why we don't think he's guilty."

"I want to know him," McCall said, "because that's the only way I can help him."

"Why should you be interested in helping him? No one else is."

"Because I don't think he's guilty, either."

"Well, hallelujah. It's nice to know that someone from one of the newspapers has some common sense. But I still believe justice is only for those that can afford it."

"Maybe so, but if I'm given the opportunity, I might be able to help Paul Broadus. It would help if I could talk to Annie."

"She isn't here."

"I didn't figure she would be, but you being friends and all, I'll bet you could put me in touch with her."

"I don't know that she'll want to talk to you."

McCall handed Chris his business card. "It has my work and home numbers. Ask Mrs. Broadus to call me, or you call if you can arrange a meeting."

"I'll try," she agreed.

"Now what about this woman who said Paul stared at her all the time?"

"That bitch. That's a crock of shit and you can quote me."

McCall laughed. "I probably will."

"The police around here are a joke," she said. "You can't find them when you need'em, but when you don't need'em, they're all over your ass."

Neither McCall nor Ramirez could help laughing at her tirade.

She smiled. "I'm not kidding. Shit, why aren't the police nailing that damn husband. He's the one who killed her. I'll bet my bottom dollar on it."

"The husband has a pretty good alibi."

"Well, the whole thing stinks if you want my opinion," she said.

"You said you weren't sure whether you talked to Paul the day before or the day of the murder."

"That's right. My children were here during the time, and they were flying in and out of the apartment so much that it's hard for me to remember."

"Your children don't live with you?"

"No, they live with their father."

McCall wasn't sure why a warning signal went off in his brain every time a mother said her children lived with their father. Maybe it was because a mother's character had to be pretty questionable, at least in Texas, before most judges would award custody to the father.

"How old are your children?" he asked.

"I have girls thirteen and ten, and a boy who's six. They were here for the whole week and we had a birthday party for my little boy. Paul and Annie came to the party."

"So, you're not sure about seeing Paul on the day of the murder?"

"No, I'm not."

"What about Mrs. Broadus?"

"I can't be certain. She works, too, and generally doesn't get home until around six."

"The day you and Paul talked about the cat, do you recall the time?"

"It was late afternoon. Maybe he had just gotten off work. I'm not sure."

"Do you recall what he was wearing?"

"If he had just gotten off work, he was probably wearing his uniform. But you know how it is when you see people a lot. You don't pay that much attention."

McCall didn't know. He had been trained to observe and remember everything, down to the most minute detail.

"What did Paul usually wear?"

"You mean around here?"

"Yeah, when he wasn't wearing work clothes."

"Most of the time he wore jeans and a western style shirt."

"What about shoes?"

"He likes cowboy boots. I think it's 'cause they make him

197

look taller."

"Did you ever see him in a suit?"

"He has a suit that he wore to church on Sundays. Annie had him going to church every Sunday."

"Do you remember the color?"

"It was dark blue, I think."

"You said you had coffee with the Broaduses on occasion. Since both of them worked, was this primarily on weekends?"

"Sometimes in the evening, but mostly on weekends."

"How long have they been married?"

"A little over a year."

"Do you know if either of them had been married before?"

"No."

"What was this church they attend?"

"Mission Drive Methodist."

"And they're regulars, huh?"

"Every Sunday."

"Where does Mrs. Broadus work?"

"Crow Realty. But she's taken a leave of absence because of this mess."

"That's understandable. Now, I'm counting on you to get in touch with her for me."

"I'll try."

"Any suggestions about who else I should talk to here?"

"You might want to try Sylvia Jenson. She's the manager."

As they were walking toward the complex office, Ramirez said, "You figure that Mrs. Broadus is with her parents, so what's the point in getting Chris Darling to be your go-between?"

"Because I want Annie Broadus to think that talking to me is her idea. Chris Darling may be able to convince her that by talking to me, she might help her husband. You know it's always better to make someone think something is their idea."

"Yeah," Ramirez said. "I can buy that."

Sylvia Jenson was busy with paperwork when they entered the office. She seemed, however, anxious to dispense with what she was doing.

"You'd have a hard time making me believe Paul Broadus is a murderer," she said. "We normally talked once or twice a week. He'd usually stay in the office thirty minutes to an hour."

"What did you talk about?" McCall asked.

Sylvia, he thought, looked like an apartment manager. She was five feet six or seven inches tall, more than filled out her blouse and slacks, had frosted hair and was mildly attractive.

"We talked about anything and everything," she told them. "We never got into where he was from or his family ties, but he's a very nice man."

"Did you know about his prison record?"

"Not until I read about it in the paper."

"Now that you know about it, does it bother you?"

"Not at all. He made some mistakes and he paid for them. As much as I talked to Paul, I never heard him swear or even raise his voice. In fact, I wish all the tenants were as nice as the Broaduses."

"So," McCall said, "you obviously think that Paul Broadus has reformed."

"I don't know that he was guilty of anything, at least nothing I can be sure about. But this thing that's happened, it will kill the man. Whatever happened to innocent until proven guilty?"

"There'll still be a trial."

"Sure, but even if he gets off, what's he going to do? He's dead in this town as far as work is concerned. Who's going to trust him?"

"You're right, of course."

"The Broaduses are good people," Sylvia said. "No one here is hysterical, because they know Paul. It's tragic about that woman and someone should have to pay, but the police don't have the right man."

"They think they do."

"Well, they don't."

In interviews with other tenants, McCall and Ramirez found that most considered Broadus innocent, a victim of the system.

"A lot of husbands get rid of their wives like that," one woman said.

"The arrest scared me," another woman said. "I had a man chase me when I was walking back from the shopping center one night. That cured me of walking anywhere at night. Now, I take my car everywhere."

On the way back to the car, after McCall had decided that they had talked to enough people, Ramirez said, "Did you notice something about all the women we talked to?"

"What?"

"It was the largest collection of big-titted women I've seen in one place."

McCall chuckled. "Sometimes you get lucky. Of course, some of them weren't much even with big tits. Big-titted ugly women don't do much for me."

"I didn't think any of them were all that bad-looking."

"That must be because you're young and horny. You'll become more selective with age."

"Well, I'll sure take any of your culls."

"I don't have any."

When they were in the car, Ramirez said, "It looks as though you might be right about Paul Broadus. From what we learned back there, he's a model citizen nowadays."

"He's a fuckin' con artist."

"I thought you were all hung up on his innocence."

"I don't think he killed Laurie Roget, but guys like Broadus don't reform. He's a sicko and ought to be put out of his misery. Chances are that he's the one who chased the woman."

Ramirez laughed. "You're unbelievable."

CHAPTER TWENTY-TWO

"**S**he's on the phone," Ramirez said the next day.

"Who?" McCall asked. He was leaning back in his chair, feet propped on the desk, nursing a cup of coffee and pondering a spot on the ceiling.

"Annie Broadus."

McCall grinned. "Chris Darling came through for us." Taking the receiver from its cradle and pushing the lighted button he said, "Mrs. Broadus, this is Matt McCall."

"Chris Darling said you might be able to help my husband," the voice responded.

"If he's innocent, I know I can."

"Oh, he's innocent, Mr. McCall. He didn't have anything to do with killing that poor woman."

"Then I can help him. What we have to do is account for his whereabouts on the day of the murder."

"Mr. Cody's supposed to be doing that," she said.

"Cody?"

"Bill Cody. He's the lawyer we hired for Paul."

Putting the name and face together, McCall recognized Cody as an often-used attorney for some of the less desirable elements in the city.

"I didn't know you hired Cody," he said. "Is there any particular reason why you retained him instead of some other lawyer?"

"No, he just came to us and offered to help. Why, is there something wrong with Mr. Cody?"

"Not that I know of." Hell, he's probably as good as any of the other ambulance chasers, McCall thought.

"I'm not sure that Mr. Cody would want me talking to you," she said. "I called his office this morning and asked him to call me, but his secretary told me he would be out taking depositions all day."

"I'd think Mr. Cody would welcome my help," McCall assured. "It never hurts to have the press as an ally."

"The press has hurt, not helped."

"You're talking about the other paper and the television stations. I don't think you've read one negative thing about your husband in the *Tribune.*"

"Well," she challenged him, "you did print that stuff about him being in prison and all."

"We had no choice on that," he defended, "and your husband's past could actually work in his favor."

"What do you mean?"

"He has no record of violence, and from what I've been able to learn, he's a reformed, church-going man."

There was a momentary silence. "That's true."

"So, if you can provide me a detailed account of his whereabouts on the day of the murder, I can clear him."

"Well, I don't know. Mr. Cody..."

He interrupted. "Where are you, Mrs. Broadus?"

"Why do you need to know that?"

"I like to talk to people face-to-face. Did your husband give you an account of where he was on the day of the murder? I'm talking about a list of the places and the time he was there."

"Mr. Cody got that from him, but he gave me a copy. It has everything Paul did that day."

202

"Do you have it with you?"

"Yes, but Mr. Cody..."

He interrupted again. "While Mr. Cody is taking depositions on some other case, a witness who could help your husband might be lost to us. Let me take the list and run with it. Mr. Cody might have his mind on several cases, but this is the only one I'm interested in."

There was a prolonged silence.

"Look," he continued, the irritation obvious in his voice, "if you don't want my help, just forget it."

"I do want your help," she stammered, "but I just don't know what to do."

"If you really want to help your husband, you know what to do. We get on with this thing and we do it now. Every minute we lose just tightens the noose around your husband's neck."

There was an audible sob. "I'm at my parents' house."

Her reservations broken, he got directions to the home of her parents. It took only thirty minutes to make the trip to the south side of the city.

On arrival, McCall and Ramirez were greeted at the door of the white frame house by a gaunt, bespectacled man with sad brown eyes. He introduced himself as Tom Lomax, Annie Broadus' father.

They followed the smallish man into a modestly furnished room where Annie was sitting on the couch with an older woman.

"This is Mrs. Lomax," the man explained. "Annie's mother."

McCall smiled. "Nice to meet you Mrs. Lomax." She was a bit fleshy, very nondescript. "And nice to meet you, too, Mrs. Broadus."

Ramirez merely shook his head in greeting.

"Sorry," Lomax said. "For some reason, I thought you knew Annie."

"No," McCall said, "we've only talked on the phone."

"Daddy, I told you no more than thirty minutes ago that I

203

didn't know Mr. McCall."

McCall noted that Annie had inherited her mother's fleshiness and bland appearance. It was hard to imagine any man being excited by her.

Ignoring his daughter, Lomax said, "I've read a lot of your stuff, Mr. McCall. I told Annie that if anyone could help Paul, it would be you."

"I appreciate that. As I told Annie, if he's innocent, I'm sure we can help."

"What do you want Annie to do?" Mrs. Lomax asked. She, like her daughter, had a kind of brownish short cut hair that defied description. Her pug nose and the dark bags under the eyes accentuated a deflated football-shaped face.

McCall directed his comments to the younger woman. "If you'll provide me that list of Paul's activities on the day of the murder, we'll check everything out."

"I have it for you," she said, reaching for and retrieving a piece of paper from the coffee table in front of the couch. The difficulty she had in making the retrieval showed that she was well into her pregnancy. She extended her arm and McCall took the sheet of paper.

"Why don't you gentlemen sit down?" Mrs. Lomax said.

McCall and Ramirez found refuge in old-fashioned, overstuffed chairs.

"I'm glad you're going to check things out," Lomax said. "I don't have much confidence in that lawyer we hired."

"About Bill Cody," McCall said, "did you say that he contacted you about representing Paul?"

"Yes," Annie replied.

"Would you mind telling me how much he's charging?"

"I don't mind," Lomax said, "since it's my money we're paying him with. He's charging us twenty thousand dollars, and we had to give him five thousand in advance. Tell me, Mr. McCall, is that normal for lawyer fees?"

"I'm not sure there's such a thing as a normal fee for a lawyer," he answered with a laugh.

Lomax saw no humor in the reply.

"We had to mortgage our house to get the money," he said.

McCall felt a tinge of pity for the man. Here he was, a working stiff with a homely daughter, one he probably thought would never marry. And when she does land a man, he's a piece of shit, a pervert with a twisted mind. What's more, the daughter's now carrying the asshole's baby, which the father will probably end up supporting. It was enough to make a grown man puke.

"I'm sorry," McCall said. "If I'd gotten to you before you hired Cody, I might have been able to save you those legal fees."

Lomax shrugged his shoulders. "No point cryin' over spilt milk. If you can help Paul out, we'd be grateful."

"What about his folks?" McCall asked. "Can't they help with the legal fees?"

"Paul's father and mother are divorced," Annie said. "Paul's father lives in Kerrville and he hasn't had any contact with him in years. His mother's remarried and lives here, but they don't have any money."

"They damn sure have as much as I do," Lomax said.

Annie gave her father a disgusted look.

Typical woman, McCall thought. She doesn't appreciate what the man is doing for her.

"Tell me everything you know about Paul's background," McCall said to Annie.

"Why do you want to know that?"

"Because we want to establish who he is and what he's capable of."

"Don't be askin' Mr. McCall why, just do what he says," Lomax ordered.

"You already know Paul's been in trouble," she said.

"Yes, but being in trouble and being capable of murder are two entirely different matters. From a character standpoint, we need to qualify him as being incapable of murder."

"I don't know that much about Paul's past."

"Just tell me everything you know."

He took notes while Annie talked. It didn't take him long to realize that Annie didn't know much. About anything.

CHAPTER TWENTY-THREE

McCall was dubious. Broadus' time and place schedule for the day of the murder, the one Annie had provided, was too thorough. Either Broadus had an uncanny memory, which McCall doubted, or the man was lying.

And the latter was more likely.

It would probably take more than normal investigative work, McCall figured, to determine what was real and contrived in Broadus' recollection of his activities on the day of the murder.

"From what I've been able to ascertain so far," McCall told Ramirez, "Broadus is one of those stupid sonofabitches who is preoccupied with screwing up. If he's not nailed for this murder, it'll be for something else."

Ramirez laughed. "You have a high regard for your fellow man."

"This asshole's not my fellow man. Mark my words. We'll get him off the hook on this murder charge and he'll run out and show his cock to some woman or child."

McCall was speeding, driving at least fifteen miles an hour faster than the posted limit. Ramirez was busily trying to find a particular station on the car radio.

"None of that heavy rock shit," McCall warned. "That's one of the things wrong with the country. People making heroes out of a bunch of damn dopeheads who play loud guitars and yell words that no one can understand."

"Damn," Ramirez said, turning off the radio, "you're in one helluva mood. I thought you'd be happy because we're getting a handle on the story."

"We've got a handle on nothing right now. And I really don't like the idea of letting Broadus back on the street. Even if he is innocent."

"He's not out there yet. And he won't be unless we can verify his alibi."

"You're right," McCall said. "Read to me again what's on that schedule Annie gave us."

"It says here that the asshole, as you call him," Ramirez teased, "got up with his beautiful pregnant wife at six-thirty on the day in question. I added the 'beautiful wife' part."

"Ramirez, you little asshole, keep up the bullshit and I'll call immigration and have them haul your brown ass south." McCall really liked the fact that Ramirez was not intimidated by his sour moods.

"Hey, man," the young reporter replied, "I was born on this side of the border. I have a birth certificate and a Chevy to prove it."

McCall laughed. "OK, so what did the scumbag do next?"

"Well, since it was his day off, he made breakfast like a dutiful husband while the little wife got ready for work. They had a breakfast of poached eggs, crisp bacon, wheat toast, orange juice and coffee. Then knocked-up Annie left for work at seven-thirty."

"There are a lot of things about that report that bothers me," McCall said. "For one thing, do you remember what you had for breakfast two weeks ago?"

"Sure," Ramirez answered with a grin. "It's easy to remember because I never eat breakfast."

"Forget it, smartass. I guess it's possible Broadus would remember. Intelligent people tend to sort out things and remember only what is important. Dumbasses tend to remember any and everything."

"So, is remembering the breakfast menu important or unimportant?" Ramirez teased.

"Since, like you, I rarely eat breakfast, what do you think?" McCall countered.

"I noticed that you asked Annie if her husband ever used Sweet'n Low. Chris Darling had already told you he didn't."

"Just double checking. I'm convinced Laurie Roget's killer uses it. I'm positive that's who had coffee with her."

"Well, if Mrs. Broadus wasn't lying, and if Chris Darling wasn't lying, and if you're right about the killer using Sweet'n Low, then Paul Broadus isn't the killer."

"I've known that all along."

"Do you think he might have used it that day just to confuse the police?"

"Anything's possible, but I doubt it. I think it was premeditated murder. Broadus might be capable of killing someone, but I think it would be in a fit of passion, if I'm reading him correctly. I don't think he'd plan a murder."

"So, you're still holding to the theory that Roget and Reynolds did a swap-out?"

"Seems logical. And guess what?"

"What?"

"Both of them use Sweet'n Low."

"So do millions of other people"

"But they're not suspects," McCall countered. "But back to Broadus' alibi, what's really incredible to me is that a woman can get up at six-thirty, get ready for work, eat breakfast and be gone by seven-thirty. If Cele had to go anywhere at seven-thirty in the morning, she'd start getting ready about midnight"

Ramirez laughed. "The prettier the woman, the more time it takes her to get ready. Annie could probably have gotten up at seven and left at seven-thirty."

It was McCall's turn to chuckle. "A shrewd observation. Now, continue with our activities report."

"Well, Paul Broadus did what any dutiful husband would do on his day off. After Annie left for work, he washed the dishes, took out the trash and began vacuuming. But in the midst of all this activity, the phone rang."

"And who was calling?" McCall asked sarcastically.

"It was Annie," Ramirez responded in sing-song fashion. "Paul had asked her to call when she got to work, so he would know she had arrived safely."

"And did she call him the minute she arrived?"

"Oh, no. There was some work that had to be done immediately, so it was eight-twenty before she called."

"And was Paul worried about the delay in hearing from her?"

"Oh, yes. According to Annie, he was beside himself. Overwrought with anxiety."

"I know this is a stupid question, but if he was that concerned, why didn't he try to call her?"

"He doesn't like to call her at work."

"That explains everything. Does she call him every day to report her safe arrival?"

"No, only on his day off."

"Makes sense," McCall said facetiously. "So, what did our boy do after Annie's call?"

"He finished vacuuming, of course. You know a house-husband's work is never done. And after finishing his household chores, he took his car down to Chuck's Automotive to get it inspected."

"And what time did he arrive at Chuck's?"

"Nine-thirty on the dot. He remembers because Chuck has a big clock above his sign."

"And there it is," McCall said, bringing the Porsche to a stop in front of Chuck's. "Let's see if Chuck remembers things as vividly as Mr. Broadus does."

210

McCall's first impression of Chuck was that he was a man with an affinity for pizza and beer. He was short, fiftyish, balding and shaped like a pear.

"Yeah, I know you," Chuck said after McCall had identified himself. "I've seen your picture on a billboard or something."

Asked whether Broadus had brought his car in on the day of the murder, Chuck answered, "How in the hell do you expect me to remember that far back?"

"You do keep records, don't you?" McCall asked.

Chuck grinned, showing yellow teeth. "It depends on whether someone pays with cash, check or credit card. If he paid with cash, I might not have a record."

"Chuck, you're my kind of guy. No point payin' Uncle Sam when you don't have to."

"That's the way I figure it."

"But even for cash customers, don't you have some kind of work order?"

"Sure. And I was just kiddin' about not keepin' records." He turned toward an inner door and called out, "Vera, get your fat ass out here and help this man.

"Vera's my daughter," he explained. "She keeps the books."

A female clone of Chuck soon appeared, waddling up to where they were standing. Chuck introduced McCall and Ramirez, then said, "Mr. McCall wants to know if a Paul Broadus was here the day that lawyer's wife was killed. What day did you say it was?"

McCall told Vera the date.

"Yeah, he was here," she said. "I know because he talked to me quite awhile, and then I saw his picture in the paper and on TV."

"Damn it, girl," Chuck warned in a raspy voice, "haven't I told you that you're going to get your ass in trouble comin' on with every Tom, Dick and Harry who comes in here?"

McCall didn't figure Chuck had too much to worry about, that very few Toms, Dicks or Harrys would be interested in Vera.

"I wasn't comin' on to him," Vera defended. "He was waitin' for his car to be fixed and just wanted to talk."

Chuck mumbled an expletive.

"Do you remember the time of day when you talked to him?" McCall asked.

"I'm not sure about the exact time, but it was in the morning," she said. "It all kinda came back to me when I saw that he'd been arrested."

"Was he a regular customer?"

Chuck gave an "I don't know" shrug of the shoulders.

"I think it was his first time here," Vera said. "I think I'd have remembered his name if he was a regular."

"What did you talk about?" McCall asked.

"Nothin' much. We talked about the weather, stuff like that. Oh, he did tell me that his wife was going to have a baby, and that they had a Siamese cat."

"Do you recall what he was wearing?"

"I think he was wearing jeans and a western type shirt. Maybe he had on cowboy boots, too. I just can't recall."

"It would really help is you could remember the time when you talked to him. Does your service manager record the time a customer brings a car in?"

"Naw, we're not like a dealer," Chuck said. "We just tell 'em when they can expect to get it back. We do keep a record of how long we work on a car."

"So, it's possible that he brought his car in at nine-thirty and that you didn't finish the work until two o'clock?"

"I don't know what we did to the car," Chuck replied.

"According to Broadus, he had a minor tune-up and inspection."

"Vera, pull the work order," Chuck commanded. "If that's what the man had done, it probably didn't take over a couple of hours. It wouldn't take that long if I had any good help. You know, it's almost impossible to get good help nowadays."

McCall sympathized with Chuck's plight until Vera returned with the work order and a copy of the bill for service

212

on Broadus' car. Chuck examined both pieces of paper thoroughly.

"Yep," he said, "we worked on the car for a couple of hours. At least that's what we charged him for."

"But even if he brought his car in at nine-thirty, you might not have started work on it immediately?"

"That's right. Most of my mechanics haven't quit pissin', shitin', and drinking coffee by nine-thirty. And if he didn't have an appointment, we just worked him in as best we could."

"Do you keep an appointment book?"

"Naw, we throw that shit away."

"Obviously," McCall said to Vera, "you didn't talk to Mr. Broadus from nine-thirty until two."

"I just talked to him for a few minutes," she said. "And I think he said he'd had coffee in the cafe across the street before he talked to me. And when he paid his bill in the afternoon, I think he said he'd had lunch at the cafe."

"So you talked to him twice?"

"We didn't really talk when he paid his bill."

"The way Mr. Broadus recalls it," McCall said, "is that he had coffee across the street, talked to you from about ten-thirty until eleven, then sat in the waiting room reading magazines before and after lunch."

"That could be," she said. "I just can't remember the exact time we talked."

"What about his statement that he spent considerable time in the waiting room reading magazines?"

"I hardly ever go in there," she said. "We use a speaker to tell customers when their cars are ready."

"Vera, I know it's a lot of trouble," McCall said, "but while we're checking at the cafe across the street, would you mind compiling us a list of customers who might have been in the waiting room when Mr. Broadus says he was there? We'll need addresses and phone numbers."

"She'll be glad to make you a list," Chuck said. "By the way, Mr. McCall, do you think Broadus is guilty or innocent?"

"Chuck, I can think either way," McCall deadpanned.

As they were walking toward the cafe, McCall asked, "From here, how long do you think it would take to get to the Roget house by bus?"

"I have no idea," Ramirez said.

"I'm going to say anywhere from thirty to forty-five minutes, but I want you to check it out. Do the whole trick, which will include a little walking."

"When do you want me to do it?"

"You can do it tomorrow while I'm in Kerrville."

"I'd like to go with you."

"I need you here. I want Broadus' alibi checked out as quickly as possible, because I think things are finally going to start popping."

As they entered the cafe, McCall immediately surmised that it was not the kind of place Cele would like to go for Sunday brunch. It seemed clean enough, though. They occupied stools at the counter.

"My guess is that Broadus is a counter person," McCall said.

"I'm not even going to ask why," Ramirez responded.

"Good, because I have no idea."

A waitress brought water and asked, "What'll you have?"

"We'll start with coffee," McCall said. "And is that pineapple pie over there?"

"Sure is," she replied.

"Good, I'll have a piece."

"Me, too," Ramirez said.

While the waitress was filling their order, McCall asked, "Do you see that sign over there? The one above the pies?"

"You mean the 'Homemade Pies' sign?"

"That's the one. Signs like that really piss me off."

Ramirez laughed. "Should I ask why?"

"Because the pies are made here or in a bakery. They're not made at home. And what's the big deal about something being homemade? Who gives a shit as long as it's good?"

The waitress was back with their order.

"Pie really looks good," Ramirez said. "What bakery makes 'em?"

"We don't get 'em from a bakery," she said. "A lady bakes them at home every day and sells 'em to us."

Ramirez started laughing. He laughed so hard that tears came into his eyes.

"What did I say that was so funny?" the watiress asked.

McCall smiled. "You didn't say anything. Mexicans often have these fits of laughter for no apparent reason. I think it has to do with the water they drink down there."

She looked puzzled. Ramirez, still chuckling, took a sip of coffee.

"What's your name?" McCall asked.

"Melba."

"Well, Melba, I'd imagine that you have some of my friend's compadres back there in the kitchen, don't you?"

"Mexicans, you mean?"

"That's what I mean."

"We have a few."

"There's no such thing as a few. If the immigration people raid your kitchen while we're here, have 'em come out front and net this one, too."

She laughed. "I'm not sure I'd want you as a friend."

Ramirez agreed with an "Amen."

"You look familiar," Melba said.

"Name's McCall. I work for the *Tribune*."

"I was talking about the other gentleman," she said.

McCall laughed. "Melba, I'd appreciate it if you'd cut me a little slack. I'm duty-bound to train this youngster in the proper way to report the news, and he's already getting a swollen ego."

She smiled. "I know who you are. I recognized you when you came in. I suppose you're here to ask me about Paul Broadus?"

"Bingo, Melba. I wasn't sure who I needed to talk to, but I wanted to talk to someone about Broadus allegedly being here on the day of the murder."

"I'm the one to talk to. I work the counter every weekday from eight to five. Let me take care of this customer and I'll get right back to you."

While she was waiting on the customer, McCall took a good look at Melba. She wasn't bad. She had a good figure, good tits and wheels. The red hair wasn't all that attractive, but the face was pretty. He figured she was about thirty.

"You know," he said to Ramirez, "if I had to guess, I'd say that Melba has three kids and is married to a truck driver."

"How do you figure that?"

"Experience. Most of the waitresses who work in cafes like this during the day have two or three kids and are married to truck drivers."

"You have a really weird mind, McCall."

"Thanks. I consider that a compliment."

Melba returned and said, "I've been reading the stuff you've written about the murder."

"From what you said earlier, I assume Broadus was in here on the day of the murder?"

"He was here."

"You're absolutely sure?"

"No doubt about it. I know Paul Broadus, I'm sorry to say. I can't stand the man."

"Why's that?"

"Because he's been hassling me for months. He's always putting the make on me in his obnoxious way."

"Sorry to hear he's been giving you problems."

"It's nothing I can't handle. I just ignore him."

"He claims that he was in here twice on the day of the murder, once for coffee and again for lunch."

"That's right."

"Do you remember what time he came in for coffee?"

"It was a little after eight, because I hadn't been here long."

McCall looked at Ramirez. So much for the dutiful househusband part of the alibi.

216

"Are you sure about the time?"

"I'm sure. He didn't stay long, either. Not like he usually does. He wasn't here more than ten minutes."

"Do you remember what he was wearing?"

"Same as always when he's not working. Jeans, western shirt and cowboy boots."

"What time did he come in to eat lunch?"

"It was after twelve," she said. "It might have even been a little after one. Our rush was over. I remember that he ate lunch faster than he usually does, too. He probably wasn't in here more than fifteen minutes.

"The reason I noticed the short time he was here for coffee and lunch is that he usually hangs around forever, especially on his day off. Even when he's working and comes by, he stays a long time."

"Maybe it just seems like a long time."

She laughed. "You're right about that. By the way, another reason I remember is that he came in here the day after the murder, too."

"He did, huh?"

"Yes, and he started talking about it."

"What did he say?"

"He said that sort of thing could happen to any woman alone, that it could happen to me. He suggested that he should come over and keep me company if my husband wasn't home."

"Any reason why he'd think you might be alone?"

"Some time ago, one of the other waitresses told him that I didn't have any children and that my husband worked late sometimes. I threatened to cut her tongue out if she ever told him anything else about me."

"What does your husband do?"

"He's a coach at Mission High School."

McCall looked at Ramirez who was acting as though he was interested in something on the ceiling.

"When Broadus came in the day after the murder, was he wearing his work clothes?"

217

"Yes, his uniform."

"Do you remember when he came in?"

"It must have been about five, because it was almost time for me to go home. He started in about going home with me and I told him my husband would break his head. He said he wasn't afraid of my husband, that he was an expert in karate.

"He was always poppin' off about how tough he was, about all the slants he had killed in Vietnam. Now I read where he spent all his service time in the states, and most of that in the stockade."

"Well, he's not what you'd call a model citizen," McCall said, "but I'm not sure he's a killer."

"I don't know about that," Melba replied. "I just know he's a creep."

After they left the cafe and picked up the names from Vera, McCall said, "I want you to check this out, Eddie. What started out looking like a good alibi for our boy is beginning to fall apart. We're in deep shit if we can't find someone who remembers all that reading he did in Chuck's waiting room."

"If Melba's telling the truth," Ramirez said, "then Mrs. Broadus is lying."

"I'd put my money on Melba. I told you Broadus was a piece of shit. In regard to this murder he may be innocent, but he's scum just the same."

They got in the car and McCall juiced it. As they sped past a topless bar, McCall said to Ramirez, "Most of the girls who work in those topless places go with guys who ride motorcycles."

Ramirez looked at him incredulously. "You know, you're really off the wall, McCall."

"Eddie, another day like this and I'll be ready for the rubber room."

They spent some more time checking out Broadus' alibi.

CHAPTER TWENTY-FOUR

The next day McCall drove to Kerrville, the small town where Broadus had been born and had spent much of his youth. It was only an hour or so drive, but enroute he had considerable time to think about what he had learned of Broadus. And while he was still sure the man was innocent, things were not falling into place as he had hoped they would.

McCall had confronted Annie Broadus with Melba's statement regarding the times Paul was in the cafe on the day of the murder. Annie said Paul had told her about Melba, how the waitress was interested in him, kept coming on to him. Naturally, faithful Paul had refused her advances, which was why, Annie, said, that Melba had lied about her husband.

Referring to Broadus' written alibi, she had admonished, "You have to believe what's on that paper."

To which he had replied, "I don't have to believe anything."

But it didn't matter what he said. Annie stuck to her story about the time she called her husband on the day of the murder. She was, indeed, a dutiful wife. Stupid, but dutiful.

"I'm not doubting that you called him at that time," McCall had told her, "but I do doubt that he answered the phone. And another thing, if he was so concerned about your welfare, why didn't he drive you to work? Why did you have to take the bus?"

Annie hadn't liked the questions, became tearful. But then her tears had turned to anger when he had showed no sympathy.

"I'm not the enemy," he had told her. "I'm just telling you that your husband had better not try to run his alibi past the district attorney. It has too many holes in it. The truth is a helluva lot better weapon than a lie."

Ramirez had contacted the customers on the list Vera had provided. And though some of them had been in Chuck's waiting room during the time Broadus claimed to be there reading, none of them could remember him.

After his encounter with Annie, McCall had also had a confrontation with Bill Cody. The lawyer was angry because Lomax had told him that McCall said he was charging too much.

He had tried to explain to Cody that Lomax had misinterpreted what he said, but when the attorney became abusive he angrily shouted, "I didn't say it, but I should have."

A shouting match ensued, in which Cody had warned McCall to stay out of his business or face the consequences. McCall had told him that he would wrap his fuckin' consequences around his head.

And to top off the evening, he and Cele had had words. She had threatened to go home to her folks, and he had told her not to let the door hit her in the ass on the way out.

Yesterday was definitely not my best day, he thought. He was a bit concerned that the current one might not be any better. Two Extra Strength Excedrin hadn't helped his aching head.

McCall started his investigation of Broadus at the Kerrville Police Station, where he met the town's police chief, Scooter Scruggs. He was a wiry little man, fiftyish, with a long nose, big ears and gray hair.

"I'll bet you got that name 'Scooter' playing baseball," McCall said.

"No," Scruggs replied, "never played baseball. I think it's a family name."

"Kind of a strange family name."

"I dunno about that. Think it came from my mother's side of the family. She was Italian."

"Have you been police chief here long?"

"Forever," Scruggs replied. "Don't know why we need a police chief, really. Seems like the sheriff's department could handle everything that happens here. Truth is, game wardens have more crime problems than I do. Big deer hunting area, you know."

"Yeah, I know."

"Of course, we did have a woman murdered here a couple of years ago. Think it happened about the same way that woman in San Antonio was murdered. There was some writin' on the wall in lipstick and so on. Guess I'm going to have to see if Paul Broadus was in town at the time."

McCall knew that Scruggs was just talking, that by the following day he would have forgotten his intention to check. But McCall asked for copies of the police reports on the murder, which Scruggs cheerfully provided.

"Not often we get anyone from one of the big papers in here," Scruggs said, "except for deer season. Then we don't get anybody but sports writers. None of 'em know shit about deer hunting."

Asked if he remembered Broadus, Scruggs said, "I think he was a pretty good football player. You might check out at the high school with some of the coaches. And you might want to check with John and Kathy Wayland. He had some trouble with the Waylands. Tried to rape their daughter, the way I remember it."

Scruggs gave McCall directions to the Wayland home and the high school.

"Even though it's summer, there'll still be some coaches at

221

the school," the police chief said. "Around here, football's a year long thing. They'll have some boys out there practicing, even though it's against the rules. "When you get through, come back and I'll buy you a cup of coffee."

McCall found four coaches at the football field, trying to look uninvolved as some of their charges ran through what was touted as 'unsupervised play'. He sought out the head coach, a burly man who looked the way a coach was supposed to look.

"Paul was a quiet, courteous and respectful boy," the man said of Broadus. "But he'd run through a brick wall if I asked him to. He was a disciplined, tough kid.

"When he first came out for football, though, I don't believe I'd ever seen a kid so scared of contact. That's when he was a sophomore. He shied away from contact and none of the other kids respected him. Frankly, I didn't think he had any future in football."

"When did that change?"

"He began to develop as a junior," the coach said, "and by the time he was a senior he was the toughest kid on the team. It was a complete turnaround. He ended up playing linebacker, started most of his junior year and all of his senior year. I thought he might even try college ball."

"What else can you tell me about him?"

"Nothing much, except that he was a leader by action. He was basically quiet, easy to deal with, respectful in every way. I never heard anything bad about him.

"I've used him as an example to other kids many times, telling them they can get over being gunshy about hitting. Him being arrested for murder really shocked me."

McCall got a different perspective at the Wayland home. John Wayland was at work, but Mrs. Wayland was quite willing to tell how Broadus had attempted to rape their daughter, Kathleen, at knife point.

"At the time he was on furlough from the Marine Corps," she said in a voice tinged with bitterness. "Kathleen had been one of his friends in high school, so he came here and asked her to drive him to another friend's house. On the way, he pulled a knife on her, forced her to stop the car, then threatened to rape her."

"But that's as far as it went?" McCall asked.

"He forced her down in the car seat and told her he'd use the knife if she didn't do what he said. She said that when she told him her daddy would kill him, he got down on his knees in the floorboard and started crying.

"Kathleen was right about one thing. John would have killed him. Both of us wanted to kill him."

McCall knew not to be deceived by Mrs. Wayland. She was a tall, shapely and attractive woman for her age. She even looked a bit fragile. But she had those "no bullshit" eyes. He figured she would be capable of killing Broadus, or anyone else, who screwed with her daughter.

"So, what happened?"

"We went to the police," she said, "but were told to drop the matter. We were told that he was sick and that we should leave him alone. Can you believe that?"

"Was Scooter Scruggs the chief?"

"Yes, it was that gutless little toad that told us we should leave Paul Broadus alone. Anyway, I understand that he left town at four o'clock the next morning and we've never seen him since, but I'm still bitter about it. If he'd been locked up, maybe that poor woman would still be alive. I wonder how Scooter feels about that?"

"Scruggs was the one who sent me here."

"I'm surprised. He knows how we feel about him."

"As for Broadus, he was locked up several times for indecent exposure and spent some time in a mental institution," McCall said.

"Why in the world did they let him out?"

"I don't know."

"I guess you already know that he used a knife to rape one girl here and tried to rape another."

"No, I sure didn't. Who were the parties involved?"

"I can't give you their names because they may not want their names dragged into this mess. But the rape is the reason Paul Broadus went into the Marines."

"What do you mean?"

"The district attorney gave him a choice of jail or the service."

McCall checked Mrs. Wayland's allegation at the county courthouse. Sure enough, several years earlier, an affidavit was filed and a warrant issued for the arrest of Paul Broadus. The affidavit stated that he had committed an assault with a sharp and dangerous weapon on one Julie East. Charges had been dismissed without prejudice on recommendation of the district attorney.

In his continued questioning of townspeople, all of whom seemed eager to contribute, McCall discovered that Julie East was Broadus' aunt by marriage. Or at least she had been after his mother's second marriage. His mother dearest was now on her third trip.

A woman who worked in the courthouse told McCall that she had, years before, known the Broaduses quite well, and that Paul always seemed a bit abnormal to her.

"It's my understanding that he tried to rape the East girl," the woman said, "but he failed. He tried to rape two or three other girls, but never succeeded. Paul never could do anything right."

The woman also said Paul had been given a choice of jail or the service.

McCall found that the district attorney who had given Broadus a choice had been elected to the state legislature and was now practicing law in Dallas.

He discovered one of Broadus' high school friends, Bubba Tubbs, working at a service station.

"Yeah, ol' Paul and me used to run around together quite a bit," Tubbs said. "I'd say he was just a typical high school kid, got along with everybody. I don't think he'd kill anybody. It don't sound like him."

Several other persons contributed to his profile on Broadus. It would be a good story. But he still wanted to interview Broadus' father.

The senior Broadus, however, wouldn't talk to him. An elderly woman came to the door and relayed his message to the old man. He was told to leave or they would call the police. Since he didn't want to inconvenience Scooter, he left.

Over cups of coffee at the police station, Scruggs told him the elder Broadus was off in the head. "Some folks say it's 'cause he was in a Jap prison camp, but hell, he was crazy as a bat before he ever went in the Army. If the truth was known, being a prisoner was the best thing that could have happened to him. He's been gettin' a pension from the government ever since he got back. And he damn sure doesn't know how to do anything. Never did."

"He obviously had Paul a little late in life," McCall said.

"The ol' man knew how to use his peter, but that's about all."

CHAPTER TWENTY-FIVE

McCall's drive back to San Antonio took very little time. That's because he rarely let the speedometer drop below eighty.

He went first to the condo because he wanted to apologize to Cele. She wasn't there. A check of her closet revealed that all her clothes were gone. He checked her bathroom and found it also had been cleaned out. She had left nothing that belonged to her.

He considered calling her parents' home, but nixed the idea. She probably needed some time to cool off. Maybe a brief separation period would be good for both of them.

Checking his watch, McCall noted that it was time for the early evening television news. He clicked on the set and watched an inane commercial that led into the news broadcast.

One of the stories was that Broadus would the next week be going before the grand jury. The jury would determine if there was sufficient evidence to bind him over for trial.

McCall perked up when Clark Ramsey appeared on the screen. Responding to questions from a television reporter, Ramsey said the state had sufficient evidence to try Paul

Broadus for murder, that the suspect's appearance before the grand jury was a mere formality.

"You sonofabitch," McCall said aloud to the television set. "I'm going to knock you on your pompous ass."

He turned off the set, grabbed his jacket and slammed the door on his way out. Even in the belated rush hour traffic, he arrived at the *Tribune* in record time.

"Man, am I glad to see you," Ramirez said.

"I'm touched."

"The powers that be are about to piss in their pants. They're beginning to think we've gone out on a limb on the Broadus thing."

"Not to worry. I'm going to nail Clark Ramsey's ass. Wait until you see the story I'm turning in tonight."

"Chris Darling called you early this morning."

"Did she say what she wanted?"

"No, but she wanted you to call when you got in."

"Well, it might be important. Tell our illustrious editors that I'll meet them in Parkham's office in five minutes. In the meantime, I'll get big tits on the phone."

When McCall got Chris Darling on the phone, she was subdued.

"What's wrong?" he asked.

"There's something I should have told you, but I was afraid of hurting Annie."

"You mean about your affair with Paul Broadus?"

"How did you know?"

"I didn't. But your defense of him was a little too strong for just a neighbor."

"I don't want Annie to know."

"Well, she's not going to hear anything from me." He was disgusted with the woman for letting a scumball like Paul Broadus get in her pants.

"With Paul going before the grand jury and all, I thought I should tell you."

"Tell me what?"

"Annie called me last night and told me that you said Paul's alibi wouldn't stand up."

"Not unless we can account for a little time."

"Well, I can tell you when he was with me."

"Tell me."

When Chris Darling had finished, McCall had accounted for all Broadus' time on the day of the murder. He couldn't possibly have killed Laurie Roget.

"Annie's not going to know, is she?"

"She may have to know, if you want to save your lover," McCall responded coldly.

"You promised."

"I'll do my best, but if it comes to life and death, all bets are off."

McCall felt like shouting. It was like being vindicated for what he already knew was the truth. Someone other than Paul Broadus had killed Laurie. And he was pretty sure he knew who that someone was.

When McCall entered the room with Parkham, Sipe and Katie, he was loaded for bear.

"In about an hour I'll have a story that will account for all Broadus' time on the day of the murder. He couldn't possibly have killed Laurie Roget. Clark Ramsey will be crying in his Wheaties in the morning."

Katie and Sipe looked at Parkham in an attempt to read his reaction. The room was silent as the managing editor pondered the situation.

"I understand," he said, "that you have material for a comprehensive profile on Broadus."

"That's right."

"Are you going to give us that, too?"

"Why not? Let's drop the big bomb and see who gets hit by the fall-out."

"By god, McCall, go for it. I'll back anything you do."

There were times when McCall thought Parkham might be OK, but he knew the man would eventually ruin that impression with some dumbass move.

"Are you going to try to talk to Ramsey?" Parkham asked.

"I'm not going to just try. I'm going to talk to him."

"Good," Parkham said.

After the meeting had broken up, Ramirez asked, "Don't you think it might be hard to talk to Ramsey? It's late and I doubt that he's at his office."

McCall looked at his watch. "He's home freshening up now, but he'll be at the LeRendezvous Restaurant in an hour."

"How do you know that?"

"Because I know a young lady who works in his office. And earlier today, I called her from Kerrville and had her check his calendar."

Ramirez grinned. "And what did you promise this young lady?"

"I promised to introduce her to you," McCall said. "By the way, do you like French food?"

"Sure, I like tacos."

"I've never known a Mexican with any class," McCall lamented.

"May your children be weaned on jalepeno peppers," Ramirez replied.

It took McCall a little more than an hour to do his story, then fifteen mintues to drive to the restaurant. They were greeted by the maitre d', who asked if they had reservations.

"We're just going to have a drink at the bar," McCall informed him.

"I thought we were going to eat," Ramirez protested.

"This rich food could be bad on that sensitive stomach of yours," he said. "We'll grab some chili dogs on the way back to the office."

"Big deal."

The bar was situated in the center of the relatively small restaurant, so it was easy to get a view of the dining area. And there was no problem spotting Clark Ramsey. He was a tall, imposing man, built along the lines of a professional football player. His facial features were granite-like, and his hair, with some gray at the temples, gave the illusion of being steel blue in color.

Everything about Ramsey was immaculate, including the wife who sat across the table from him. McCall thought she looked more mannequin than human, as though she had been taken out of a store window. He wondered if she had a pulse beat.

Another picture book couple was with the Ramseys. Ramsey seemed always to be surrounded by people, McCall thought, which was the way it was with a politician. And that's what the district attorney was, a politician.

McCall was certain that the young man with Ramsey was one of his many proteges, probably a recent graduate of a prestigeous law school.

McCall and Ramirez had ordered light beer. When the bartender delivered it, McCall took his and said, "Wait here. I'm going to do my thing."

Ramsey saw him coming and rose to his feet. He extended his hand and said, "McCall, I didn't expect to see you here."

McCall shook his hand and responded with, "You probably thought this was a nice place."

Ramsey laughed.

"I could say that I was just in the neighborhood, but we both know that would be a lie," McCall added.

"I believe you've met my wife, Colette."

"Yes, we've met a number of times at dinners I didn't want to attend. You look beautiful, as always, Mrs. Ramsey."

Her automatic smile flashed on, then off. "Thank you."

"And this is Mr. and Mrs. Brian Parker," Ramsey said. "Brian's just recently joined my staff."

McCall shook hands with Parker, greeted his wife and thought, all Ramsey's flunkies look like they were cloned from the same Greek god.

"I notice that you haven't been served yet," McCall said.

"We haven't ordered," Ramsey said. "We were just having a

230

pre-dinner cocktail."

"I hate to bother you, but I do need to talk to you for a few minutes. Privately, if possible."

"No problem," Ramsey said. "The manager will let us use his office."

They excused themselves, checked with the manager, and entered his small office.

"OK, McCall, what can I do for you?" Ramsey began.

"Maybe it's what I can do for you."

"What do you mean?"

"Maybe I can tell you who killed Laurie Roget."

If his statement shocked the district attorney, the man didn't let it show. McCall had always credited him with having a calm demeanor. He was difficult to rattle, at least outwardly.

"Unless you've been away from all contact with civilization, you know that we already have Laurie Roget's killer," Ramsey replied.

"What if I told you that I could prove Paul Broadus couldn't have killed her?"

"I'd say you were crazy. We have an airtight case against Broadus."

"You don't have shit, Clark, and you know it. Your people put together a hodgepodge of circumstantial evidence."

"And, as usual, you have the truth," Ramsey grumbled. "It must be an awesome responsibility, McCall, always being the only one who's right."

Ramsey's sarcasm made McCall realize that he had struck a nerve. It was good to know that his adversary had a few.

"I'd think you'd be interested in the truth, Clark, no matter who or what the source."

"I only know that for some reason, you're out to get me."

"You're being a bit paranoid, aren't you? I came here to give you some information."

"Bullshit. If you have something to tell me, it's for your own benefit, not mine."

"You sure have me pictured as a cold bastard. Where did

231

you get that impression of me, from Bob Winnow?"

"Let's not play games, McCall. You don't like me and I don't like you. You've been trying to nail my ass for years, even before you came up with this Webster thing."

"I wasn't going to mention that, but now that you've brought it up, I won't deny that I think you screwed the Websters. And another thing that might be of interest to you. I've unearthed some evidence that Harold Webster's death was not an accident. He was murdered."

"Are you accusing me of having something to do with it?"

McCall waited a few seconds before replying. "Of course not. You're a man who solves murders. You don't commit them."

There was no problem in interpreting McCall's sarcasm.

"If this is the kind of shit you want to talk about," Ramsey said, "I'm going back to my table."

"Don't get your ass in an uproar, Clark, because I'm trying to give you a preview of what's going to be in tomorrow's *Tribune.*"

"If this is a threat, McCall..."

"No threats, "McCall said, "just a profile on Broadus along with all the facts on where he was the day Laurie Roget was murdered."

"Don't be stupid, McCall. We've checked, and there's no way you can account for all Paul Broadus' time."

"Don't count on it, Clark. When I decide to get stupid, I go all the way."

"You can't sell the public on Broadus' innocence."

"Wanna bet? Clark, my friend, we have accounted for all Mr. Broadus' time on the day of the murder. We have sworn testimony that'll blow your case right out of the tub."

"And you think you know the identity of the so-called real murderer?"

"Murderers, plural. You see, Annie Reynolds' death is tied to Laurie Roget's, but they weren't killed by the same person."

"Annie Reynolds? She died of natural causes."

"How do you know anything about Annie Reynolds' death?"

"Francis Reynolds is a friend of mine. So was Annie."

"If you'll get her body exhumed and have an autopsy performed, you'll discover that Mrs. Reynolds was murdered."

"Pure speculation on your part."

"So, I can't count on your support in getting the body exhumed?"

"Of course not. Besides, she died in Jones County."

"But she was buried here."

"I don't know what you're leading up to, McCall, but you're skating on very thin ice."

"You know exactly what I'm leading up to. We're talking swap-out murders here. Roget kills Reynolds' wife so Reynolds can have an airtight alibi. Reynolds kills Roget's wife so Roget can have an airtight alibi."

"That's ridiculous. I know both men."

"I know you do. But what have they done for you that makes you so protective of them?"

"Why do you say I'm protective?"

"What would you call it, Clark? I'm referring to your interference in the Roget case."

"I call it my job."

"You haven't gotten involved in any other murder cases. You usually leave that sort of stuff to the police."

"Special circumstances called for my involvement."

"That's what I mean."

"This is really an exercise in futility, McCall. You're not interested in facts. If you were, then you'd see that you're barking up the wrong tree."

McCall decided to put all his cards on the table.

"You know what I think, Clark? I think you're afraid to do anything about the murders of the two women because of that land swindle you pulled off. That's when you got real dirty. Dirty enough that you have to ignore murder."

"That's it, McCall. I've listened to all I'm going to."

He started out the door, but McCall blocked the entrance.

"Don't try to go past me, Clark, or I'll shove those pearly whites right down your throat."

"I could have you arrested for this."

"Could you now? I just have one last thing to say, Mr. District Attorney. The *Tribune's* going to be filled with questions about you and your lawyer friends. I'm going to keep plugging until I get Roget and Reynolds put away. And I'm going to find out who killed Harold Webster, too."

"Are you through? I'd like to get back to my guests."

"Be my guest," McCall said, stepping aside. "And be sure to read the *Tribune*. I'll always make sure your name's spelled right."

McCall retrieved Ramirez from the bar where he was working on a fourth beer.

"You want me to drive?" Ramirez asked as they approached the Porsche.

"I wouldn't let you drive my car if you were sober."

"You're one helluva buddy."

"We're not talking the Cisco Kid and his sidekick here. By the way, what was his faithful companion's name?"

"Damned if I know," Ramirez replied. "I never watched any of those Mexican shows."

"Not even Zorro?"

"Cisco and Zorro, they were before my time. But you'd make a good Zorro, McCall."

"Why's that?"

"You like to carve people up."

"Only the bad guys."

"Maybe. What did you get from Ramsey?"

"Just the standard bullshit." He stomped the accelerator and the car lurched forward. There was, McCall thought, no point in involving the kid in his threatened expose of Ramsey and friends. The D.A. might get nasty and he didn't want Ramirez burned.

"What now?" Ramirez asked.

"Let's get those chili dogs and go home."

When he finally got home, McCall experienced the emptiness of the condo without Cele. It didn't feel good.

He couldn't sleep, so he sat drinking scotch and thinking. He drank most of the bottle before falling asleep. It had been a long time since he had been drunk.

CHAPTER TWENTY-SIX

The next day brought sunshine and a headache. McCall was awakened from a fitful sleep by what he interpreted as chimes going off in his head. As he achieved a degree of consciousness, he realized the sound was too fast for chimes. It was the telephone.

"McCall, you've outdone yourself on this one," the voice on the line said. It was Ed Parkham.

"What does that mean?" He needed a cup of coffee.

"I mean it's great," Parkham lauded. "I don't know if you've ever done anything better."

"Thanks, Ed." He wasn't in a mood for praise, expecially from the managing editor. For one thing, he suspected there was some underlying reason for the man being so laudatory.

"Where are you going from here?" Parkham asked.

"I'll be down in a little while and we'll talk about it then, OK?"

"Sure," Parkham agreed, "but I think we've got an award winner here."

The statement didn't surprise McCall. He already knew that was all the story meant to the man, just another plaque to adorn the wall at the *Tribune* Building. To Parkham, the murders and the reason for them were just an inconsequential part of the entire scenerio.

"I'll be down in an hour or so," McCall said.

The story in the morning paper was one of his best. He often did his best work when depressed. And, while he didn't like to admit it, Cele's departure had left him in a black mood.

His story was full of questions, many of which were going to be difficult for Clark Ramsey and associates to answer. There were no libelous statements, only a call for further investigation into the murder of Laurie Roget. It was also stated that a *Tribune* investigation had proved that Paul Broadus could not have been Laurie Roget's killer.

The story was not complimentary of Broadus, going into every sordid detail of his past. McCall implied that Broadus' past made him the perfect patsy for a sinister coverup.

And for the first time in any of his stories on the Roget murder, McCall mentioned Annie Reynolds; how tragic it was that the wives of best friends had died within so short a time of each other.

The questioning nature of the story would cause people to think. They would have to wonder about Clark Ramsey's involvement in a routine murder investigation. McCall had spelled it all out.

After making himself a cup of coffee, McCall sat pondering the sunlight filtering through the living room drapes. He couldn't get Cele out of his mind, the emptiness of the bed without her. How in the hell had he let this happen?

A shower, shave, his usual morning routine, did little to clear the cobwebs. It was going to be a long day. He swallowed a couple of Extra Strength Excedrins before heading for the *Tribune*.

Ramirez was his chipper self, but McCall cautioned him with a wave of the hand. "No loud noises," he warned. "I feel like hammered shit."

Ramirez laughed. "You don't look much better than you say

you feel. How about a cup of coffee?"

"Fine. Just don't make any waves with it. Today, I couldn't stand the sound of splashing against styrofoam."

"You might be feeling worse in a few minutes. Look who's here to see you."

Across the newsroom at Sipe's desk, McCall saw Bob Winnow. He was talking to the city editor. When he saw McCall look in his direction, he waved. McCall waved back.

"Oh boy," he told Ramirez. "Tell the sonofabitch to come on over. And we might as well be courteous. Ask him if he wants a cup of coffee."

Moments later, Ramirez escorted Winnow to McCall's desk. The lawyer was holding a cup of coffee. McCall offered him a chair, which he accepted.

"I suppose I should commend you for writing that narrative of half-truths so skillfully," Winnow began.

McCall took a sip of coffee. "You can commend me if you like, Bob, though to tell the truth I don't give a rat's ass about your commendation. As for the half-truths, are they really?"

"You smeared the integrity of a very fine man."

"If you're talking about Ramsey, he screwed himself when he couldn't wait to put an innocent man behind bars. And I think you sort of encouraged him on that, Bob."

Winnow's face flushed crimson. "I handle some of Clark's legal work, but I certainly don't advise him on how to run the district attorney's office."

"Be that as it may, what in the hell are you doing here?"

"I'd like to say that I'm here to reason with you, but with you reason does little if any good. So, I'm here to warn you that further harassment of Mr. Ramsey, Mr. Roget or Mr. Reynolds will result in legal action against you and this paper."

"Go for it, Bob. It may have escaped that keen legal mind of yours, but Ramsey is a public figure. And in that capacity, he's subject to public scrutiny in everything he does.

"As for the other two clowns, I would welcome legal action. It would enable me to bring out a lot more than I've been able

238

to print thus far.

"Bob, you can probably scare the hell out of the *Tribune's* lawyers, but with me you're just pissin' into the wind. And if the *Tribune* decides it can't take the heat of printing my stuff, someone else will."

"I wish I could make you see that Paul Roget and Francis Reynolds are fine young men, not deserving of the kind of character assassination that you intend."

"You have no idea about what I intend. If Roget and Reynolds are clean, they have nothing to fear. But if they're dirty, I'm going to nail their asses. Count on it."

Winnow stared at McCall for a few seconds, then said, "You'd misunderstand, I'm sure, if I suggested the possibility of making a deal."

"You're right. I'd misunderstand."

"So, I guess we're at a stalemate. We'll just have to let the chips fall where they may."

McCall laughed at the melodrama Winnow was trying to impose. "Was there ever any doubt?" he asked.

After Winnow had left, McCall met with Parkham and discussed the approach he would take on future stories. He told Parkham the stories would continue to question and pressure police into continuing the murder investigation. He also said that he would continue investigating the deaths of Laurie Roget and Annie Reynolds on his own, looking for the threads of evidence that would prove his theory.

And he said he would keep the pressure on Ramsey, keep asking in print why the district attorney's office had been so quick to arrest Broadus on such flimsey evidence; also question why Ramsey had become involved in a murder investigation normally handled by police.

Parkham liked what he was going to do. He liked the prospect of increased circulation and possible journalism awards; evidence he could provide top management regarding his effectiveness.

McCall found it interesting that Sipe and Katie had, for the first time, been excluded from their meeting.

With Ramirez's help, McCall spent the next few hours going over all the material they had gathered on the Roget murder. He called and tried to set up an interview with Laurie's parents, but they refused. He planned to interview everyone involved again, to try to find that elusive piece of the puzzle that would make the picture complete.

As the day's sun gave way to afternoon shadows, Ramirez asked, "Is there a chance for lunch today, or should I just plan on breakfast tomorrow?"

McCall laughed. "That stomach of yours is going to be the death of you yet."

"I can't help it. I'm a growing boy."

"I could stand a little chow myself," McCall said. "Why don't you go over to the Coney Island and get us some chili dogs?"

"My car's in the shop."

"Hell, it's not that much of a walk."

"It damn sure is."

"Well, you can take my car."

Ramirez couldn't believe it. "You're going to let me drive your Porsche?"

"That's what I said. And as long as you're driving, stop somewhere and get us a six-pack of light beer."

"You know there's a rule against drinking in the newsroom."

"Fuck the rule. I want a beer."

"As long as we're breaking the rule, how about a couple of six-packs?"

McCall handed Ramirez his car keys and a twenty. "I don't care how many you get, but there is something I want to warn you about."

"What's that?"

"When you get back with my car, I don't want to find any of those big dice hanging from the rear view mirror. And I don't want a plastic Jesus sitting on the dashboard."

Ramirez laughed. "Hey, man, those are options for

240

Camaros and Firebirds only.

When Ramirez exited, McCall began restudying the police report on Laurie Roget's murder. He had almost finished it when an explosion rocked the building, shattering panes of glass in the newsroom.

Oh, my god, he thought.

CHAPTER TWENTY-SEVEN

"**I**'m sorry about the kid," Haloran said.

It had been a couple of hours since McCall's car had exploded, killing Ramirez and injuring a number of other persons in the vicinity. Now the detective and reporter were in the diner having coffee.

McCall sighed. "Damn it, Bill, I should have realized they were capable of this. It should've been me, not the kid."

"You can't blame yourself."

"Hell, I'm not blaming myself. I'm blaming the sonofabitches who did it, and you know who they are as well as I do."

"The bomb was the work of a pro."

"I'm sure it was. And we both know that pros only do this kind of thing for money."

"You do have a lot of enemies, McCall. You've stepped on a lot of toes over the years."

"Yeah," he replied sarcastically, "so I'm not supposed to assume this was the work of Ramsey or any of the Roget murder suspects."

"You can't believe the district attorney is mixed up in this?"

"Why not? The bastard's dirty. I know it and so do you."

"I can't deal in wild speculation," Haloran said defensively.
I have to deal in facts."

"Facts can sometimes be deceiving."

"My men are hitting the streets," Haloran said, "trying to get
a lead on the bomber. Maybe someone saw him messing
around your car. We're running checks on Winnow, Roget and
Reynolds, too, but I doubt that we'll come up with anything."

"I'd almost guarantee it," McCall said. "But now that I
know I'm a target, the bastards have their work cut out for
them."

"Maybe we ought to give you police protection for awhile."

"Are you kidding? The D.A.'s got some of your cops in his
back pocket."

"C'mon, McCall, don't give me a lot of shit."

"Well, I don't want any of your fuckin' police protection. I
can take care of myself."

"I don't doubt it. But at least let me give you a ride home."

"I'd appreciate it."

During the drive to the condo, neither man spoke. McCall
was deep in thought and Haloran respected his meditation.
The detective was sensitive to the feeling of pain and loss that
McCall was enduring.

While McCall was feeling remorse in thinking about
Ramirez's death, inside he was also seething with a cold,
calculating anger. He was determined that Ramirez's killer be
punished, no matter what the personal cost.

Haloran interrupted his thoughts with, "Here we are."

"Thanks, Bill. Listen, I hope you don't think I'm ungrateful
for what you're doing. This kinda hit me hard and I might have
said some things that I shouldn't have."

"I know."

"I just want you to know that I think you're a damn good
cop, and I also think you know what you're doing."

"Hell, McCall, I guess going by the book does seem a bit
cold and uncaring when you know the victim, but I just don't

243

know any other way."

"It may not be the wrong way. I just get impatient."

"Do you have a gun?"

"Why do you ask?"

"Well, it's not 'cause I think you're going to go out and shoot somebody."

"I guess there's always that possibility."

Haloran reached beneath the car seat and brought forth a pistol in a shoulder holster. "This is one of my spares."

"I don't think I'll need it."

"Take it anyway. I'll take care of the paperwork authorizing you to carry it."

McCall took the gun and Haloran handed him a box of shells.

"Just remember that this is for your protection, not to use on people you don't like," Haloran said.

"If I was going to use it on people I didn't like, you didn't give me enough shells."

Haloran laughed. "You need any company? Want me to come in for awhile?"

"I'm fine. Get on with your rat killin' and I'll see you tomorrow."

As he approached the door of the condo, he heard music inside. He was sure that he hadn't left the stereo on, which meant that either Cele or some uninvited guest had been there.

He took the pistol from its holster, checked to make sure it was loaded, then unlocked the door. He stood out of the doorway while pushing the door open.

Cele was standing in the middle of the abbreviated hallway, staring wide-eyed at the open door. It was obvious that she was frightened. Her shocked eyes traveled to, and focused on, the pistol in his hand.

"Thank God, it's you," she said, moving toward him. "You scared the puddin' out of me."

They embraced tenderly, passionately.

"I guess I'm surprised to see you," he said. "When I came

back and found you gone, I didn't know what to think."

"You can think I'm stupid if you like. I just know that I don't want to be apart from you. And when I heard on the news what happened, I thought maybe you'd need me and forgive me."

"I always need you. And there's nothing to forgive."

"Are you OK?" she asked.

"I'm fine."

"I know you liked Eddie a lot."

"Yeah, he was a good kid."

They walked to the couch, his arm around her, and sat down. They kissed and embraced.

"I missed you," she said.

He smiled. "You weren't gone all that long."

"It doesn't matter, it seemed like a long time. Didn't you miss me?"

"Isn't it obvious? I was dreading coming home tonight because you weren't here."

"I know it sounds cruel and selfish," she said, "but I'm glad it was someone else who died and not you." She put her arms around his neck, buried her face in his chest and started crying.

"Take it easy, baby. Everything's going to be OK."

She stopped sobbing, raised her tear-streaked face from his chest, looked into his eyes and said, "Matt, don't you understand? Someone tried to kill you and they might try again. I couldn't stand it if something happened to you."

He smiled. "Nothing's going to happen to me. I'm not going to let anyone kill me."

"You're not invincible, Matt McCall."

"I know, but the guy who planted the bomb hasn't got a prayer of getting away."

"You mean the police know who he is?"

"They'll probably have him in custody within the next twenty-four hours," he lied. "He's on the run so he's not going to be bothering me."

"Then why are you carrying a gun?"

"Just a precaution. There's no point in taking anything for

245

granted. In fact, I want you to go back and stay with your parents until they arrest the guy."

"No way," she said. "You can't pry me away from here. I belong with you."

"You sure do, baby, but I'd feel a lot better if you'd stay with your parents for a few days. Just until this thing cools down."

"Forget it."

He could see that her mind was made up, that there was no hope of changing it. Her mind was like a steel trap. She was as hardheaded as they came, as if there was any other kind of woman.

"Do you want something to eat?" she asked.

"Such as?"

"How about some fried chicken?"

"Fried chicken? In the entire time I've know you, you've never offered me fried chicken."

"Well, I'm offering it to you now. Do you want it or not?"

"Sure," he said. "I didnt' know you knew how to fry anything."

"Of course, I know how to fry things. But in this case I don't have to. I picked up a bucket on the way over here."

He was obviously pleased. "Will miracles never cease?"

"See how exciting life can be with me. Shall we have a nice bottle of wine with the chicken?"

"Sounds good to me. But I warn you that I get very horny after eating fried chicken."

"So, what else is new?"

"While you're getting things ready, I have a couple of quick phone calls to make."

"Do you want to watch TV while we eat?"

"No way. Let's have a little candlelight and music and see what transpires."

"I think I can guess," she replied with a smile.

He really had only one call to make, and that was to Haloran. "About that police protection, Bill. I need it for Cele."

The detective agreed to station a man outside the condo while McCall was at work.

"I'm trying to get her to go stay with her parents for awhile," McCall said.

"That would be best," Haloran replied.

After dinner and lovemaking, Cele fell asleep. Slumber was, however, impossible for McCall. The diversion Cele had created was nice, but it didn't blot out the events of the day. Eddie's death, how it might have been prevented, shrouded his mental processes.

Careful not to disturb Cele, he eased out of bed and went to the kitchen where he made himself a cup of coffee. It had begun to rain. It was light at first, but then intensified until large drops were pounding at the windows in staccato fashion. He took the coffee in the living room and sat down in his favorite chair.

Then he cried.

CHAPTER TWENTY-EIGHT

There was a pallor of gloom over the newsroom the next day. McCall wasn't sure why, but everyone seemed compelled to express their sympathies to him about the loss of Ramirez.

He figured they were all in the same boat together, all made aware of their own mortality by the kid's death, and all awkward in the art of expressing sorrow. He also knew that with Ramirez's burial, all expressions of grief would quickly come to an end. The kid's memory would fade like yesterday's news.

That's the way it was.

But he wouldn't forget. Nor would he rest until Ramirez's killer was brought to justice.

Most of the sympathizers also praised McCall for the story he had written about Ramirez's death, one he had pieced together shortly after the explosion occurred. It always amazed him about how impressed people in his own profession were at a writer's ability to string a group of words together. And as for him writing the story about the death of a person he was close to, it seemed the natural thing to do. It certainly wasn't an act of dedication to the profession of journalism.

Katie, of course, was trying to make Ramirez's death some sort of minority issue, attempting to take the reason for it out of its true context. McCall listened to her illogical verbage as long as he could stand it.

When she was in the midst of a treatise to a group of reporters and editors at the city desk, he interrupted with, "You dumb bitch. Eddie's not some minority issue. He was a man."

His outburst sent the group scurrying in different directions. Katie slouched at her desk, where she began shuffling papers in sullen silence.

McCall went back to his own desk and called Arnold. "I want you to run a check on a guy's military background," he told the agent.

"Glad to," Arnold said.

McCall told Arnold the name and said, "I'd appreciate it if you'd get right back to me on this."

Arnold agreed to give the request priority treatment.

It was just one of his hunches, but after having thoroughly checked the files on the major and minor characters in the Roget murder scenerio, he realized that one man had more or less remained in the shadows. Yet, that man had been a major player in the Webster land swindle.

About an hour later, Arnold called with the information he had requested. McCall then contacted Haloran and set up a meeting at the diner.

He had driven Cele's car to work, but it was such a nice morning that he decided to walk. The night's rain had washed the city's streets clean. And there was an unseasonable coolness to the air.

As he walked past the spot where the explosion had occurred, he couldn't help but wonder what the weather would be like in two days. That's when Eddie Ramirez would be buried. Rain would be appropriate, he thought. Tears from heaven.

249

Haloran was already in a booth when he arrived. The detective greeted him with a question he was sure that he'd been asked a hundred times during the morning. "Are you all right?"

"I'm fine," he replied with a slight irritation. "In fact, I couldn't be better. I wasn't the one killed."

"Hell, I don't know what to say," Haloran admitted.

"Bill, just talk to me the way you always have. Call me an asshole. Argue with me. I can't stand all this niceness."

Haloran laughed. "My god, I haven't been nice to you all that much. Counting yesterday, I haven't seen or talked to you on the phone for more than an hour since the kid was killed."

"Even an hour of niceness is too much. Today, I've had enough sympathy expressed already to last a lifetime."

"OK, asshole," the detective said. "You told me you had some important information. What is it?"

"Damn," McCall complained, "don't I even get a cup of coffee before we start conducting business?"

Haloran took a drink from his cup. "Shift for yourself. I have my coffee."

McCall signaled the waitress to bring him a cup, then said, "I ran a check on David Darden."

"Why? And what kind of check?"

"I checked his military record. As to why, I was just playing a hunch."

"And?"

"He was a demolition expert."

"Strange field for a lawyer."

"He didn't go to law school until he got back from 'Nam."

Haloran seemed to be pondering the information. "The job on your car was a professional one," he said, "but hell, some of the best explosives people I've had the displeasure of knowing were trained by Uncle Sam. But why in the hell would Darden rig your car?"

"He's one of them. And it goes back to that real estate scam Ramsey was involved in."

"Here we go again," Haloran muttered.

"Listen up you silly fucker and you might learn something."

"I'm listening."

"You'll remember that I told you Darden was Harold Webster's lawyer, but that he sold out and joined Winnow's law firm. Winnow, of course, was representing Ramsey."

"I remember."

"Then Webster has this fatal and mysterious automobile accident. And Darden even ends up as a beneficiary because Webster owed him legal fees. Webster was using most of his Army pay to take care of his mother's nursing home expenses.

"Another strange thing is that the pittance Ramsey allegedly paid Mrs. Webster for the land disappeared."

"What's amazing to me," Haloran said, "is how you got into all this shit while you were covering the Roget murder."

"Somehow it all ties together. The land scam and the murders of Harold Webster, Annie Reynolds and Laurie Roget."

"Whoa," Haloran said. "The only one we're sure was murdered was Laurie Roget."

"Maybe there's no official proof, but Webster and Annie Reynolds were murdered. Maybe even old Mrs. Webster."

"Without proof, you've got nothing, McCall."

"I'm going to get the proof, Bill. I'm going to put the pieces of this puzzle together if it's the last thing I do."

"I don't guess I have to remind you that yesterday could have been your last day."

"You don't have to remind me."

"If you're right in your theory that all these lawyers, the district attorney, and God knows who else, are involved in a series of murders, all I can say is that you either have a vivid imagination or a criminal mind."

McCall grinned. "Maybe both. C'mon, Bill, you know that what I've put together is logical."

"Some of it is."

"It's all logical."

"OK, let's say that it is. Now, in some of your articles you've questioned certain things relating to the Roget murder. But how much of your entire theory do these alleged murderers know about?"

"All of it."

"What do you mean, all of it?"

"I mean they know my theory. I told part of it to Ramsey and part of it to Bob Winnow. And believe me, they compare notes."

"You didn't tell me you had told them any of this stuff."

"I'm telling you now."

"Damn it, McCall, if your theory's right, you set yourself up. You're not invincible, you know."

"So I've heard."

"What in the hell did you hope to accomplish?"

"I guess I was trying to panic them into doing something. I just didn't figure on it getting Eddie killed."

"I'll say again, you can't blame yourself for that."

"I doubt that his folks will take much consolation in that. But what are you going to do about Darden?"

"Well, it gives us a possible suspect. We'll do some serious checking on him."

"You know what bothers me?"

"What?"

"The fact that Ramsey probably has access to all your files. He probably knows every move you make."

"We don't try to hide our moves from him, but I can't recall him asking for any information lately."

"Why should he? He probably has a plant in the department who gives him everything he wants."

"Damn it, McCall, you're going to make me paranoid."

"Good. One of your problems, Bill, is that you're too trusting. And why shouldn't Ramsey have a plant in your department? I have one in his office."

Haloran laughed. "I figured that."

On his return to the newsroom, McCall answered some

telephone messages and then called Cele. After several rings, a sleep-laden voice answered.

"Sorry to wake you," he said, "but I wanted to tell you that I'll be home at a decent hour."

"I'm glad you called," she said with a yawn ."I needed to get up to catch up on one of my soaps. What time will you be home?"

"No later than six."

"Anything special that you want for dinner?"

"Whatever."

"How about a steak, baked potato and salad?"

"What are you trying to do, spoil me? I figured we'd be back on the wagon tonight. You know, all that diet stuff."

"I want you to eat a good meal, because I have an evening of strenuous exercise planned for you."

"Sounds interesting."

"It will be. I have this very seductive nighty I want to try out."

"Something you'll look good out of, I presume."

"You'll have to be the judge of that."

"Keep up that kind of talk and I'll be home in a few minutes."

"If you think that scares me, you're wrong," she teased. "I'll bet you thought I'd tell you to wait until I got some makeup on."

"That thought occurred to me."

"Well, you're going to find that I'm a changed woman."

"I didn't find anything wrong with the way you were."

"The new me is going to be much better. Take my word for it."

"I'm just looking forward to seeing for myself."

"Good, you can start tonight," she said.

After they had exchanged words of endearment and said their goodbyes, McCall began working on a followup story about Ramirez's death. He had been working on the piece for about an hour when Buz Cramer, one of the police reporters,

253

came to his desk and asked, "Don't you live on Live Oak Lane?"

"Yeah," McCall answered, "Why do you ask?"

"Well, I was monitoring the police radio and heard them talking about an explosion on Live Oak Lane. I thought you ought to know."

A chill enveloped McCall's body. A lump of fear pounded inside his chest.

"Did you get the address?"

Cramer consulted his notepad and said, "Nine eighteen Live Oak."

McCall rose to his feet and started forward. His legs were weak, his body numb.

"Are you OK?" Cramer asked.

"It was my place," he replied calmly. "The sonofabitches blew up my home." Then he yelled, "If they hurt her, I swear to God I'll kill'em all."

Anger had replaced the initial fear and weakness. An almost uncontrollable strength surged through his body. He was suddenly running through the newsroom, past the rows of desks and VDTs, past the shocked expressions on the faces of his colleagues. He ignored the slow elevator and raced down the stairs.

He ran all the way to Cele's car, weaving his way through the slow-walking pedestrian traffic on the sidewalk. There was a momentary delay in finding the right key to the vehicle's door, but once inside the motor responded quickly when he turned the ignition key. The tires squealed as he wheeled away from the curb and pushed his foot down on the accelerator.

Traffic was light, so there was no problem negotiating the winding streets in record time. As the condo came into view, he saw the police cars with their lights flashing. He also saw the ambulance.

When he exited the car, Haloran intercepted him and said, "You don't want to see her." He fronted McCall and grasped his arms.

254

Any resistance McCall might have offered was drained when he saw the black body bag being carried from the building.

"What happened?" he asked.

"A controlled, directional explosion," Haloran replied. "It was planted in the television set. The best I can figure is that when the bomber missed you yesterday, he made a beeline over here and rigged your set. We've had a man on guard since you left this morning, so I know that no one went in your place today."

It made sense. When the bomber saw that he had gotten Ramirez instead of his intended target, he simply laid another trap. And again, the target had eluded him at the cost of another person's life.

"The guy is definitely a pro," Haloran droned on, "because there's very little damage to your apartment."

McCall half-listened to the detective's words. He didn't give a damn about the condo, didn't care if it had been blown to hell. All he cared about was the girl in the body bag, and in exacting punishment on those responsible for her death.

"From now on you've got police protection," Haloran said, "whether you want it or not."

"No," McCall protested. "I don't want to scare the sonofabitches off. I want them to come after me. And I'm not going to be hard to find. They've all bought the farm."

Haloran knew it would do no good to argue.

"Now, if you'll excuse me, Bill, I'm going to ride with Cele."

255

CHAPTER TWENTY-NINE

The trunk had been locked for a long time. Cele had always been curious about its contents, questioned him about it on numerous occasions. But he had always been evasive with her, usually making a joke about her curiosity.

In thinking about it, keeping the stuff in the trunk hadn't made all that much sense. Especially since he had planned never to open it. It contained too much of a past that he wanted to forget.

But now, as he was turning the key in the lock, he had to wonder. Had he really wanted to forget the past? He had to think that if he had really wanted to forget, he wouldn't have kept these damn relics from the past.

When he lifted the lid, the first thing he saw was the nine-milimeter Browning automatic. There was an ugly beauty to the weapon, a kind of strange charisma not present in the gun Haloran had provided him. This gun had been his mistress in Vietnam. He had grown to love its deadly venom, to be as dependent on it as he was on a cup of morning coffee. It felt comfortable in his hand, and its fourteen-shot capacity had spelled death to any enemy who ventured into range.

He took the gun from its camouflage holster and caressed it. The cold steel sent a chill up his spine.

How easy it would be, he thought, to let the gun take care of his enemies. But that would provide them too gentle a death. It would be too clean.

He remembered a time when he had planned to use the gun on himself. That was when he had been wounded, left in a swamp with Viet Cong searching frantically for him. He would have blown his brains out rather than be captured.

Maybe he'd have to go that route this time. That is, if things didn't go according to plan.

He was a bit startled to realize that he was glad it was coming down to this. Them against him.

The very thought of the confrontation sensitized every nerve in his body. For the first time since Cele's death, he began to feel very much alive. He was once again going into battle. And the anticipation stimulated him.

There was still much to do, much planning before initiating action. He had to be sure that his intellect and body were synchronized in perfect harmony. When that occurred, he would once again be the consummate jungle warrior.

CHAPTER THIRTY

For two days and nights, McCall did not leave the condominium. He slept sporadically and neither ate nor drank. He was seemingly in a trance, though in reality he was honing his senses for the project to which he had committed himself. His concentration level was high, his mind contemplating every move. There could be no mistakes. Nothing could be left to chance.

Such preparation for a project was not new to him. Developing the proper state of mind for a mission was something the Company had taught him well. And he had been a willing pupil. From the first, he had understood that proper preparation was the key to staying alive.

However, for this project, staying alive was not all that important to him. Being successful was all that mattered. Once his task was completed, he didn't care whether he lived or died.

Still, he would take all the precautions, all the necessary steps taken by a man intent on survival. Maybe it was his training. Maybe it was something else. Whatever, he was determined to succeed at all costs.

Never had there been a mission in Vietnam as important as

this one. And never had there been such a desire for vengeance.

In the aftermath of Cele's death, he had been able to quell the initial anger and frustration that swelled up in him. It had been replaced by the cool assurance that the murderers would pay the price for their sin. And he didn't want to trust their destruction to anyone other than himself.

There was, of course, no lack of hatred and anger within him, but the combination burned like a controlled fire. The emotions were intense, but sharper still was the logic and cunning of a jungle warrior. There would be time enough for emotion. Time enough after he had finished what he had to do.

The phone had rung numerous times over the past two days, but he had ignored it. Now he picked it up and dialed a familiar number.

"Let me speak to Arnold," he told the voice that answered. "Tell him it's McCall."

When Arnold came on the line, he said, "God, I don't know what to say, McCall. I don't guess there's much to say, is there?"

"No, there's not much, but I appreciate your concern. What I need, though, is a favor."

"Name it."

"I need a van and an alibi."

"Is that all?"

"That's it."

"No problem. Where, when and for how long do you need the alibi?"

"Let's start it a couple of days from now. Give me about a week of cover."

"I assume you'll want to be a considerable distance from San Antonio."

"Yeah, but I'll leave the site up to you."

"I'll get back to you within the hour."

While waiting for Arnold's call, he considered eating something. He negated the idea, however, because for some reason he still wasn't hungry. He did drink a glass of milk, then sat patiently waiting.

Arnold's call came fifty minutes later.

"You're going to Athens," the agent said.

"That's nice, I've always liked Greece at this time of year."

"We have an airline ticket in your name and a double to use it. He has a bogus passport and plenty of credit cards carrying your name. I'll provide you a list of all the places where he'll use the cards along with the dates and times. I've even instructed him to bring back souveniers for you to give to friends.

"We also have people in Athens who'll testify to spending time with you. You're covered for your entire stay.

"You're scheduled to depart at ten o'clock Wednesday morning. Drive your car to the airport and park it. Your double will follow you in the van.

"Have the van back at the airport when your double returns and he can pick it up. What you pay for parking your car at the airport will further verify your alibi."

"It sounds like you've taken care of everything," McCall said.

"If I don't take care of you, the Ol' Man will hand me my balls on a platter. He's still trying to get you back in harness."

"No way."

"That's between you and him. I've scheduled for your double to return on a Friday, but just to confuse things he'll be coming back on Thursday on a different airline. That's in case someone decided to meet your return flight."

"That's a nice touch, Arnold."

"I'll get all the written details to you right away, but for now your airline ticket calls for a ten o'clock departure Wednesday and a return to San Antonio a week from Friday at seven o'clock in the evening."

"What if I decide to take the double's place in Athens?"

"That won't be a problem. We can pick you up in one of our private aircraft and get you there."

McCall knew Arnold would tend to every detail of his alibi.

The man was a real pro. He figured Arnold might have an idea why he needed an alibi, but he would never ask why. He had been trained to do, not to question. For McCall, that had been the hardest part of working for the Company.

He hadn't talked to Haloran since Cele's funeral, so he called.

"Bill, do you have time for a cup?"

"Sure," the detective answered. "Do you want to come by here or just meet at the diner?"

"Let's just meet at the diner. I'll be there in twenty minutes."

When McCall arrived at the diner, Haloran was already entrenched in a booth. He looked more somber than usual, which was understandable, given the tragic events that had occurred in McCall's life during the previous week.

"Any clues?" McCall asked.

"None."

"But we know the murderers, don't we?"

The detective stared into his coffee cup. "I know that you think you know who did it. But I can't make a case on speculation. I have to have evidence."

"And you don't have any?"

"Not yet."

"You know they're going to get away clean, don't you?"

"No, I don't know that. All I know is that we're doing the best we can to find the murderer."

"Murderers," McCall corrected matter-of-factly.

Haloran was surprised by his friend's calm demeanor in talking about Cele's death. He was too calm, not like the McCall he knew. And that worried the detective.

"Are you OK?" he asked.

"Sure," McCall responded. "I'm getting myself together. In fact, I'm going to take a little trip starting Wednesday."

"That's a good idea. Where arc you going?"

"Athens."

"Greece?"

"Yeah."

"I hear it's beautiful. The wife's been after me to take her there for years."

"You should."

"You've been before?"

"Yeah. I have a few friends there, but that's not why I'm going. I want to be alone."

"Well, you need to be around some people. You don't need to be spending a lot of time alone."

"I just want to spend some time thinking. Or are you going to tell me I shouldn't be thinking?"

"Would it do any good?" Haloran asked with a chuckle.

"There's no doubt I'd be better off if I left the thinking to someone else. My thinking gets people killed."

"C'mon, don't start that."

"It's true. If I'd let well enough alone, Cele would be alive today. So would Eddie."

"McCall, there's no way you can know that for sure. Besides, you're the way you are. You always go all out on a case."

"Well, I'm beaten on this one."

"No, you're not. With a little time off you'll regroup and get back after the bastards."

"Does that mean you agree with my theory?"

"Let's just say I can't totally disagree with it. But as you know, I'm not any more objective than you are. I wouldn't mind seeing Clark Ramsey nailed."

"Well, I doubt that I can do it."

"That sure doesn't sound like you."

"When it comes right down to it, what difference does it make. The assholes of this world control everything, and that's not going to change."

"It does seem that way sometimes, but all we can do is keep pluggin' away."

"You plug away. I say to hell with it."

"That's what you say now, but after a little time in that Greek sunshine you'll change your mind."

McCall didn't respond. He sipped some coffee, then stared

nto the cup. His seemingly defeated attitude bothered Haloran.

When he did speak it was, "What do you want me to bring you from Greece, Bill?"

Haloran shrugged his shoulders. "Hell, don't worry about bringing me anything."

"I'm not going to worry about it, but I did think I'd pick up something for you and your wife."

"That's nice of you, but hell, I wouldn't know what to tell you."

"I'll just use my judgment then."

"Don't go overboard."

"How in the hell can you go overboard on a two dollar gift?" McCall kidded. "I hope you didn't think I was going to get you something nice, shithead."

"Well, fuck you very much," Haloran replied with a laugh. The fact that McCall had injected a little humor in their conversation made Haloran feel better. But the feeling was shortlived. The reporter immediately fell back into a state of melancholy.

"If I'm going to leave Wednesday, I guess I'd better get my shit together."

"When will you be back?"

"A week from Friday."

"Be sure to give me a call."

"Sure."

"And, McCall..."

"Yeah."

"You can count on me to do everything I can to find Cele's killer."

"I know that."

"You want to leave me a number where I can reach you if anything breaks?"

"Good idea. I don't have the number of the hotel with me, but I'll call and give it to you when I get home."

CHAPTER THIRTY-ONE

Haloran didn't feel all that easy after talking to McCall. He couldn't buy McCall's defeatism. It was totally alien to his personality. And he remembered McCall's threat to avenge Cele's death.

From what Haloran knew of McCall, the reporter was not one to make idle threats. Of course, he might have made the threat while in the throes of grief. But it was hard for the detective to imagine McCall emotionally out of control, no matter what the circumstances.

He had seen his friend's eruptive anger in some situations, but he always figured McCall's temper was calculated. He had always thought McCall showed only the emotion he wanted seen, nothing more.

Haloran knew a former army colonel who claimed to have known McCall in 'Nam. His assessment of the reporter was that he was the coldest, most calculating jungle fighter he had ever known. The former colonel had told him McCall didn't operate under the auspices of any branch of the military service, that he was more a mercenary in command of a group of highly trained killers who operated behind enemy lines.

When Haloran had asked McCall if he knew the colonel, he drew a blank. McCall had simply said, maybe, that he'd known a lot of people in 'Nam, most of whom he didn't care to remember.

Maybe McCall was planning something. Maybe his proposed trip was a ruse.

Haloran couldn't blame McCall if he did take matters in his own hands, but he hoped that he wouldn't. He liked McCall, but first, last and always, he was a cop. He had his duty.

CHAPTER THIRTY-TWO

After leaving the diner, McCall returned home to complete his preparation. A messenger was waiting with an envelope from Arnold. The messenger was, of course, a local agent. He had been instructed to wait until McCall returned home, to give the envelope to no one other than the addressee.

McCall entered the condo and checked the contents of the envelope. It was a complete itinerary of his double's activities in Greece. The details were unbelievably exact. It detailed the specific times the double would be in his hotel room, where and when he would eat, and with whom. There were photos and biographical sketches of the people with whom the double would have contact, plus statements regarding McCall's alleged relationship with them.

Arnold had done one helluva job.

McCall's job was to memorize all the information, then destroy the papers. He had never had a problem with memorization. In fact, he was capable of putting himself in such a state-of-mind that he would, for all practical purposes, believe he had actually been to Greece.

He had that kind of mind control.

After about an hour of studying Arnold's master plan, he torched it and flushed it down the toilet. Then he called Celeste.

"I wanted to call you," she said, "but I didn't know whether I should or not."

"I haven't been answering the phone, so even if you had called you couldn't have reached me."

"It's hard to know what to say."

"It's not necessary to say anything. If it had happened to someone else, I sure as hell wouldn't know what to say."

"But you're OK?"

"Yeah, fine. I need to get away for awhile, so I'm leaving for Athens on Wednesday."

"Greece?"

"Yeah. As long as I'm going away, it might as well be far away."

"I don't guess you'd consider company?"

"Any other time, Celeste. The timing's all wrong now."

"I know."

"I suppose your boss is doing well?" he said with disdain.

"They're here, if that's what you mean."

"I don't know what I mean. Listen, could you meet me at The Plum at about five-thirty? I'd like to see you before I leave."

"I'll be there."

McCall wasn't particularly interested in seeing Celeste or any other woman. Cele's death had left a void in him that, for the moment, no one could replace. But he figured Celeste might have some information that would be helpful.

After making himself a cup of coffee, he called Haloran and gave him the phone number and name of his hotel in Athens. His double would not answer the phone, so if Haloran called he'd have to leave a message. Through the Agency, he could return a call to Haloran that would be routed through Athens.

He noted that it was just three-thirty, still plenty of time to pack before meeting Celeste.

McCall packed as though he was actually going to Athens. His double would, in fact, take McCall's packed suitcase on the trip. Some of his clothes would even be sent to the cleaners there, then repacked along with items he supposedly purchased on his trip. Clothes for his double were being sent under separate cover.

He left the condo at five o'clock, arrived at The Plum at five-twenty. While having a scotch and water, he observed that the crowd looked the same. The usual three-piece suits, open-neck shirts with gold chains, secretaries dressed to look business-like, and a few women in unusual outfits that were supposedly fashionable. All, he thought, searching for that elusive ingredient to life that was called happiness.

It was an ingredient, he was quite sure, that he would never find.

Heads turned when Celeste entered the bar. The men eyed her with longing, the women with envy. She was truly beautiful and, under normal circumstances, he would have wanted her very much. But for him there seemed to be nothing normal left in life. His life had turned into a hodgepodge of strange and unrelated dreams.

"Hi," Celeste greeted with a smile.

"Hi, yourself." He kissed her lightly on the lips. "You look beautiful, as usual."

"Thank you."

"What'll you have?" The waitress was there, pen at the ready.

"I'll just have a glass of white wine."

McCall pointed to his almost empty glass and said, "I'll have another of the same."

Celeste, stating the obvious, said, "You know, this was the first place we ever had a drink together."

"Yeah, you'd think I'd have taken you to a nicer place."

"This is nice."

"The place is always full of shitheads."

"No one can ever accuse you of being judgmental," she

ased.

"I'm just discriminating."

She changed the subject with, "I've been thinking about you. Of course, that's nothing new. I think about you all the time."

"That's nice." He was glad she wasn't being morbid, feeling sorry for him.

"I wanted to tell you," she said. "I've sort of been into honesty lately."

"Where you work, that must be tough."

"It is, but I'm not going to be working there much longer."

"You're not?"

"No, I've already given my notice. I'm starting to work for another law firm next week."

"Yeah, which one?"

"Austin and Barrett."

"I'm sure Bob will miss you."

"Who cares. Besides, I think they'd just as soon I left anyway. They know I can't stand any of them."

"Tell me, how are the boys getting along?"

"Since you're off their backs, they seem contented and happy."

"I'm glad," he said sarcastically. "I certainly wouldn't want to cause them any discomfort."

"Well, you did. I thought the phone lines from Clark Ramsey's office to ours would burn up from so much use."

"Clark called Bob a lot?"

"Not as much as Bob called Clark. But he did call a lot."

"And that's no longer the case?"

"They still talk, but things are more normal now."

They must figure that Cele's death stopped me, he thought. They have a real surprise coming.

"How are Reynolds and Roget getting along?" he asked. "Still lovey dovey?"

"Oh, yes. When Reynolds visits the office, Roget looks at him like he was a cheeseburger."

McCall laughed. "Well put, Celeste. By the way, do you

know whether the boys are back to doing their Wednesda
night thing?"

"If I'm not mistaken, tomorrow night's a big night. I hear
Mr. Winnow talking to Paul about something they're going t(
do. But they stopped their conversation when they saw I was ir
hearing distance.

"My glass is empty, Matt."

McCall signaled the waitress and said, "You'd better ease u¡
on that stuff. You know how passionate it makes you."

"That shows how little you know. It's you who makes m
passionate, not the wine."

"Well, under different circumstances, I..."

She interrupted. "You don't have to explain. I understand.'

"Thanks."

"But just because I understand, doesn't mean I want you an
less. I think I want you more now than ever before."

"I don't know what to say."

"It's probably best that you not say anything. But if yo
want me when you're in Athens, all you have to do is call.'

"Thanks. And I really mean that."

After saying goodbye to Celeste, he returned to the condo tc
continue with his preparations. Having had opportunity tc
better define his plans, he called Arnold.

"When I've finished what I have to do here, I probably
should go on to Athens," he said.

"As I told you earlier, it's no problem," Arnold replied. "We
can pick you up in a private aircraft and you can travel using
the identity of your double. Then you can assume your rea¡
identity when you get to Athens. Just call me when and if you
decide to go."

Arnold was being more than accommodating, but McCal¡
knew that somewhere down the line he would be required to
repay the help he was getting. The Company, more than any
other organization he knew of, adhered to the philosophy that
"there's no such thing as a free lunch." But he didn't care. They
could extract a pound of flesh later. It was now that mattered.

For some reason, he felt the need to call Mary Murphy. It emed important to let her know that he hadn't forgotten his ledge to avenge Laurie.

"I've prayed for you, Matt," she said. "You've been through lot lately."

McCall couldn't remember the last time someone told him ey had prayed for him.

"Mary, I appreciate your concern. But I didn't call for ympathy. I called to tell you that I haven't forgotten about aurie. I still intend to find her killer."

"I never doubted that for a minute."

"I also wanted you to know that I'll be gone for awhile. I just eed to get away and regroup."

"That's certainly understandable."

"Anyway, I just wanted you to know that I'll be out of touch or awhile."

"It was nice of you to think of me."

He thought about calling Lanelle, then decided against it. He figured that if he was honest with himself, it would be better ever to call her again.

It would be best for her, too.

He unplugged all the phones. He wanted to spend the emaining hours without interruption. He wanted to sharpen is mental processes to a fine point.

CHAPTER THIRTY-THREE

Paul Roget was excited about what promised to be an entertaining evening. Bob Winnow had suggested that they all go to a new club some forty miles west of the city, a club away from the scrutiny of any prying eyes in San Antonio.

Bob thought it now safe for them to engage in some evening activity, something they had done little of since Laurie's death. And the lack of activity had been rough on Roget, because he was a man who genuinely liked to party.

The bitch, he thought, made life miserable for me while she was alive. And lately she's made life miserable for me even though she's dead. But all that's about to change.

Roget hurriedly completed his afternoon's work, leaving the office earlier than usual in order to beat the rush hour traffic. The drive home seemed much faster than normal, perhaps, he thought, because of his anticipation at what the evening might offer. Whatever the reason, he was in an exceptionally good mood when he wheeled the car in the garage and cut the engine.

Glancing at his watch, he noted that he had ample time to get ready before Francis arrived. They would be going to the club in Francis' car.

When he entered the coolness of the house, he was grateful for its solitude. No Laurie, no baby. He hoped her parents could keep the baby permanently. Regardless, he was going to invite Francis to move in with him.

Entering the bedroom, he couldn't help but smile. It was here that Laurie had known the sensation of having the life strangled from her. The thought of her strangulation excited him. He wondered what she must have been thinking as the life escaped her body.

The thought of her body made him frown. He detested her body, felt sick at the thought of it being pressed against his. He recalled how often he had wanted to kill her, especially when she tried to hold him close.

Roget removed all his clothing and admired his nakedness in full-length mirror. After several moments of rubbing various parts of his body, relishing its softness and smoothness, he went to the bathroom and turned on the shower. He adjusted the water temperature until it felt right to his hand, then stepped inside the glass-encased stall.

The heat of the water steamed the glass as he soaked his body in it. He soaped himself thoroughly, then rinsed. Turning off the water flow, he reached for and found a large pink bath towel.

While drying himself, he thought about what he would wear. He decided on a black silk shirt, which would accentuate the gold chains he planned to drape around his neck.

As he stepped from the shower, still toweling himself, his eyes immediately picked up the image of a man in the mirror. An attempted cry of anguish died in his throat and his knees turned to jelly. He dropped the towel as a speechless fear numbed his body.

Though the man was dressed in military camouflage clothing, though his face was splotched with a paint that blended with the clothing, he had no problem knowing his identity. And that knowledge was more frightening than the way the man was dressed.

Weak with fear, he looked for a weapon with which t
combat his adversary. Finding none, he attempted to run pa
the formidable figure. The attempt was rejected by a crushin
blow to his skull. Then darkness overcame him.

CHAPTER THIRTY-FOUR

Francis Reynolds was convinced that his supervisor was looking for an excuse to fire him. For that reason, he didn't dare leave work early, even for a night as important as the one upcoming, a night in which they would all be together again. His paranoia actually kept him at work a bit past the normal quitting time.

Reynolds didn't consider himself a good lawyer. He'd done well enough in law school, even passed the bar exam with flying colors, but he was never really able to comprehend exactly what he was supposed to do. He didn't even like being a lawyer, but he couldn't think of another field that interested him, either.

By the time he cleared his desk and started home, rush hour traffic was at its worst. So, by the time he parked his car in the garage, he was hot, angry and mentally cursing the fates that made his current work predictament unbearable. He was also a bit frantic because it was getting late, and he wanted to clean up before going out.

After unlocking the door and rushing into the house, he was totally unprepared for the man who suddenly stood before him. He gasped in astonishment, turned and tried to run. But a strong arm encircled his neck, pressure was applied to a vital area, then everything went black.

CHAPTER THIRTY-FIVE

David Darden was not all that excited about an evening with his lawyer friends. He would have preferred to have gone his own way, to have found his own form of entertainment. What his colleagues considered fun was too tame for him. He wanted the joy of hurting someone, to possibly even have someone hurt him.

But this place Bob had selected for the evening, it was not the right kind of place for that kind of activity. It was a hangout for those he considered weak. His only hope was that someone like himself had also been coerced into visiting the club.

Darden was a fitness buff, a student of karate. He was muscular, but had the suppleness of a dancer. He prided himself on his strength, was very competitive, and enjoyed any form of physical combat.

So, when he walked into his apartment and came face-to-face with a man in camouflage clothing, he reacted differently than Roget and Reynolds. Recognizing his adversary, he laughed and prepared to do battle.

The laughter died when the man walked through his blows and brought him to his knees with crushing fists. He tried to fight back, but his muscular arms turned limp in response to the savageness of the man's attack. He saw the blow coming that would render him unconscious, but was helpless to stop it.

CHAPTER THIRTY-SIX

Bob Winnow was becoming increasingly impatient. It was already twenty minutes past the time he was to have been picked up by Francis Reynolds. Repeated calls to Reynolds' home went unanswered. Calls to Paul and David netted the same results. He surmised that the threesome were on the way, that they would be arriving at any moment.

He was anxious for them to see his new dress, one he had saved for this special occasion. It was red dyed leather, which was a bit unseasonal, perhaps, but he was reasonably sure that the club would be cold.

To accentuate the dress, he was wearing more jewelry than usual. He was also wearing matching red shoes with less of a heel than he liked, and black silk hose. For some reason, which he didn't himself understand, he had always preferred hose and a garter belt to pantyhose.

The wig he was wearing was jet black, the hair fluffed and just above the shoulders. He had fussed with his makeup for more than an hour, but still wasn't entirely satisfied with it. He had applied more base than usual, and he was using a bright new lipstick that was new to him.

He was admiring himself in the vanity mirror when he heard the door open and close. He had left it unlocked and, since his wife was on vacation, he guessed the person entering was one of his three friends.

With a smile on his face, he turned to face the bedroom door. The smile dissipated when the man appeared in the doorway. Fear replaced an earlier happiness in Winnow's eyes, and a sense of dread overwhelmed his entire body.

On rubbery legs he rose to his feet, knowing that he no longer controlled any part of his destiny. It was all in the hands of the man standing in the doorway.

With no thought of struggle, he submitted to the silent commands of his captor, following him through the house and to the garage driveway. There he got inside a black van and meekly allowed the man to bind his hands and feet.

He saw that he was not alone in the van. Paul, Francis, David...they were all there.

Winnow could not judge the amount of time they drove, but it really didn't matter. He was so paralyzed with fear that it was impossible to think. He wanted to talk to his friends, but they were gagged.

The van finally came to a halt. Their captor got out, opened its sliding side door, took the bindings off their ankles and commanded them to exit. When they were outside the van, Winnow recognized their location. They were at Francis' lake home.

The camouflaged man now had a gun in his hand. He ordered them onto the porch of the house and, while they stood waiting, he opened the door with ease.

When inside the house, he ordered them to sit. Then he removed the gags.

Winnow couldn't understand why Paul was nude, but he didn't say anything. He felt as though he had swallowed his ability to speak.

The man said they were going to have a trial of sorts, that he wanted to know who was responsible for the deaths of Laurie

280

Roget and Annie Reynolds.

None of them responded.

Their captor stared at them, his face impossible to read beneath the splotches of paint. Finally, after what seemed an eternity, he retied the ankles of all but Francis. While they watched in horror, he took a knife from a sheath attached to his belt. Then he pulled and dragged the struggling, crying Francis to another room of the house.

They could hear snatches of Francis pleading and crying for awhile, but then there was silence.

CHAPTER THIRTY-SEVEN

McCall had selected Francis Reynolds, because he thought the man would be the weakest of the quartet. Now, in another room of the house, the man was shaking with such fear that McCall was afraid that he might not be able to talk.

"Would you like to save your life?" he asked.

"Yes," Reynolds whimpered.

"The only way you can save it is to tell the truth. Do you understand?"

"Yes," Reynolds whimpered again.

"First, I want you to calm down. No matter what you tell me, if it's the truth, you'll live."

He had no intention of letting any of them live. They had sealed their fate when Cele was murdered. But he lied to Reynolds about his fate in order to find out who killed Laurie Roget and Annie Reynolds.

Reynolds continued to shake, but the whimpering ceased. He was so preoccupied with fear that he didn't notice when McCall turned on the voice-activated tape recorder in his shirt pocket.

"Did you kill Laurie Roget?" McCall asked.

"No," he stammered.

"You're lying."

"No, I swear to God, I'm not."

"Who killed her?"

Reynolds didn't answer, so McCall put the blade of the knife on his throat.

"Bob did it," he whispered.

The fact that he said Bob Winnow was the murderer shocked McCall momentarily.

"Who did you say killed her? Speak up."

"Bob Winnow. Bob Winnow killed her."

"You're lying."

"No, no I'm not. Bob killed her. I swear it."

"And who killed your wife?"

"Bob killed her, too."

McCall was sure Reynolds was telling the truth. He was too frightened to lie.

"Why did Bob kill them?"

"He just wanted to. He said we'd be better off without them. He said they were holding us back."

"Holding you back from what?"

"What we really wanted to be."

"And what's that?"

Reynolds dropped his head. He didn't want to answer, and McCall saw no need in pursuing a response.

"But you and Paul Roget knew Bob was going to kill your wives, didn't you? I mean before he actually did it?

Reynolds hesitated before answering, but looking into McCall's eyes, he knew that he had better not lie.

"We knew," he admitted.

"What about the bombings?"

"David did those."

"You mean David Darden, don't you?"

"Yes."

Did David ever kill anyone else?"

"I don't know?"

"What about a man named Harold Webster?"

"I don't know."

"But you knew that David was going to plant a bomb in my car, didn't you?"

Again, Reynolds looked in McCall's eyes and was afraid to lie.

"We all knew," he admitted.

"I'm going to untie your hands for a few minutes and I want you to write down and sign just what you've told me."

"I can't. They'll kill me."

McCall placed the point of the knife against Reynolds throat and said, "You didn't have a part in the murders, so what do you have to fear."

"I'll go to prison."

"But you won't get the death penalty."

McCall knew what Reynolds was thinking as he felt the cold steel against his throat. He was thinking that if he did escape from his current situation, he could claim that he had been forced to make a false confession. Under those circumstances, he would have a chance at freedom.

"I'm tired of waiting," McCall said.

Reynolds started crying, but said, "I'll write it down."

With McCall making sure he didn't leave out any details, it took the lawyer only a few minutes to write the confession.

After he had finished, McCall retied his hands and told him they were going back to join his friends.

"Do we have to go back in there?" he whimpered.

"Afraid so," McCall said.

CHAPTER THIRTY-EIGHT

When the man and Francis returned, Winnow was sure that he knew. He was sure that Francis had told him. The sureness caused chills of fear to run the length of his spine.

But the man didn't say anything. He just untied Paul's feet and took him to the other room. Paul went whimpering and crying as Francis had done.

Winnow wondered why none of them had called their captor by name. They all knew him. It was as if they thought that by ignoring the reality, by feigning ignorance, they would somehow have a better chance of survival.

The fact that Francis was still alive triggered some hope within him. But what if Francis had told him. He wanted to ask Francis, but he couldn't talk. A chalky dryness filled his mouth.

David should be the one the man wanted. It was David who had tried to kill the man. It was David who had killed another reporter and the man's girlfriend by mistake.

If I could only talk, Winnow thought, I'd tell him about David. I've never liked David.

David was sitting there now, snarling, trying to be macho.

Winnow thought he was probably as scared as any of them, bu
afraid to admit it. There was nothing about David's bravadc
that he envied.

CHAPTER THIRTY-NINE

It was, perhaps, fifteen mintues later when McCall returned to the room with Roget. He had gotten pretty much the same taped and written story from Roget that he had gotten from Reynolds.

He addressed Darden first, venom in his voice.

"Your friends have spilled their guts. Is there anything you want to say?"

"Yeah," Darden snapped. "Go to hell."

"You're close to being there, Mr. Darden. Your bombs didn't get me, but now I have you."

"But I sure as hell killed your fuckin' girl..."

McCall's fist smashed into Darden's nose, causing blood to spurt.

"You sonofabitch," McCall said, "I'm going to make sure you die slowly and painfully."

Darden slowly brought his head upright, the blood still pouring from his nose.

"That's great, you bastard," the lawyer said. "It's pretty easy to beat up a man who's tied up."

McCall used his knife to cut the cords binding Darden.

"You're free now," he said, "and I'm putting my gun and knife aside. Now, come get me."

Darden lunged at McCall in football-tackle style, only to be chopped on the back of the neck. He went sprawling to the floor. As he attempted to get to his feet, McCall kicked him in the face. As he rolled over on his back, McCall pounced on him and beat his face brutally, unmercifully, with his fists. It took only moments for all the fight to go out of Darden.

McCall rose to his feet and with gritted teeth said to Winnow, "What about you, Bob? Do you want some of this, or do you just stick to killing women?"

Winnow opened his mouth, but he couldn't speak. There was too much fear lodged in his throat.

"Maybe if I pounded you a little bit, you'd tell me what you have on Clark Ramsey," McCall said. "You do want to tell me don't you, Bob?"

Winnow nodded his head affirmatively.

"You have the floor, Bob, go ahead and speak."

The older lawyer's mouth came open, but nothing came out. His body started shaking and then he keeled over in a dead faint.

McCall sat down in a chair and looked at the four men; Darden groveling on the floor, Winnow slumped over on the couch, Reynolds and Roget watching him in wide-eyed fear.

They all deserved to die, and he had fully intended to kill them. But they were such a pitiful lot. They seemed unworthy of his plans for executing them.

He then realized that he was looking for an excuse not to kill, trying to disguise his aversion by playing mental games about their worthiness to die by his hand. They all deserved to die because of the parts they played in the deaths of Laurie, Annie Reynolds, Eddie, Cele and Harold Webster. But McCall was finally forced to admit to himself that he was incapable of killing them in cold blood.

He had never killed anyone who was not trying to kill him. He had never killed an unarmed man.

Maybe, he thought, it would be better if they all suffered shame and punishment. With the tape recordings and written confessions, he had the means to impose that shame and punishment.

Darden had regained consciousness, and Winnow was now sitting upright on the couch. McCall could see that he was still incapable of speech, but he could hear. He was sure of that.

"Gentlemen," he said calmly. "In a few moments I'm going to walk out that door and I'm going to drive to the sheriff's office. And I'm going to let the sheriff listen to a tape recording."

He then turned on his recorder and let them listen to Reynolds' confession.

Before it was over, Darden was screaming at Reynolds, "You sniveling coward. I'll kill you for this."

As the recording went into Roget's confession, Darden shouted threats and obscenities at both men. They sat close together, cowering in fear.

When the recording was over, McCall went to the phone and called the Jones County Sheriff's Department. He told the deputy who answered the phone that he was coming into town to talk to the sheriff, and that someone should come to the Reynolds' lake house to pick up four murderers.

Initially, the deputy was dubious, thinking it was possibly a crank call. But McCall convinced him to verify his identity with Bill Haloran of the San Antonio Police Department. He got a lucky break because the deputy was Haloran's contact, the one the detective had talked to about Annie Reynolds' death.

The deputy told McCall that he would contact the sheriff, who would be waiting for him at his office.

McCall walked past his four captives, paused in the doorway and said, "Gentlemen, I'm going to see to it that you all roast in hell."

CHAPTER FORTY

Sheriff Chuckles Garland was a heavyset, amiable man, one whose cigar looked as though it was growing out of his mouth. He was, perhaps, as tall as five-feet nine-inches, but part of the height might have been because of his snakeskin cowboy boots.

He listened with intent interest to the recording of Reynolds and Roget's confessions, injecting an "I'll be damned" intermittently.

After the recording ended, he glanced at the two written confessions McCall also provided and again said, "I'll be damned."

When McCall began to wonder if the sheriff's vocabulary was limited to three words, Garland asked, "How in the hell did you get these confessions, Mr. McCall? Did you beat 'em out of those ol' boys?"

"You don't hear any threats on the tape, do you?" McCall answered.

"No," Garland responded.

"And you'll note that each wrote that their confession was of their own free will."

Garland grinned. "We've gotten a few like that ourselves, but we've kinda had to help'em know what their own free will was."

"Well, I don't think you'll have any problem getting Reynolds and Roget to talk. Now Darden, he's another matter."

"What about this Bob Winnow fellow?"

"He seems to have lost his voice."

"You know, Mr. McCall, I've been readin' what you've wrote about this Roget murder in San Antonio, and when ol' Bill Haloran called down here checking on Mrs. Reynolds' death, I'll admit it got my curiosity up."

McCall smiled. "Well, sheriff, I think you got yourself a few headlines on this deal."

Garland chuckled. "It sure can't hurt anything come election time."

The phone rang and Garland answered. He listened for a few moments, then said, "I'll be damned."

More listening, then he said, "Hell, get the rest of the boys out of bed and we'll try to find the sonofabitch. He can't get far.

"Hell no, I'm not comin' out there. Call Doc Davis and get back to me when you have something. Me and Mr. McCall are goin' to make us a pot of coffee and talk awhile.

"That's your job, damn it. I don't need any shit, get me some results."

When he hung up the phone, Garland said, "You're not goin' to believe this."

"Believe what?"

"That damn Darden killed the other three."

"What?"

"A couple of my deputies caught him in the act and still let the sonofabitch get away. They'll get'em, though. He can't get far."

"How did he kill'em?"

"The sonofabitch castrated 'em, stuffed their mouths with their testicles, then taped their mouths shut. None of 'em died easy. Darden must be one mean mother fucker."

McCall laughed. "I can't help laughing," he apologized, "because in a way I think it's poetic justice."

Garland grinned. "Hell, I feel the same way. Saves the taxpayers a bit of money, too."

The sheriff had made no mention of the way McCall was dressed. Nor had he bothered to ask how McCall had come to be with the four lawyers in Reynolds' lake house. There were, the reporter decided, some advantages to the way the law operated in Jones County.

They sat drinking coffee and talking about the Roget murder for awhile, about the bombings that killed Cele and Eddie, and about Annie Reynolds' mysterious death. McCall didn't hold anything back. He told Garland all that he knew. The sheriff interrupted occasionally with an, "I'll be damned," but mostly he just listened. He seemed to be enjoying the story, grateful, perhaps, that he was an insider to the information.

After some length of time, the phone rang again. Garland was obviously, McCall surmised, talking to the doctor who had been summoned to the scene. After they had concluded their conversation, the sheriff said to McCall, "The doc just verified what my man said. The bastards were castrated and had their privates shoved down their throats."

"Any word on Darden?"

"Not yet," the sheriff answered.

"Mind if I use your phone?" McCall asked. "I need to make a collect call to the paper."

"Be my guest."

After finally convincing a night editor that he wasn't in Greece and just playing a prank, McCall filed a story detailing the events of the evening. Much to the delight of Chuckles Garland, he made the sheriff and his deputies the heroes of the story; said they had played an integral part in solving the murders.

He gave a graphic portrayal of how the trio of lawyers had met their end, causing the editor to ask, "Do you think we ought to use this kind of stuff, McCall?"

"Just use it, asshole," he replied. "And don't change a word."

He also told how David Darden was being sought in connection with the slayings, and that the Jones County Sheriff's Department expected an arrest within hours.

Then he told how Bob Winnow was dressed, and identified him as being Clark Ramsey's legal counsel.

"We can't do that," the editor protested.

"The hell we can't," McCall said. "I want it in there. And if it's not, I'll be in tomorrow to personally kick your ass."

In the background, Garland laughed.

But having warned the man, McCall knew that not one word of his prose would be changed. He would probably call Parkham about it, tell him of McCall's threat. And Parkham would tell him to go with the story as it had been dictated. It was, after all, the big story that the managing editor had wanted. And the *Tribune* had a leg up on everyone in reporting it.

After he had finished dictating the story, Garland laughed and said, "I like your style, Mr. McCall."

The reporter smiled. "Yours isn't so bad, either, sheriff. How about another cup of coffee?"

CHAPTER FORTY-ONE

"**Y**ou had a lot of people fooled, McCall," Bill Haloran said, "including me."

They were in the diner having coffee.

"I will admit, though," the detective continued, "that I was a little suspicious about your attitude."

"What do you mean?"

"I mean, hell, I've never known you to give up on a story, McCall. And I also couldn't believe that you were taking Cele's death as calmly as you let on."

"You know, I really did plan to kill them, Bill. I wanted them to die slowly and painfully. I wanted to be the executioner."

"But you weren't. And I'm really glad."

"I set things in motion, though."

"Let's not get into that. Sheriff Garland isn't one to ask a lot of unnecessary questions, so let's let sleeping dogs lie. Besides, the sheriff's enjoying being a big hero and thinks you're the best thing to come along since the King Edward cigar."

"When it came right down to it, though, I couldn't kill them in cold blood."

"Well, I know you had every right," Haloran sympathized,

'but I'm glad you couldn't do it."

"On my part, I consider it a character flaw," McCall said.

Haloran laughed. "For your sake, for all our sakes, I'm glad t's over."

"But it's not."

"You mean Darden?"

"He's still out there running around somewhere. And I think he's proved that he's dangerous as hell."

"He'll be caught soon. There's no place for him to go."

"He's the one I really thought I could kill. I sure as hell tried. But even when he's caught, it's not going to be over."

"You're talking Clark Ramsey again, right?"

"I am. The man's dirty and I'm going to get him."

"Those confessions you obtained by dubious means didn't mention him."

"That's because Winnow couldn't talk and Darden wouldn't. Those are the two who were tied to Ramsey."

"Well, you're sure not going to get anything out of Winnow. Maybe we can get something from Darden, if he's taken alive."

"You know one of the things that kind of bothers me about myself, Bill?"

"What?"

"The fact that when I was about to kill those assholes, I started thinking 'story.' Maybe I would have killed them if I hadn't gotten those confessions. When I got those, I wanted to write the damn story."

"You talk a good game, McCall, but you have a book you go by just like mine. They're different books, but they're the rules you live by."

"I think that subconsciously I was thinking that if I killed them, I'd have to go to Greece or lie low and that someone else at the *Tribune* would write the story. I didn't want that. I wanted to write it. Just like I want to write the final end to Darden and Ramsey."

"There's nothing wrong with that."

McCall glanced at his watch. "It's getting late. Do you want some dinner, Bill?"

"I know this is gonna surprise you, but not tonight. The little lady's fixing some of her famous pineapple pork chops and rice, and she insisted that I get home at a decent hour. Why don't you come over and eat with us?"

McCall made a face. "Pineapple pork chops and rice? Sounds kind of gross to me."

"To tell the truth, it's not the best thing I've ever eaten," the detective said. "But it's about the only thing she can fix that's worth a shit. I'd appreciate it if you'd come home with me, because that way I won't be forced to eat so much."

McCall laughed. "It's hard for me to believe there's something you don't like."

"There's a lot of stuff she fixes that I don't like. Now damn it, are you goin' to come with me or not?"

"Hell no. Your wife's not expecting company. I'm not going to barge in on her."

"I can handle that with one phone call," he said.

"Never mind."

"I insist."

They argued for a few more minutes until McCall relented. He really didn't want to be alone.

After Haloran made the phone call, they exited the diner and started walking along the street toward the police station. McCall's car was parked there, along with Haloran's.

Simultaneously, they saw David Darden rise from the seat of a parked car and point a pistol at them. The first bullet caught Haloran in the side, the second grazed McCall's shoulder.

As Haloran fell to the sidewalk, McCall fell alongside him. He then reached inside the detective's coat and took Haloran's gun from his shoulder holster. Rising to his feet with bullets ricocheting around him, McCall charged the parked car from which Darden was firing.

One of Darden's slugs caught McCall in the upper part of the chest, but he kept coming until he was within almost arm's

ach of the man. Darden fired again, only to hear a click as the
ring pin fell on an empty chamber.

His gun was empty.

McCall looked at him fumbling for more shells. When he
oked up at McCall, he took a bullet right between the eyes.

Through hazy eyes, McCall could see people running
oward him from several directions. Then he collapsed and
verything went black.

CHAPTER FORTY-TWO

When McCall regained consciousness, both he and Haloran were being wheeled into a hospital emergency room. There was no pain, so he knew the paramedics had given him something.

"You OK, Bill?" He could see that Haloran's eyes were open and that the detective was looking at him.

"Hell yes. I've had worse mosquito bites."

"You'll go to any lengths to keep from eating your wife's pineapple pork chops, won't you?"

Haloran laughed. "They told me you were going to live, asshole, but they've gotta get that bullet out of you."

"Not until I call the fuckin' paper. I've got a story to file."

"Don't you ever quit?"

"Not until I get Ramsey."

"Oh, shit," Haloran said.

❋ ❋ ❋ ❋